Also by Phillip Finch

Diving into Darkness: A True Story of
Death and Survival

Fatal Flaw

F2F

Paradise Junction

Sugarland

DEVIL'S KEEP

PHILLIP FINCH

POCKET BOOKS
New York   London   Toronto   Sydney

Pocket Books
A Division of Simon & Schuster, Inc.
1230 Avenue of the Americas
New York, NY 10020

This book is a work of fiction. Names, characters, places, and incidents either are products of the author's imagination or are used fictitiously. Any resemblance to actual events or locales or persons, living or dead, is entirely coincidental.

Copyright © 2010 by Phillip Finch

All rights reserved, including the right to reproduce this book or portions thereof in any form whatsoever. For information, address Pocket Books Subsidiary Rights Department, 1230 Avenue of the Americas, New York, NY 10020.

First Pocket Books paperback edition April 2010

POCKET and colophon are registered trademarks of Simon & Schuster, Inc.

For information about special discounts for bulk purchases, please contact Simon & Schuster Special Sales at 1-866-506-1949 or business@simonandschuster.com.

The Simon & Schuster Speakers Bureau can bring authors to your live event. For more information or to book an event, contact the Simon & Schuster Speakers Bureau at 1-866-248-3049 or visit our website at www.simonspeakers.com.

Interior design by Esther Paradelo
Cover design and illustration by Tony Mauro

Manufactured in the United States of America

10 9 8 7 6 5 4 3 2

ISBN 978-1-4391-6856-1
ISBN 978-1-4391-6951-3 (ebook)

For Daniel
who was there on Day One

PROLOGUE

As their outrigger *banca* skimmed across the rolling swells beyond the Sulu Sea, JoJo and Rasul Pangulag came upon the most amazing sight they had ever encountered.

Somebody was feeding the fishes off Berbalang Island.

The brothers were Badjao, water gypsies. They roamed the wild Sulu archipelago that stretches hundreds of miles from Borneo to the southern Philippines. Their families lived in shacks set on stilts above tidal waters, but the brothers spent days at a time in the slim twenty-foot *banca*, occasionally smuggling, usually fishing.

They rarely visited the waters around the island. Few Badjao ever did. The *berbalang* was a dreaded shape-shifting ghoul of Sulu myth, said to feed on the corpses of its victims. Most Badjao didn't really believe that the island was home to the *berbalang*, but they didn't exactly disbelieve it, either.

There were more practical reasons to avoid the island. It was beyond the Badjao's natural territory, the placid shallows of the archipelago where one could travel three hundred miles without losing sight of land. Berbalang Island was a solitary place, with ferocious tides and wind-driven seas, the last chunk of land before several hundred miles of open water.

But the brothers' catch had been poor for several days, and they were venturing out in hopes of changing their luck.

The island was a craggy hump of volcanic rock, forested with coconut palms and banana trees. JoJo and Rasul approached it from the west. They headed for a steep bluff that plunged down into the sea, an area where mackerel were known to run. The *banca*'s single-cylinder engine clattered as it labored through high swells. Rasul sat working the tiller. He watched JoJo standing easily at the prow, peering out across the open expanse of water, which blazed under the midday sun. Rasul was twenty-nine years old, JoJo twenty-seven. They were both small and lithe, brown-skinned men, although JoJo was perhaps an inch taller, his skin a tone or two darker from the hours that he spent in the hot glare of the sun, while Rasul sat in the shade of a canvas canopy.

They were about half a mile off the island when JoJo shouted over the engine's noise and pointed out across the water. Rasul followed the line of his brother's arm and finger. A speedboat was rounding the rocky point at the far end of the island. This was no hand-built native boat. It rode high, the sharp white bow uplifted, throwing up twin plumes of spray as it banged through the waves.

It was a wonderment. Neither of them had ever seen such a craft in these waters.

The speedboat slowed and stopped, settling into

the water. At the wheel was a pink-skinned man with light hair. A foreigner, Rasul realized. It was stunning. No foreigner ever ventured within a hundred miles of these waters. The man at the stern stood up, and Rasul got another shock. He was huge, the biggest man Rasul had ever seen: tall, wide, and solid. His chest and upper arms bulged against a white T-shirt. To Rasul he looked like a pink bear.

He stood near the stern and lifted a tall white bucket. He tipped the bucket forward, and something spilled out over the side, splashing into the sea.

The *banca* was still pushing across the water, on a course that would take them about one hundred yards from the speedboat. As they closed the distance, the pink-skinned giant picked up another white bucket. Rasul shaded his eyes against the sun, looking through the glare, as the huge foreigner lifted the second bucket over the side and upended it. Solid chunks of something slithered out and down into the water. Food. Meat. *This can't be true,* Rasul thought. *Nobody throws away food.*

The foreigner dumped out a third bucket. Now the *banca* was closer, and Rasul could see the water simmering around the stern of the speedboat. Fish were surging up, dimpling the ocean as they ate at the surface. Gulls were flapping in from perches atop the cliff, circling low over the speedboat and diving toward the water.

JoJo and Rasul shared a glance of bewilderment. The foreigner was actually feeding the fish.

Not just that. From the eager way the fish were rising, they seemed to be expecting food. So this wasn't the first time they had been fed this way.

Unbelievable.

The foreigner now picked up a fourth bucket and lifted it. But he didn't tip it over the side, not right away. He cocked his head and looked toward the *banca*, seeming to notice them for the first time. Rasul sensed that the look was not friendly. Instinctively, Rasul pushed the tiller, turning the *banca* away from the speedboat, and cut the engine down to idle.

He watched with JoJo as the big man dumped out the fourth bucket and put it down. The water was alive now, the fish in a frenzy. Their silvery flanks flashed in the sun as they attacked the food.

The foreigner could have easily scooped up a boatload of fish with a few dips of a hand net. But he didn't; he just put down the bucket and went forward to the wheel, throttling up the engines. The speedboat made a throaty burbling sound. It pulled away quickly, leaving a broad wake as the foreigner turned the wheel and cut back toward where he had first appeared. In less than a minute he was gone, vanishing around the point.

The patch of sea where he had spilled out the buckets was still alive with the feeding fish, the surface almost boiling now with greedy movement.

And *that* clearly was the most amazing sight JoJo and Rasul had ever seen: a feast of fish left for the taking.

Rasul didn't hesitate. As soon as the speedboat was out of sight, he gunned the engine, full power. The *banca* began to move forward. Rasul, back at the tiller, couldn't see the feeding fish from where he sat. But he let JoJo guide him in, steering by the small motions that JoJo flicked with a hand held behind his back as he stood at the prow. Right. Right again. Easy left. Steady. Easy right. Slow. Stop.

Rasul turned off the engine, and the boat glided to a halt. Up front, JoJo was staring down at the water. Rasul expected him to snap into action—grab a net, something—but for a few seconds JoJo remained fixed on the water.

"Jo?" said Rasul.

JoJo didn't answer. He crouched on one knee and got low to the water. Still staring.

Then he abruptly recoiled, straightening at the waist.

He turned back to Rasul. His face showed shock. Fear.

"What is it?" Rasul said.

"Turn around. Now."

"What?" Rasul began to rise out of his seat, to get a look at what had startled his brother.

JoJo's head blew apart.

In the same instant, time began to parcel itself out in excruciating segments.

There was the part where JoJo's face ruptured in ghastly slow motion.

There was the part where Rasul heard a wet spattering on the deck and felt a stinging mist on his face and arms, and heard a thunderclap from above, and thought, *Rain?*

There was the part where JoJo's body began to topple forward and Rasul looked into the top of JoJo's head and saw just a bloody husk, and then the part where Rasul heard himself keening a mournful *"Jo!"*

And then Rasul realized that the mist was blood and tissue, and the stinging was pieces of bone, pelting him, and the thunderclap was not thunder but a gunshot from somewhere up at the top of the cliff.

JoJo's lifeless body thumped down hard into the *banca*, sending a shudder along the deck.

Now time began to move in a hurry, and Rasul moved with it. He pushed the throttle all the way forward, and leaned into the tiller to turn the *banca*. The bow came around; the island swung out of sight behind his back. The *banca* picked up speed, headed back the way they had come.

Rasul twisted the throttle hard, trying to squeeze every bit of power out of the engine, and for several seconds the *banca* plowed straight westward, banging into the waves. Rasul fought against panic. Dark blood was spilling from JoJo's head, pooling on the deck, and Rasul flashed on that last moment of his brother's existence, the startled and stricken expression on JoJo's face the instant before he died.

What did he see? Rasul thought. He glanced back over one shoulder, but there was only the wake that the *banca* made, and the fish still thrashing at the surface.

Rasul looked forward again, westward to where the archipelago lay. Home.

A heartbeat later, Rasul found himself sprawled inside the boat, facedown, as if he had been flung to the deck. He was aware of having been struck from behind, a hard and heavy blow at his back. He dimly heard another thunderclap from the island.

He had been shot.

The *banca* was still churning forward. Rasul knew that without a hand on the tiller it would soon begin turning in circles. He tried to get up, get back to his seat, but he couldn't move. His arms, his legs—they didn't respond.

Another gunshot cracked from the island. A bullet smacked into the deck a few inches from Rasul's face.

Another gunshot. The bullet ripped through the plywood on one side of the *banca* and blew out a fist-sized hole on the other side.

More gunshots, more gaping holes. Some of them were below the waterline, and the sea rushed in, mingling with the blood. The *banca* was swamping now, slowing as it filled. Rising seawater sloshed into Rasul's face, and he struggled to push himself up. But he couldn't move: he felt pinned by a great weight. He gagged at first on the water, but it quickly became all too much to resist. He surrendered and let the seawater course down his throat. He tasted it, the salty tang that he had known every day of his life.

Rasul knew that he was dying. He thought of their families, wives and children, waiting. They

would never know what happened. He thought of
bright sunlight on the sea, a cooling breeze on his
face as he steered the *banca* over crystal green water.
He thought of JoJo standing up at the bow, agile and
complete.

And as the light faded, he saw JoJo peering down
at the water where the fish were feeding, then almost
jumping back in fright, the shock on JoJo's face.

And again the question, now the very last
thought that ever passed through Rasul's mind:

What did JoJo see?

What?

HARVEST DAY
–10

ONE

In the cool darkness before a Sunday morning
dawn, Marivic Valencia stood beside the coastal
road that ran beside Leyte Gulf and waited for the
Manila-bound bus that would carry her away from
her family. She was eighteen years old, slim and
pretty and demure, with long black hair bound in a
ponytail behind her head. She used no makeup. She
wore denim jeans and a loose T-shirt.

A large duffel, stuffed full, sat in the gravel beside
the road. Marivic had never been more than an hour
away from home; now she was beginning a journey
that would take her to a job thousands of miles away,
and she didn't expect to return for at least a year.

Her family huddled around her. Lorna, her
mother, held her tight. The five little ones, arrayed
from fourteen to two years old, clung to her. They at-
tached themselves wherever they could find a hand-
hold: one at each elbow, one at a shoulder, the two
smallest wrapping their arms around her legs. Her
twin brother, Ronnie, stood a couple of steps away,
looking perplexed and helpless.

She and Ronnie had always been close. Each
understood the other like nobody else. They hardly
needed words. Marivic met his eyes and shot him a

smile that was supposed to say *It'll be all right,* and Ronnie nodded and smiled back weakly.

Now others were appearing, aunts and uncles and cousins wandering over from the small village across the road where she had grown up, the place called San Felipe. They gathered around Marivic and her family, murmuring low, sad words. Marivic felt dampness at her cheek: her mother was weeping. A couple of aunties began to sob too.

Marivic wished the bus would hurry and get there. She wasn't eager to leave, but she wanted this to end. It felt too much like a funeral, and it was all too familiar.

Departures were a way of life for San Felipe, as for all other small towns and villages in the rural Philippines. People left all the time. They left to find work, to make money. Some headed for Manila. Others, more adventurous and more fortunate, were hired for jobs abroad. At least a dozen of the sons and daughters of the village worked overseas, sending home remittances that sustained their families. Marivic's father had been one of those. The duffel was his old sea bag.

Until his sudden death two years earlier, he had been a seaman, a chief mate who spent nearly a year at a time on a Norwegian freighter, returning home for only a few weeks before going out to sea again. Each time he left, the family had gathered here beside the road, just like now, weeping and clinging as they waited for the northbound bus.

Marivic could remember each of those departures.

Until this moment, she had never realized what an ordeal it must have been for him.

Now twin lights appeared down the road, growing bigger and brighter. A breeze from the south carried up the rumble of a diesel engine. "Here it is," somebody said, and Lorna wailed.

The bus loomed up, slowed, and chuffed to a stop. The door swung open, and the crowd parted and made a path for Marivic to the open door and the steps beyond. But Marivic couldn't move. Lorna had tightened her embrace, and the little ones were clinging even harder.

The driver ended it. "We have a long way to go," he said, in a tone that was stern but not unkind.

Lorna squeezed her once more, kissed her, released her. Marivic kissed each of the younger children, then Ronnie. She picked up the duffel. Her ten-year-old brother, Ernie, was carrying a string sack with bananas and snacks for the long trip ahead. He held it up to her; she took it and climbed up, and the driver shut the door behind her.

She walked about halfway down the aisle, lifted the duffel onto a rack overhead, and dropped down into an open seat. The engine rumbled, the bus pulled away. Marivic got just a glimpse out the window of her family and the others, and then they slid out of view.

She was on her way.

As the bus rolled up the coastal road, with dawn lifting over the gulf to the east, Marivic felt lonely, excited, scared—and very lucky. Manila was just a stopover. After a couple of weeks of processing her passport and paperwork, she was headed abroad to help care for the children of a wealthy Arab family in Dubai. She would be paid the equivalent of eight hundred dollars a month, plus room and board. The Philippines had millions of unemployed college graduates who gladly would have left home and family to earn that kind of money, doing even the most menial labor.

And Marivic didn't even have a high school diploma. After their father died, she and Ronnie had left school and gone to work. Ronnie harvested copra from coconut trees on the steep mountainside behind the village. Marivic got a job as a waitress at a roadside restaurant near the village. Long hours, hard work, and awful pay didn't add up to much: in the past year, she had earned the peso equivalent of $750. Now she would be making more than that every month, and sending most of it home to support her family.

It was miraculous.

The opportunity had presented itself when a customer left behind a newspaper at one of her tables. She brought the paper home and read it by the light of the single dim electric bulb that her mother allowed to burn after dark. At the back of the newspaper were ads for overseas employment agencies. One caught her attention: OPTIMO. She liked the name; it sounded bright and cheerful. And she saw that Optimo had a branch office in Tacloban City, the provincial capital, about an hour up the highway.

She went there on her next day off. The address was a shabby three-story office building, a single small room at the top floor. As Marivic entered, she found half a dozen metal chairs along walls with flaked and peeling paint. Five of the chairs were occupied by people filling out forms on clipboards. At the front wall, a plump middle-aged woman sat at a desk. A nameplate on the desk read: REGIONAL MANAGER. She impatiently motioned Marivic inside and gave Marivic a clipboard and a form—BIOGRAPHICAL DATA AND APPLICATION FOR REPRESENTATION, the form said— and Marivic took it to the last empty chair and began to fill it out, balancing the clipboard on her knees.

The air in the room was dense and torpid. An electric fan turned lazily overhead. Marivic wiped her damp forehead with the back of one hand to keep the beads of sweat from dripping onto the form. When she was finished, she brought the clipboard to the desk and stood waiting as the plump woman examined the form. Finally the woman sent her to a clinic on the first floor for a physical exam. A doctor took her medical history, examined her eyes and ears and throat, listened to her heart and lungs, and drew a blood sample. Marivic trudged back up to the top- floor office. The woman curtly told her that the application would be sent to the head office. Whatever happened would come out of Manila.

It didn't sound encouraging.

Marivic felt foolish as she walked out. What chance did she have? *Everybody* in the Philippines wanted to work abroad. She had wasted a day off.

Three days later, the Manila office called. They had a job for her, but it had to be filled quickly. Could she be in Manila in two days?

Marivic stammered a yes.

She was instructed to return to the Tacloban office, where the regional manager gave her a reserved-seat bus ticket and one thousand pesos—more than a week's wages at the restaurant—for incidental expenses. The plump woman told her that an agency employee would meet her at the bus terminal in Manila. While Marivic waited for her passport, she would stay free of charge at the agency's dormitory.

"Be sure that you're on that bus," the woman told her.

Marivic hurried home to pack. The next morning she was headed north, stunned by her good fortune.

The journey to Manila was twenty-two hours, nearly a full day and a night.

Marivic stayed awake through the daylight hours, eagerly taking in the countryside she had never seen before. It included a crossing of a spectacular bridge high above the San Juanico Strait, terrifying but thrilling, and a two-hour passage on a large ferry that carried the bus to a landing at the southern tip of the island of Luzon.

Manila was on Luzon, so the rest of the trip was overland. Something about that thrilled Marivic, knowing that there was no more water between her and the big city. MANILA 670 KM said a road sign at the ferry landing. Marivic pulled her cell phone from the pocket and powered it up. It got a signal, three bars.

This didn't surprise her. In the past ten years, cell service had proliferated throughout the country, with towers appearing even on remote mountaintops. The Philippines was cell crazy. All but the very poorest owned a phone with a prepaid SIM card. Airtime for conversations was relatively expensive, beyond the budgets of most, but a text message cost only a few centavos. For the price of a scoop of steamed rice at an outdoor food stall, you could send dozens of texts. So Filipinos were now a texting nation, universally adept, able to walk, talk, eat, drive—sometimes even make love—while their thumbs danced on the phones' numeric pads.

Marivic, seeing the three bars, thought about Ronnie. He had always wanted to make the journey to the big city.

She sent him a text:

manila 670 km

Moments later, the reply flashed back:

lucky u

The bus ground on. Twice more that day, as road signs passed her window, Marivic sent texts to her brother.

manila 512

Ronnie answered:

:-(

And just before dark:

manila 402

That got no answer at all. Ronnie was pouting, she thought, and was missing her. She would feel the same in his place.

She slept on and off after nightfall, waking when the bus stopped in towns and small cities. Then after midnight the stops were more frequent, the populated areas bigger and closer together, until finally there was no more countryside, just an endless sprawl of streets and homes and shops and buildings, with Manila glowing in the sky ahead.

She didn't know exactly when they entered the city. But some of the streets became wider, and there were trucks and cars and taxis waiting at traffic signals—even at 3:30 a.m.!—and she knew they must be close. She turned on the phone and tapped out a quick message to Ronnie:

arrived

He would be asleep, but he'd find it first thing in the morning.

The bus terminal was on the south side of the metropolitan area, along a broad boulevard. Most of the passengers seemed to know that they were getting close, because they began to gather their bags. Marivic stood, took down her duffel, and sat with it in her lap.

On impulse, she unzipped it and dug down into the clothes. She brought out a small drawstring bag of red velvet with a braided cinch. She looked around, saw that nobody seemed to be paying attention to her, opened the bag and let the contents fall into her palm.

It was her most treasured possession: a gold herringbone bracelet with a centerpiece of red rubies forming the letter "M," encircled by a ring of small diamonds. Nothing else she owned was even remotely so expensive, but this wasn't the real significance. The bracelet was a gift from her father, bought in Brazil for her sixteenth birthday. He had always brought thrilling surprises when he returned from his voyages, but this one was really special. It was a grown-up gift. It had made her feel like a woman.

Marivic had intended to keep the bracelet out of sight in Manila. She had heard stories of robbers who stole gold chains and even rings, ripping them free and then running. But she had also heard of bus station thieves who snatched baggage from the hands of unwary travelers, and she could just as well lose the bracelet that way.

Marivic folded her hand around the bracelet. She thought about her father. She imagined him shopping for it and thinking of her and carrying it halfway around the world to place it on her wrist. Just touching it now made her feel confident and secure, as if it carried some of her father's strength and love.

She draped the bracelet over her left wrist, and fastened the clasp.

Some of the passengers were standing in the aisle now, impatient. Marivic looked to the front and saw that the bus was pulling into the terminal. It rolled to a stop. The front door huffed open.

Marivic waited until most of the passengers had left. Then she grasped the handle of the bag and stepped out into the aisle. She walked up to the front of the bus and into the thick, pungent air of Manila.

Two

A rap on his bedroom door woke Ilya Andropov. He had given orders to be awakened as soon as the deed was done. Within a few seconds he was conscious and aware, ready to operate.

"Done?" he asked.

"Done," said the voice on the other side of the door.

"Coffee," Andropov said.

He came out several minutes later, a red silk robe over black silk pajama bottoms. Andropov was an elegant man, nails manicured, his stylishly cut hair maintained with a weekly trim. But his lips pursed in a perpetual sneer, and his eyes and his manner were completely without warmth. He had the appearance of a man both prim and vicious.

He walked down the hall to his office, in a walled residential compound in the Malate district of Manila. Waiting on his desk was a glass French press filled with dark coffee. He poured out a cup and picked up the telephone. He punched in a call to a number in the United States. But the routing was indirect. It ran through an Internet connection, into a landline relay from Chechnya to Moscow, again across an Internet trunk to London, from where it followed the usual pathway into the domestic circuits in the U.S.

Though the call quality was often poor, with a lag of several seconds, this arrangement ensured that the call could not be tracked to its source.

A woman's voice came through from the other end, a curt "Yes." Formalities were not required. She was speaking on a cell phone reserved for this purpose.

"We have what you are seeking," Andropov said. His English was crisp.

Her reply came back several seconds later: "I'll make the transfer."

"The price is now fifteen."

"What? We had an arrangement!"

"That was for an item of ordinary quality. This one is exceptional. It's literally a one-in-a-million specimen. You can't do better."

Because of the transmission lag, speaking on the connection was like using a two-way radio. When Andropov stopped talking, he found that the woman at the other end had already launched into a diatribe. He caught the last few words:

"—filthy thieving motherfucker, I'm not paying it! Do you know what I can do with fifteen million dollars?!"

"If you don't complete this sale, I suppose you can do anything you want with the money. At least for as long as you are able."

This stopped her. Andropov knew that it would. He often had this discussion with prospective clients, and it always ended the same: with Andropov getting what he wanted.

"How do I know it's true, about the quality?" she asked. "All I have is your word."

"We both depend on mutual trust and discretion," Andropov said. This was an exaggeration: Andropov and his group were much less vulnerable than his clients. But it sounded good, and it always seemed to soothe those who needed reassurance.

Andropov heard a long silence, longer than the circuit lag.

"I can't get it right away," she said finally. "It'll take a couple of days. I'm not that liquid. Fifteen million, I wasn't ready for that."

"I'll be watching for it," Andropov said.

He ended the call, sat back, and lifted the cup of coffee to his lips. Still hot. Fifteen million in less time than coffee needs to cool. Given the choice between life and cash, even those who truly love cash will always choose life. Just a chance of life was good enough. The choice had to become real, that was all. Then things became clear.

What a business, he thought.

THREE

Lorna Valencia was already awake, fixing breakfast for Ronnie before he left to harvest copra on the steep mountainsides beyond the village. She kept her phone in a pocket of her housedress, expecting that Marivic would call at any time, as soon as she arrived in Manila. This should have happened already, she thought. But perhaps the bus was delayed.

When Ronnie woke and came to eat, he showed her the last text from Marivic:

arrived

The message was almost an hour old. This irritated Lorna. An hour in Manila, and the girl couldn't find a few moments to contact her mother? Her brother, but not her mother?

She tapped out a brief message to Marivic, trying not to seem upset, and brought Ronnie his usual breakfast: a plate of fried eggs, fried rice, and fresh fruit. As Ronnie ate, Lorna waited for a reply. Nothing.

The boy scooped up the last of the food, swallowed, and stood. He left his phone on a wicker stand by the front door—there was no signal up on the mountainside—and picked up his bolo knife, which hung from a peg beside the door.

"She's probably asleep already," Ronnie told Lorna as he left. "She'll send another text when she's awake."

"I hope you're right," she said.

The entire day passed. No text, no call.

When Ronnie came home, Lorna waggled her phone in his face.

"You were wrong," she said. "Nothing."

"She's probably busy," he said. "Wait until she has some time tonight."

By 9:00 p.m.—their bedtime—there was still no text.

"Something must be wrong with her phone," Ronnie said.

"She could borrow someone's phone for a text."

"Maybe she doesn't know anyone yet."

Lorna laughed out loud at this: the idea that Marivic, friendly and vivacious, could be in Manila for an entire day and not make a single acquaintance.

That night she slept fitfully, woke earlier than usual, and immediately reached for the phone, hoping to find a message from overnight.

Nothing.

"Mommy, she's there, she's all right," Ronnie said as he left the house. "You'll hear from her today."

She heard doubt in his voice, though. Something was wrong, and he knew it too.

That morning, after the little ones had gone to school, Lorna put on a Sunday dress. She dropped Ronnie's phone into her purse, along with her own, in case Marivic called him first. She walked out to the highway and caught a local bus to Tacloban.

She found the Optimo office and took a seat at the desk across from the plump woman.

"It's about my daughter. Marivic Valencia is her name."

"You're her mother?" the woman said. "I'm glad to see you."

"Why? Is something wrong? It's more than a day since she got to Manila, and I haven't—"

The woman put up a hand. Stop. She reached for a phone, punched in a speed-dial number.

"The main office thinks I stole the expense money and the fare," the woman said as she waited with the phone against her ear. "They chewed my ass yesterday, now they can chew yours."

She spoke into the phone: "Yes. About the Valencia girl. Her mother is here."

The plump woman handed the phone to Lorna, but before Lorna could speak she heard a female voice in the earpiece, commanding and brittle.

"You're the mother of Marivic Valencia? That little thief is your daughter?"

"Marivic is not a thief."

"She took expense money and a bus ticket, but she never went to Manila."

"Of course she did. I watched her get on the bus," Lorna said.

"So you say, but she wasn't there when it reached Manila—"

"She sent a text—"

"—and now I'm out the cost of the bus ticket and the cash."

"Someone was supposed to meet her at the terminal. Maybe they missed her. Maybe they were late."

"That was me," said the voice on the phone. "And I wasn't late. I was there when the bus pulled in. I was waiting. There was no Marivic."

"Something's not right."

"Yes. A girl takes bus fare and a thousand pesos and promises to arrive on the bus, then never arrives—*that's* not right."

"So what happened to her?"

"Who knows? Maybe she met a smooth-talking pimp on the bus and decided that his job sounded easier."

"Not my Marivic!"

"It wouldn't be the first time."

"What am I supposed to do?"

The voice on the phone said, "I should hold you responsible for our loss. But what good would it do? So just go away now. Stop harassing my employee. This matter is at an end."

The voice clicked off in Lorna's ear, and she handed the phone across the desk.

"You have to help me," Lorna said.

"What can I do?" the plump woman said. "They say she wasn't on the bus. They were there, I wasn't. Neither were you."

"I want to speak to someone else," Lorna said.

"Who?" said the woman. She spread her arms wide, taking in the small room. "Who else do you see? There is only me and my boss in Manila, and you just spoke to her. You have to go. Now."

The woman glared at Lorna, adamant.

Lorna got up and walked out. She stood on the sidewalk and considered her options. Really, there was just one place left to go. She had hoped that she wouldn't need it. Like most Filipinos, she avoided contact with the Philippine National Police, believing that no good could come of it.

But she saw no choice.

The Tacloban headquarters of the PNP was three blocks from the Optimo office. From the front desk, Lorna was shunted to the office of a PNP sergeant who—to her surprise—seemed friendly and receptive. He took notes and nodded sympathetically as she told him her story. Lorna showed him the series of texts on Ronnie's phone and related what the plump woman at Optimo had told her.

"It's now more than thirty hours since Marivic arrived in Manila. And I know that she arrived."

"But no contact in that time?" the sergeant asked.

"None at all. No calls, no texts. I'm worried sick."

"I'm sure that you are," the sergeant said. "My oldest is fifteen. I can just imagine."

"You'll help?" Lorna said.

"I'll put together a report today and send it to Manila. If there's any mischief, that's where it occurred."

"Thank you. And what will Manila do?"

"Ah, Manila, that's the problem." The sergeant gave a small, pained grimace.

"What problem?"

"In Manila they are very busy. Many, many reports and requests." He gestured toward his notes. "And in this case, we don't even know that there has been a crime. Not that I doubt you. But I don't think this will get much attention. Sorry to say it, but you shouldn't expect much from Manila."

"That's all? You can't do anything more?"

"I will pray for the safe return of your beloved child," the sergeant said, and he got up and showed her to the door. And that was it.

That evening, when Ronnie returned home from work, Lorna told him about her trip to Tacloban and what had happened there at the agency office and with the police.

"This is so frustrating!" she said. "The truth is in Manila, and here we are in Leyte!"

The night was long and tortured. Lorna, in her bed, kept imagining Marivic alone and frightened and beyond her reach. She could feel Marivic crying out for her. It was like a fever dream, endlessly repeated, but it had no details because she had no idea where Marivic could be. All Lorna could see was Marivic's face, pleading with her, surrounded by a murky, threatening cloud.

Lorna was already exhausted when she woke before dawn. She reached for her phone, checking for messages. Nothing.

She shuffled across the hall to the small room that Ronnie shared with his younger brother, Ernie.

She said, "Ron. Wake up. I'm making breakfast."

Ernie answered: "Ronnie isn't here. He left already."

Lorna went to the front door. Ronnie's bolo still hung from the peg. But his phone was gone.

Up on a shelf was the old coffee jar where he kept his copra money. She looked inside: empty.

She stepped out into the cool darkness.

Out toward the highway, a diesel engine thrummed softly. Then a mechanical groan, and a chuff of compressed air. She knew that sound: it was the Manila bus stopping for a passenger, throwing open its front door.

"Ronnie . . . ? Ronnie, *no*!"

She began to run toward the highway.

"Ronnie!"

The door banged shut. In a few seconds, the diesel sound picked up, louder, rising and falling, growling up through the gears as it pulled away.

Lorna hurried back to the house. She found her phone and immediately dialed her son. After a few rings, he finally answered.

"Ronnie, come back. Tell the driver to stop, you come back!"

"No, Mommy. I can't do that."

"What are you doing?"

"Don't you know?" he said. "The truth is in Manila. I'm going to find Marivic."

HARVEST DAY

–7

FOUR

———

In an office suite on the top floor of a lodge on the south shore of Lake Tahoe, Nevada, Raymond Favor stood beside the desk where Arielle Bouchard was working. He looked down and picked up a framed snapshot.

Arielle was astonished. The photo had sat there for several years, and Favor had never taken notice. She knew he was aware of the photo. Favor missed nothing. He had just never chosen to acknowledge it.

Now he was studying it, giving it full attention.

The photo had been taken sixteen years earlier, on a very hot July afternoon. It showed Arielle and Favor—then twenty-two and twenty-eight years old—with two other men at an outdoor bar, all four of them grinning at the camera and hoisting their drinks high in a boozy salute.

"That was a great day," Arielle said.

Favor nodded almost imperceptibly as he peered down at the photo in his hands.

"You think about those times?" Favor said.

"I think about the good parts."

"I would do that if I could," Favor said. "But it doesn't work for me. So I try to just leave it alone."

"We have plenty to be proud of."

"That's getting into dangerous ground," he said. "If you tally the right and the wrong, I'm not sure we come out looking so good."

"Done is done, Ray. My advice, let go of the bad parts, hang on to what made you feel good."

He said, "That's where I run into trouble. Because the really bad stuff, the shit that keeps you awake at night if you dwell on it . . . I loved it. I mean, I *loved* it. I was doing what I was born to do. I was a natural."

Favor gave the photo a last long look and replaced it on the desk. He said, "So you see my problem. The feel-good times, the nightmare scenes—I can't tell 'em apart. For me they're one and the same."

The four in the photo could have been a study group of graduate students relaxing after a successful round of final exams, or longtime friends toasting a wedding engagement. They seemed that familiar together, standing hip against hip, free arms draped over one another's shoulders. In fact, they had met as a group just the day before and were celebrating their first collective success as clandestine agents in training.

Arielle was second from the left in the photo, standing tall and straight even after three beers. Born and raised in Boston, she was the daughter of a French mathematician and his Senegalese wife. Arielle had dazzling green eyes, a mocha complexion, and a regal profile.

To Arielle's right was Alex Mendonza, Oahu born, with the typically Hawaiian riot of ancestral blood: Irish, Polynesian, Japanese, Filipino. He was twenty-five years old on that afternoon, squat and thick necked and muscular, with a face like an Olmec head come to life.

To Arielle's immediate left in the photo was Winston Stickney, the son of Virgin Islanders who had emigrated to Brooklyn. At thirty-one, he was the oldest in the group. A receding hairline added a few more years to his apparent age. He wore glasses with thick black rims and stood in a slightly awkward slouch, and his clothing was exceptionally unstylish, a white shirt over baggy gabardine trousers. It was the look of an ascetic intellectual, and this wasn't deceiving: he held advanced degrees in engineering and Russian literature. But Stickney was also a warrior, a former U.S. Army Ranger, an expert in high explosives and demolition, a decorated marksman with pistol and rifle.

To Stickney's left stood Ray Favor. He was an inch over six feet, broad shouldered and trim. His face was taut, with a sharp jaw and angular brow over deep-set eyes. His ruddy complexion and straight black hair were legacies of a Nez Percé grandmother who had married into a family of ranchers in eastern Oregon. Like Stickney, Favor had an impressive military background, with eight years in the U.S. Marines, the last five of them in the USMC Recon battalion. Ray Favor was the most focused person Arielle had ever known, and his intensity was obvious in the photo. Even in celebration, Favor's eyes had a predatory glint, feral and fierce. He seemed ready to pounce.

After a year of individual preparation, they had been brought together as a group for the first time that weekend to take part in a mock field exercise, and they had performed beyond all expectations. It was a critical moment for their future in the covert Bravo Cell program.

Bravo Cell was a rarity among America's security and intelligence agencies. It was a secret entity that actually remained secret. Its funds were skimmed from the discretionary budgets of the better-known agencies, allowing Bravo to operate off the official ledgers, invisible to committees and commissions. Beginning in the early 1970s, Bravo sent teams of three to five agents into foreign lands under deep cover to undertake the nation's riskiest and most sensitive tasks, the darkest of black ops: kidnapping, sabotage, assassination. Bravo agents were multilingual, highly intelligent, adaptable, and resourceful. They were also fully deniable. They traveled plausibly under the passports of various nations, performing missions that often required them to remain undercover for weeks.

The program's name was never officially explained, but the dry inside joke was that Bravo—the military's phonetic "B"—actually stood for "buried." It could refer to a team's operational status, so deep undercover that it disappeared. But for an unsuccessful cell, "buried" was literally the outcome. No rescue was forthcoming if Bravo agents were exposed and captured. From the U.S. government, a compromised Bravo agent could expect only disavowal.

When a Bravo cell went undercover, it was cut off

from outside aid, its members totally dependent on one another. A mistake by any one of them usually meant torture and death for all. The arrangement demanded absolute trust and loyalty within the team. The directors of the program studied individual trainees for about a year before matching them to prospective teams for a second year of training as a group. These assignments were tentative, and the trainers often tinkered with team rosters, seeking the elusive personal chemistry that was essential to a cell in the field.

But from the first day they met as a group, nobody tinkered with the team of Bouchard, Favor, Stickney, and Mendonza. Their collective strength as a team—their *rightness*—was obvious to all who observed them.

After a year together in training, completing a series of increasingly difficult mock assignments, they received their first actual mission. This was a noteworthy event. In more than twenty years, Bravo trainers had sent only eighteen teams out into the world on their missions of deception and mayhem and death. From that day forward, the team of Bouchard, Favor, Stickney, and Mendonza would forever be known among themselves, and to their few handlers and superiors, as Bravo One Nine.

After he put the photo back on Arielle's desk, Favor went into his office and shut the door.

Something was wrong with him. Arielle could sense it.

He had been acting oddly for about a week and a half, preoccupied and distant. It was totally out of character. In the sixteen years that she had known him, Favor was always fully engaged, always completely in the moment. Always.

And now this unreal exchange as he held the photo in his hands. *The shit that keeps you awake at night if you dwell on it.* He had never before spoken this way about his time with One Nine.

Two hours passed, and Favor didn't come out.

The office building had once been a lodge, the main residence of a luxury vacation compound. Favor had bought the property six years earlier and converted the lodge to an informal office building, the headquarters of his private investment holding company. The company had five full-time employees, of whom Arielle was by far the most important. It was a minuscule staff relative to the company's revenues, which for the previous twelve months totaled nearly thirty million dollars.

Ray Favor was a very rich man.

His career as an investor had begun ten years earlier, when the members of Bravo One Nine resigned after five years of service, a consensus decision.

Favor was then thirty-four years old. He had a modest inheritance and some savings from unspent salary that had accumulated during his time undercover. He also owned a quarter share of $2.6 million in Krugerrands that the cell had acquired and secretly cached several years earlier, during one of their missions. It was money that no living soul would

ever miss. Covert operations occasionally created
such opportunities. When they disbanded, the stash
of gold became a severance bonus for the four members of One Nine, none of whom had ever known
any employer besides the U.S. government.

Favor used part of the money as down payment
on an apartment block in Seattle. Within weeks, he
sold the building and tripled his investment. He
tripled it again with a quick series of land swaps
and purchases. Favor found that he had an uncanny
sense of impending value in real estate. His cunning
and guile and unshakable nerve, developed over
years under deep cover, also served him well. They
made business almost too easy.

He continued to prosper. After about a year, Arielle accepted his offer to work with him. The salary
was generous, and she received a ten percent share of
his newly formed holding company. And she earned
it. Arielle ran his office, kept his books, hired his staff,
dealt with his bankers and attorneys.

When Favor bought the Tahoe property, he chose
a corner room in the lodge for his personal office.
The room had a magnificent westerly view that took
in the lake with the gray granite ramparts of the Sierras on the far side. It was a few steps from Arielle's
office, a larger room with a slightly less expansive
view.

From her desk, Arielle looked across a hall to the
half-open door of Favor's office. Now three hours
had passed since he had disappeared inside. Not a
word, not a rustle. This was unusual. Favor didn't

like to be desk-bound. He often ducked in and out of his room a dozen times a day, prowling the building, pacing around the property outside.

She shuffled through a stack of folders, chose one, and walked out and across the hall.

She paused at his door.

Favor's office was dark and completely still. She must have somehow missed him slipping out.

Then she noticed a shadowy figure at one edge of the big window, standing so quietly, so completely motionless, that she had to look twice to be sure. At first she thought that he was gazing outside, absorbed in the view. But the slump of his shoulders and the cant of his head, and his eerie stillness, made Arielle think that he wasn't really seeing the lake at all.

Ray Favor was zoning out. She paused at the threshold, expecting him to notice her at any time. Favor was always alert to the presence of others, and Arielle knew that his hyperawareness had preserved his life more than once. But now he seemed oblivious. Several seconds passed, and he still didn't move. She felt like an intruder, a voyeur to some private, unguarded moment.

She stepped into the office, moving briskly, making more noise than necessary as she crossed the hardwood floor. This finally got his attention. His head turned toward her as she approached his desk.

"Appraisals on the Santa Barbara purchase," Arielle said, showing him the sheaf of papers. "No surprises, but you might want to review it anyway."

He watched her as she put the folder on his desk.

"And the Tulsa boys will be here in forty-five minutes," she said. "You want something to eat first?"

After a pause that seemed much too long, Favor shook his head.

"Nothing?" she said.

"I'm not hungry."

"Hey, Ray," she said. "You okay?"

"Sure," he said.

"Something on your mind?"

"No more or less than usual."

"Right," she said. She started to leave and was almost out the door when he spoke again.

He said, "Life's a bitch—you know that, Ari?"

She stopped and manufactured a smile as she turned to look back at him.

"That's the rumor," she said, trying to keep her tone light. But she was thinking: *Who are you? And what have you done to Ray Favor?*

It happened again an hour later.

They were in a conference room on the second floor. Favor sat in a leather swivel chair at one end of a long table with Arielle beside him, taking notes, as three developers from Tulsa made a presentation at the other end.

The developers wanted to build a luxury hunting retreat and gun club on 2,800 acres of scrubland in southeast Kansas that Favor had owned for about a year. Rough and rocky, the land had never been cultivated. This had made it inexpensive for Favor to buy, and it was perfect for the developers' plans. Favor had declined their offer to buy the land at what would have been a quadruple profit. Now they were back with an offer of an equity position, part ownership. It would be a windfall for Favor.

One of the developers, a man named Terry, was pitching the proposal, ticking off details as he paged through a PowerPoint deck on a wall-mounted LCD.

He stopped halfway through one of the screens.

He said: "Mr. Favor? Sir?"

Arielle looked at Favor and saw that he was leaning back in the chair, fingers laced behind his head.

His eyes were closed.

"Mr. Favor? Should I repeat that last part? I'll be glad to go back a couple of screens," Terry said. He sounded slightly peevish.

Favor didn't respond right away—at least, not so that anyone else would notice. But Arielle caught the slight rumpling of his mouth and the tightening at the corners of his eyes. He was back in focus now. And he wouldn't like that tone.

Favor had an intimidating presence. It was in his growl of a voice, in the intensity of his stare. He usually tried to mute the intimidation. Most times he was exceedingly polite, almost courtly. But he could also use the effect to his advantage. Some women—many women—swooned for that air of menace. And it gave him an edge in business negotiation.

Arielle knew that he was about to turn it on.

He opened his eyes. His expression was blank as he unlaced his fingers and slowly brought his hands down to the armrests of the chair. He began to lean forward, gradually bringing his gaze down until he was eye to eye with Terry.

Favor squared his shoulders. The impatience drained out of Terry's face as Favor fixed him with an unblinking look.

Terry blinked and nervously licked his lips.

That'll cost you, Arielle thought.

"This is all in the proposal, right?" Favor said. "Anything here that's not in the package?"

"No," Terry said. "This is just a more visual presentation."

"I don't care about visuals," Favor said.

"I'm sorry," Terry said.

"I read the proposal. I liked it."

"That's great," Terry said.

"You did your homework. You have a good idea; I think it'll fly."

"We have a deal?" Terry said.

"I want three and a half points at the front end," Favor said. "Then we have a deal."

"That's a lot, three and a half points."

"I don't need an answer right away. You take a little time, talk it over. Give me your answer by six o'clock."

"Three and a half points seems excessive," Terry said. "Can we meet somewhere in the middle?"

"Three and a half points, nonnegotiable. I know that sounds tough, but I think you'll see there's enough left to still make it worth doing." Favor stood. "Or not. I really don't give a shit."

The three developers were staring at him. Arielle was staring at him.

"Excuse me?" Terry said.

"Do it, don't do it, it's really all the same to me." He looked at Arielle. "I'll be out the rest of the day." To the developers he said, "You guys have a good one."

He turned and walked out of the room.

The developers left grumbling, but less than an hour later they called back to accept the deal. Arielle took the message and phoned Favor with the news.

"You now have three partners in Tulsa," she said.

"I figured."

"That was quite a move. 'I really don't give a shit'—that's playing some hardball."

"It wasn't a play," Favor said. "I mean it. I really don't care if we do it or not."

"Ray, this is a nice deal. Could be extremely nice."

"Uh-huh. How nice, you think?"

"You're asking me?" she said. "I think in a year you make back what you already have in the land. After that, you have a nice, steady revenue stream. I'd say six hundred K per annum as a floor, maybe a million a year in a good year, with no obligation for you except to cash the checks. Not bad for some raggedy-ass trash land that you bought with fifty thousand down."

"That's about how I read it," he said.

"You're complaining about that?" she said.

"Not complaining. It just doesn't matter."

"I don't understand."

"What does it change?" Favor said. "Does my life get better? Will a million a year let me do anything I couldn't already do?"

"I guess you already do whatever you want."

"There you go," he said. "I mean, it sounds great, six hundred K, a million a year. There was a time when that would have mattered. Not anymore. Not even close. Ergo, it doesn't matter. Ergo, I really don't give a shit whether the deal happens or not."

Arielle didn't know what to say.

"You want it?" Favor said after a few moments. "Take it, it's yours."

"No. It's not my deal."

"Up to you. I'll see you tomorrow, Ari. I'll be in around noon. We get to do this all over again. The wheels on the bus go round and round."

He clicked off.

Arielle listened to the silence in her earpiece, then called two numbers in quick succession.

In a workshop surrounded by a redwood forest outside Mendocino, California, Winston Stickney was bent over a bench where two vises gripped a shaft of burnished blue steel. He was peering through a welder's mask as he used a plasma arc torch to burn a precise curving cut across the shaft. Stickney was now an artist and sculptor, best known for his intricate installations of welded steel. He was nearly finished with his cut when the phone rang on the wall of the workshop. He heard it dimly over the loud hiss of the torch, but he kept working. When the cut was complete a few seconds later, he put down the torch head, flipped up the mask, and went to pick up the phone.

The second call went to Alex Mendonza at the personal protection company in Los Angeles. Mendonza was in a meeting with the representative of a hip-hop recording artist, working out the security details for the rapper's visit from New York. Mendonza's assistant picked up the call but sent it through to Mendonza when she recognized Arielle's voice.

Arielle linked Stickney and Mendonza in a conference call.

She said, "Something is up with Ray. He's not being Ray. Maybe it's nothing, but it bothers me, and having you two around for a couple of days might do him some good."

"I can be there tonight," Mendonza said. "Let me find a flight."

"Five hours' drive for me," Stickney said. "I just need to lock up here."

"Tomorrow is fine," she said.

"Okay," Mendonza said. "Tomorrow."

"Tomorrow it is," Stickney said.

When he spoke with Arielle, Ray Favor was headed west on Highway 50, into the mountains, behind the wheel of a four-wheel-drive pickup truck. A few miles beyond the summit, he turned off the highway and went down a narrow road. Ahead, a vertical rock wall rose five hundred feet into a cloudless blue sky.

A mile and a half farther down the road, he reached the small campground at the foot of the wall. Favor was glad to see that the campground was empty so far. The Sierras were his refuge, his getaway, and he got away as often as possible. Lake Tahoe was only a few minutes away from the heart of the range. But the accessibility had a big draw-back: it meant that the trails and peaks were easily available to everyone else who lived and worked in the area, and to all of Lake Tahoe's annual millions of visitors. Highway 50 was a main route across the mountains to the San Francisco Bay Area, and this campground was often full by the mid-afternoon of a summer day.

Favor parked as far as he could get from the campground entrance, got out, and walked to the back of the truck. He unlocked the rear window of the fiberglass shell that covered the bed, and let down the tailgate. The bed was full of camping equipment and outdoor gear. He kept it ready to go.

Favor changed into a T-shirt and a pair of run-ning shorts and slipped on a pair of rock-climbing shoes. They were of heavy nylon fabric, cut to an exaggerated point around the big toe. The soles were a smooth, soft black rubber that wrapped around the heel and up the sides of the foot and toes.

Favor had been a climber since he was a teenager, scaling boulders and short buttes on his grandpar-ents' ranch in eastern Oregon. Favor rarely visited a gym or weight room. Climbing shaped his body and his mind. It developed strength and balance and ingenuity. He usually climbed alone, without ropes. When he was clinging to a rock wall without protection, fifty or a hundred feet or more above the ground, he entered a state of calm that he could find no other way.

He had been craving that calm all day.

Favor tied the shoes tight, strapped on a belt that carried a pouch of powdered chalk, and walked to the base of the high wall. Lover's Leap, it was called, a Tahoe landmark. It was a sheer reef of granite, laced by fractures and ribbed by sills of dark igneous rock. For several minutes he stretched and flexed while he studied the webwork of cracks and protrusions on the face.

Favor walked a couple of paces to one side. An inch-wide sill ran about waist high. He jumped, seeming to throw himself at the rock face. His left foot caught the sill, and the fingertips of his right hand found a narrow seam.

He began to climb.

Favor traversed the face for about an hour, back and forth, up and down, as much as two hundred feet above the ground. He didn't go higher. That was for the morning. He planned to make a predawn ascent, climbing by the light of a full moon that would still be high in the sky, reaching the top in time to watch the sunrise.

As he worked across the face, a car rolled into the campground below and stopped. Favor was splayed against the wall, legs spread, arms extended in a wide V above his head. But the handholds were secure, and his feet had found a shelf nearly as wide as his shoes. He paused to rest his aching calves.

Favor glanced down at the car. Two teenage girls and a boy had gotten out and were standing around a picnic table. Giggles and loud chatter filtered up from below.

The noise would have grated on him if he had been down there with them. But from up here they belonged to a separate universe, and they ceased to exist for him the instant he shifted his attention back to his body and the space it occupied. The fires had burned out in his calves, and his breathing was under control.

He began to move again.

Sarah Jean Athold knew it would be trouble: her friend Missy, and Wallace, the semi-geeky senior from biology lab, and the fifth of Captain Morgan that Missy had coaxed Wallace into buying. Trouble—Sarah Jean could see it coming. But she went with them anyway. They bombed out of Carson City in Missy's Grand Am, heading straight up to the lake after their last class of the day. They brought Wallace because he had the ID and looked twenty-one, kind of. But Sarah Jean knew that Wallace had been invited for another reason too. He was going to be Missy's admiring audience. Or helpless victim, depending on how you looked at it. Missy was a huge flirt, nonstop and indiscriminate. Sarah Jean sometimes joked that Missy would flirt at a funeral. With the corpse.

That was just the usual everyday attention-whoring. After a couple of drinks, Missy would turn strip-club raunchy. Always just teasing. Missy never actually went hard-core. They had a word for it. Sarah Jean called her Lut. That was slut without the "s." One letter short of all the way.

They had headed into the mountains because Wallace said he always had good luck at a liquor store in South Lake Tahoe. The ID worked. Wallace came out with the Captain and a two-liter of Coke and a bottle of butterscotch schnapps. He led them to the campground, where he said they could party without getting hassled.

Wallace passed Sarah Jean a rum and Coke in a plastic cup. Sarah Jean drank it in a hurry, then got a second. While Missy and Wallace laughed and hooted at the picnic table, Sarah Jean took her drink and wandered around the campground, smelling the lodgepole pines that surrounded the campground, feeling small as she craned her neck to look up at the big cliff.

That was when she saw him, the crazy dude way up on the endless slab of rock. Like a bug stuck to a windshield. He was going to fall any second now, Sarah Jean just knew it, and she told herself that when it happened she was going to turn away because she didn't want to see it happen, and she would cover her ears because she didn't want to hear him hit.

But he didn't fall. He was moving. At first it was

just one leg sliding a few inches to one side, then an agonizing reach with an arm, then suddenly a quick burst of scuttling across the rock, arms and legs shooting out at crazy angles.

Sarah Jean was going to point him out to the others, but when she looked over at the picnic table, Wallace was throwing his head back and whooping as Missy humped a butt grind against his crotch. Sarah Jean walked over and poured herself another drink. They weren't going anywhere for a while.

Soon the lodgepole pines were throwing long shadows across the campground. The climber on the rock came down and walked to his truck, put on a sweater, and cooked a meal over a camp stove. Sarah Jean went to get one last drink and found that the Captain was gone, the schnapps was gone.

Missy was lap-dancing Wallace.

"We should go," Sarah Jean said.

"No. I'm having fun."

"Lut! Come on, let's go home."

"Not a lut. Tonight I'm a four-letter girl."

"Sweety, it's getting late."

"No!"

"She's right," Wallace said. "We can't drive yet. We're blasted. We have to sober up some."

"I don't want to sober up," Missy said. "I'm just getting started."

Now she was rubbing her chest in his face. Wallace pulled back and looked at Sarah Jean.

"It'll be all right," he said. "Give me an hour, I'll be good to go."

The sun was all the way down now, and Sarah Jean was getting chilly. She went into the Grand Am and sat there alone. She watched the climber take his sleeping bag into the woods. She watched Missy and Wallace making out at the picnic table. *They'll get cold soon,* she thought. They would come into the car, they would all sit and wait for a while until one of them was able to drive, and she would soon be home.

No problem, she thought.

Then the Demons arrived.

Favor was still awake in his sleeping bag, about fifty yards back in the pines. He recognized the sound of Harley engines barking through unmuffled pipes. At least four bikes, he thought as he listened to them turn off the access road and roll through the campground. He counted five for sure as they shut down one after the other.

A couple of minutes later the music started, Hank Williams Jr., amp-driven through big speakers, the bass cranked up high.

Shit, he thought.

He wondered whether he should get up and go home. He didn't want to lie awake here for hours. But he had been planning the early-morning climb for a long time. A late-rising full moon, perfect weather—he didn't know when he would get the chance again.

And if tonight was like other recent nights, he would be lying awake at home anyway. At least here he had the sky and the stars.

He rolled over onto one side, turning his back to the bass that was thumping through the trees. With one ear pressed to the ground and the sleeping bag pulled over his head, the noise wasn't so bad. He willed himself to block out what remained. He promised himself that nothing would disturb him tonight. Not noise, not doubts, not nagging memories. He imagined himself rising in a few hours, refreshed and full of energy, walking to the base of the cliff in the moonlight and beginning his ascent. The image brought him peace. He could feel himself getting drowsy, and he let go and fell away to deep sleep.

But he woke right away when the girl screamed.

Sarah Jean saw that there were five men on motorcycles and two women in the van that followed them in. The men wore grubby denims and leather vests with patches on the back that read in Gothic lettering:

DEMONS M.C.
Stockton

The women threw open the rear doors of the van and set out coolers of beer and bottles of liquor. Music began to boom from speakers in the van's rear doors. The men scattered around the campground, gathering firewood, and in a short time they were standing around a bonfire that blazed flames as high as their heads, lighting up half the campground.

Sarah Jean watched it all from the car. She saw

the Demons riding in, gawking at Missy straddling Wallace as they kissed at the picnic table. The first rider in the pack pulled in just a few camp spots from Missy and Wallace and the Grand Am, and the others followed. Sarah Jean didn't like having the bikers parked so close to them when nearly the entire campground was empty. It seemed to bother Wallace too. He lifted Missy off his hips and stood, took her by the arm, and tried to lead her to the car.

Mistake, Sarah Jean thought. Missy did not like to be pushed around. She yanked her arm away. Wallace grabbed her arm again, Missy shook him off harder. He reached a third time. She was ready for it. She swung and hit him, a hard slap that landed square on his cheek, loud enough that a couple of the bikers looked over and grinned.

Wallace left Missy and got into the car.

"Well, this sucks majorly," he said.

Missy perched at the end of the picnic table, her legs drawn up in front of her, resting her chin on her knees. She looked cold.

Sarah Jean got out and walked to her.

"Missy?" said Sarah Jean. "It's time to go."

Missy didn't answer. She was looking over at the bikers. A couple of them were watching her. They were silhouetted against the campfire. Its flames licked high, throwing up tiny embers that glowed briefly against the sky before they flared out. Sarah Jean had to admit that the fire looked pretty good right now.

Sarah Jean said, "Missy, I want to go home. Now."

Missy turned and flipped the keys at Sarah Jean's feet.

"Then go," she said, and she hopped off the table and started toward the Demons. One of them held out a beer to her, and she took it and joined them around the campfire. She stepped into an open space between two of the men.

Sarah Jean returned to the car, and when she looked back Missy was dancing at the fire, head thrown back and swaying.

One of the bikers stepped behind her, moving in close. Missy didn't seem to notice until he wrapped his thick arms around her. She squealed an uncertain laugh. He squeezed her, she started to fight loose, he picked her up. Now she was yelling, kicking her legs, as he carried her to the open rear of the van, with the second biker following.

In the car, Sarah Jean turned toward Wallace. He was staring out the window, stunned and transfixed.

"Do something," Sarah Jean said. "Wallace, *do something.*"

Missy shouted, *"Help!"* Shrill, sober, scared.

The bikers threw her into the van and clambered in and pulled a curtain across the back.

Like that she was gone, swallowed up. The other three Demons, even the two women, acted as if nothing had just happened. As if nothing were happening now behind the curtain.

Wallace was staring out the window, at the empty space beside the campfire where Missy had been a few moments earlier.

"Wallace," Sarah Jean said, trying to stay calm. "We have to get her, Wallace. You hear?"

Wallace didn't look at Sarah Jean. His face was zombie blank.

"Holy shit," he was murmuring. "Holy shit, holy shit, holy shit."

"Wallace, I'm going out there."

Wallace reached and stopped her as Sarah Jean started to open her door.

"No," he said. "Stay."

He got out and sleepwalked toward the van. The three Demons formed a line in his path, blocking him.

Wallace stopped in front of them.

Missy screamed. It was like nothing Sarah Jean had ever heard, a long scream, sheer terror piercing the night.

One of the three Demons drove a fist into Wallace's gut. Wallace folded and crumpled.

Sarah Jean got out and ran. She headed toward the far end of the campground, the dark end. The bikers and the campfire were at her back. She was running toward the last place she had seen the crazy climber guy before he disappeared into the woods with his sleeping bag. She was thinking that she would have to search through the woods, shout for him and stumble around in the darkness.

But no. He emerged from the pines before she got there.

He said, "Is she playing?"

"No way," Sarah Jean said.

He ran to his truck, opened the door, took out a metal baseball bat from behind the front seat. Seeing this, something in the way he held the bat, Sarah Jean got a funny feeling. A good feeling. That he was not a ballplayer but that the bat was there just for a time like this, and he had an idea how to use it.

He took off at a lope toward the campfire. *She's in the van,* Sarah Jean wanted to say, but then Missy screamed again, and there was no question about where she was or what was happening to her.

Sarah Jean ran after him. She saw the three Demons poising for a fight, one of them holding a length of chain that reached from his waist almost to the ground.

The climber kept moving toward the three bikers, now just a few strides short of where they stood.

The Demon with the chain stepped forward and whipped it in a vicious chest-high arc. The climber dropped in mid-step, ducked under its sweep, rolled. He popped up in a crouch, suddenly behind them, and swung the bat, one-handed, and caught one of the three behind a knee.

The biker fell as if shot through the heart.

The chain swinger turned around, drew his arm back for another swing. From down in his crouch the climber sprung up, the bat in both hands, holding it upright. He drove it straight up, the thick end finding a spot beneath the chain swinger's jaw as if it belonged there, then continuing upward, jacking the Demon's head back at an impossible angle.

Down he went.

The third one—

The third one had a knife. He was coming in from behind, blocked from the climber's view, slashing the knife up as the chain swinger's body fell away. The tip of the blade swept across the climber's upper torso. To Sarah Jean this looked like something from a ballet, choreographed, the biker's momentum twisting him around, the climber leaning away to avoid the knife, somehow keeping his balance, then bringing the bat around and shoving it forward so that the knob at the handle connected with the back of the biker's skull. It was almost a gentle tap, controlled and precise.

Down he went, number three.

The climber turned toward the van.

The biker women were squealing. Their screeches brought the last two from the van. They came out one after the other, almost too easy. One popped out to look—the bat smashed down across the back of his shoulders, and he tumbled out in a heap. The second one appeared. The climber grabbed him by the hair and pulled him out and rode him, shoving him toward a flat piece of granite embedded in the earth. Sarah Jean was running hard, going for the back of the van, and she was close enough to hear the crunch of bone as the last Demon's face smashed into the stone.

The climber's shirt was torn along a diagonal that the knife had traveled, and blood was spreading from a cut. He spun, looked back at the three on the ground.

No, Sarah Jean saw. Two on the ground. One was rising to his knees, coming up with a pistol in one hand, a black revolver that he brought up at the end of his arm, pointing it at the climber.

Sarah Jean couldn't say exactly what happened next. At least ten or twelve feet separated the two men. Three good strides. Up came the gun, the climber spun and looked down the barrel. And then . . .

. . . then the climber exploded into some wild fast-forward version of movements he had made on the rock, but a thousand times faster now, body twisting, arms and legs shooting out, a water-bug skitter that closed the distance before the biker could react.

All Sarah Jean knew for sure was that on one side of a heartbeat the climber was looking up the barrel of the gun, and before her heart could thump *he had the gun* and the biker was down on the ground, the climber pinning him with a knee against his back while mashing his face into the dirt.

That was with his left hand. His right hand held the pistol. He straightened his arm and thumbed back the hammer as he held the end of the barrel against the biker's head.

Sarah Jean screamed, *"NO!"*

Although the members of Bravo One Nine were broadly trained, each also had an individual specialty. Arielle was an expert in computers and electronics. Alex Mendonza was a master of vehicles: cars, planes, boats—he could fix them and he could drive them. Winston Stickney knew explosives and demolition.

Ray Favor was a killer.

Up-close kind of killing, swift and vicious and personal. To an outsider this might have seemed a trivial ability, but it was prized in fieldwork, and few did it really well. Even trained warriors often feel an internal blink of resistance when the killing takes place within the zone of body heat.

Not Favor. He killed with the ease of flipping a light switch.

Sarah Jean didn't know any of this. But as she watched the climber straighten his right arm and cock the revolver, she knew that he was about to put a bullet in the biker's brain, no problem. And she knew that she didn't want to see it.

Her *"NO!"* stopped him.

He paused, turned his face toward her. She could see him clearly in the campfire light. His eyes were hard, so terrible that she almost couldn't look at them, but she forced herself to do it, make that connection.

She said, "Don't, mister. Please."

He stared at her. His face softened a little. Just enough. He lifted the pistol, carefully eased the hammer down.

Sarah Jean ran to the van to put her arms around her friend.

The wound was superficial. Favor knew it as he sat on a table in the emergency room at South Lake

Tahoe. He might need some stitches along the pectoral, where the blade had sliced in about an eighth of an inch deep, but otherwise the wound was hardly more than a deep scratch.

The ER physician was an attractive Pakistani woman about thirty years old. She cut away his T-shirt and revealed a road map of scars. Three were several inches in length, one bisected by the fresh cut. None were in the usual places for a surgical incision. She also found a small circular indentation at the abdomen, with a matching perforation in his back. They were the scars from a through-and-through bullet wound.

"You've been making a habit of this," she said.

"Not lately."

She swabbed the cut.

"And how are you feeling?" she said.

Favor smiled. "Pretty damn great," he said.

HARVEST DAY
−6

FIVE

About twenty-four hours after Ronnie left for Manila, about the time that he should be reaching Manila, Lorna Valencia was seated at her kitchen table. A woman from the village came to her door and entered the house without knocking. Erlinda was her name. They had known each other since childhood.

"You're awake early," Erlinda said.

"I can't sleep."

"You have a problem."

Of course, everyone was aware that Marivic had disappeared and that now Ronnie was gone. The villagers knew one another's lives down to the aching bunion. A disaster like this would travel on the wind.

"Yes," Lorna said.

"I know someone who may be able to help."

Erlinda was clutching a small, grimy, spiral-bound notebook. She opened it on the dining table. Inside were handwritten names with addresses and telephone numbers.

She had no reading glasses. She leaned so close that her nose nearly touched the paper.

She ran a finger up and down the pages.

"Here!" Erlinda said. "Give me your phone."

Lorna held out the cell phone.

"How much load do you have on here?" Erlinda asked. She meant the balance left on the phone's pre-paid SIM card.

"About two-fifty," Lorna said.

"We'll have to make it quick so you don't run out."

"Run out? Two hundred and fifty pesos?"

"You'll need it all," Erlinda said. "We are calling the United States."

"Nothing's wrong with me," Favor said. "I'm fine. I'm glad to see you—it's been too long—but if that's why you're here, you wasted a trip."

He was sitting with Mendonza and Stickney and Arielle in a gazebo that sat on a wide lawn between the lodge and the shoreline of the lake. It was late afternoon, the day after his encounter at the Lover's Leap campground, and a strip of white bandage showed around the open collar of his shirt.

Favor wasn't talking about his wound, though. He meant his state of mind.

"Ari is concerned," Stickney said. Stickney's voice was quiet and low, with a hint of honey-smooth Caribbean vowels. It was a voice that could have belonged to a midnight deejay on an FM jazz station. Cooler than cool.

"If Ari is worried, *we're* worried," Mendonza said.

Favor said, "Ari is an alarmist."

"Ray," she said. "Mooning around like a sick hound. Crapping out in a meeting. Blowing off a million-dollar deal. Multimillion. Please."

They were watching him, waiting for his response. Mendonza and Stickney sat on either side of Arielle, around an octagonal table in the center of the gazebo. Favor realized that although they spoke on the phone several times a year, he hadn't seen either Mendonza or Stickney in almost four years.

The two men had always been physical opposites: Mendonza blocky and muscular, Stickney slim and spare. Favor, looking at them now, thought at first that the years hadn't changed them much. But he realized this wasn't exactly true. They had become even more intense versions of themselves: Mendonza, an avid weight lifter, was now truly bull-like, with a thick, corded neck and a powerful upper body; Stickney was now completely lean and angular, without an ounce of excess flesh on his bones. His face was drawn, almost ascetic.

Favor said, "I've been in a little funk, that's all," he said. "It happens."

Mendonza gave a derisive snort. "Never saw it happen to you, stud."

Stickney said, "A funk, Ray? Can you be more specific?"

Favor didn't like explaining himself, but he was enjoying the moment, the four of them together again. He couldn't imagine talking this way with anybody else.

"It's like this," he said. "When I started investing, I got some advice from an old fart. He told me that banking the first hundred million is always fun. After that, making money starts to feel like real work. He said that's when you find out if you want to be just rich or filthy stinking rich."

Mendonza said: "And he was . . ."

"Oh, he was filthy stinking rich for sure," Favor said. "I laughed at him. At the time, I couldn't believe that making lots and lots of money would ever be anything but lots and lots of fun."

"You're telling me you hit a hundred mil?" Mendonza said. "Nine figures?"

"Probably about two years ago. I never knew it at the time, though."

"Jesus, Ray. I knew you were doing okay. But a hundred million?"

"It's up around one-sixty now," Favor said.

"Jeeee-zus!"

"And he was right," Favor continued. "It hasn't been fun for a while now. I just never slowed down long enough to realize it."

Stickney was nodding. "I understand that," he said. "You're at a point, you start to sort things out. You wonder how you want to spend the rest of your life."

"Exactly."

"You could give it all away and start over," Mendonza said.

"I've considered that. I might do it. But the point isn't how much money I have. It's how much time is left, and what I'm going to do with it."

Nobody spoke for a couple of minutes. The day was bright but chilly. A steady breeze rippled the water along the shoreline and raised a chop out on the lake. To Favor, the sunlight seemed startlingly bright, and the wind had a delicious bite on the skin. The day was almost painfully beautiful, as if his senses and perception were amplified.

Favor hadn't felt this way for years, and he knew why he felt it today: it was the action in the campground, the swinging of the biker's chain and the sweep of the knife's tip across his chest, the loathing and then the fear in the eyes of the bikers. Climbing provided some of the same jeopardy, but not the pure kill-or-be-killed intensity. As he sat in the gazebo and felt the breeze on his face and watched the sharp glint of sunlight off the rough water of the lake, Favor recalled that exquisite moment when the third Demon had pulled the pistol. Oh, the malevolence in his eyes as he brought the gun up. The surprise, the shock, as Favor sprung across the packed dirt of the campsite and disarmed him, and held the muzzle to his head. No rock wall ever gave him that. Not even close.

Stickney broke the silence: "Ari also says you were talking about One Nine."

"Apparently Ari is a goddamn bottomless fountain of personal intel."

"Looking back? Taking stock?" Stickney said.

"Don't go there," Mendonza said. His tone was bantering, but Favor knew that Mendonza genuinely didn't like this tack. The differences between Mendonza and Stickney were not just physical. Stickney had always been introspective, analytical. A thinker. Mendonza, though intelligent, was most comfortable in the concrete, the here and now.

"Taking stock, yeah, something like that," Favor said to Stickney.

"Worried about how you stand in the karmic ledgers?"

"Don't go *anywhere* near there."

"I don't know about karma," Favor said. "But you look back, you'd like to think that you've left the world at least in no worse shape than it was when you arrived. I can't say that."

Stickney was nodding, his face serious. He understood. Mendonza was shaking his head, arms folded across his big chest. Mendonza really didn't like this kind of talk.

Favor said, "What we did, a lot of it, you never know. Somebody gives you a job, tells you it has to be done. You do the job, they say you did a good thing. But you're never sure. All you see is the blood on the floor. That's real, the rest is guesswork. And some of it, you *know* that it was bad juju. That bothers me. It does, I won't lie."

Mendonza's phone chimed. He took it out, looked at it, and said, "My mother. I have to take this one. Ray, no shit, don't torture yourself over things you can't change."

Mendonza got up and walked some distance away, standing out of earshot as he spoke on the phone.

"Seems you were quite the badass last night," Stickney said.

"A taste of the old times."

"Havoc was wreaked. Bones were broken. Heads were cracked."

"So I'm told."

"Ray Favor at his best," Arielle said.

"At my best, he never would've gotten near me with that knife," Favor said. "But yeah. That was me."

"How was it?" Stickney asked.

"I have to admit, I haven't had so much fun in a long time." Favor found himself grinning.

"No misgivings?" Arielle said.

"Hell no. They were raping that girl. And the way it went down, I'm sure it wasn't their first time. They had it coming. Unmitigated assholes."

"You see our point," Stickney said.

"What point?"

"Favor being Favor isn't necessarily a bad thing. It's all in the situation. Just make sure you're right. I mean locked-down sure, no questions, no gray areas. No goddamn ambiguity. Then when you're clear about that, go out and joyfully be the fearsome badass that you are. You'll have no second thoughts."

"But how often does *that* come along? I only had to wait ten years for last night."

"Some would say that opportunities to do good will come your way when you commit to a righteous path," Stickney said.

"Who says that?"

"It's been said."

"You made that up."

Favor laughed. Arielle laughed.

"Yes, I did," Stickney said. He was laughing too. "But I believe it."

"Tell you what *I* think," Favor said. "I think it's

goddamn cold here. I want to go someplace warm. We ought to get on a jet and fly someplace where we can bake. Seychelles or Koh Samui or Raiatea or wherever. And then raise some decadent hell for a few days."

"When do you want to do that?" Stickney said.

"Tonight. Just go. I can have a G550 sitting on the flight line at South Lake Tahoe in three hours. One thing about money, it makes things happen in a hurry."

"I have no plans," Stickney said.

"Beautiful," Favor said. He looked at Arielle: she grinned and shrugged. Mendonza was walking back to the gazebo, putting his phone away.

"Pack your bags," Stickney said to him. "Apparently Ray wants to sponsor a disgusting blowout at some place you can't spell, and we're going there in style."

"I'd like to," Mendonza said. "But I can't. I'm on a midnight flight to the Philippines. And it's not in style, it's on standby."

"An emergency?" Favor said.

"I have no idea. A kid, a teenage girl, is in trouble. I've been conscripted to help out."

"Your family?"

"Her father is the second cousin of my mother's uncle by marriage. Something like that. Don't laugh. Please. It's a Filipino thing. There is no such thing as a distant relative. Something else about Filipinos. When Mom says you get on a plane, you don't argue, you look for a ticket counter."

"Want me to come along?" Favor said.

"I wouldn't mind a little company," Mendonza said.

"I'm going if Ray goes," Arielle said.

"I'm in," Stickney said.

"You don't have to do this," Mendonza said.

"We were just going to fart around and get a sunburn anyway," Arielle said. "We can do that in the Philippines."

"Okay," Mendonza said. "Great. But I don't think we'll all get on the flight."

"I wouldn't worry about the flight," Arielle said. "We have an alternative."

"What's the story on the girl?" Favor said.

"The girl went missing; nobody knows what happened. Mom was getting this thirdhand, and she was vague on the details. All she said was 'You must go to Manila, the truth is in Manila.' Quote unquote."

Six

Far from Manila, and half a world from Lake Tahoe, Marivic Valencia lay on her cot in a small room with high concrete walls. She was waiting for the sign that would reassure her, tell her that her situation was not as desperate as she feared.

It would be a few bars of a beautiful melody, whistled pitch-perfect by someone who really knew how to whistle. She had been waiting for it almost half a day. But she heard only the incessant churning of the ocean against a shore, and the soft whisk of the ceiling fan, the broad blades turning overhead.

No melody.

It should have happened by now. Every minute that passed, she became more certain that she would never hear it and that she was in a deep pit of trouble, with no way out.

Her ordeal had begun when she stepped off the bus in Manila six days earlier.

She didn't realize it right away. She was aware only of the thick, pungent air that leaves its impression on all first-time visitors to Manila. It was like walking into a wall. All her life, growing up beside the gulf, she had known only fresh air and ocean breezes, nothing like this viscous stew of diesel fumes and sweat and rotting garbage and fish fried in hot oil.

The odor stunned her—that, and the mob of people milling around the concrete apron, and the sounds, and the activity. So much happening at once.

A woman was calling her name.

"Marivic Valencia? You are Marivic, yes?"

The woman stood a few feet away. She was about fifty years old. Slim and well dressed. Gold bangle earrings, too much makeup on a bony, pinched face. An overpowering perfume. Marivic recognized her as a *matrona,* a middle-aged woman with some money—a formidable type.

"Yes," Marivic said, and walked over to the woman. "Are you from Optimo?"

"Were you expecting someone else?"

At first this remark struck Marivic as abrupt, almost sarcastic. But the *matrona* cocked her head and waited for Marivic to speak, and Marivic realized that it was an actual question.

"No," Marivic said. "Only the representative from the agency."

"That's me," the woman said. "Do you have any other bags?"

"Just this one."

The woman crooked a finger over one shoulder, summoning a man who stood waiting behind her. Late forties, hair shorn close to the scalp, stocky, face impassive. He stepped forward and reached for her bag, and Marivic saw that his face was badly pock-marked. His eyes were heavy lidded and unfriendly. He was terrifying without even seeming to try. Marivic stepped back involuntarily as he approached, and he took the bag and turned and began to walk away with it. The woman started after him.

Marivic hesitated. This was all happening so suddenly. The woman stopped and looked back to Marivic and said, "Well? Aren't you coming?"

Marivic didn't know what to say. Something here didn't seem right.

"What? Don't tell me you're scared. Yes, you are, you're frightened," the woman said. "I can tell."

Her tone wasn't so abrupt now. She sounded almost kind.

"I'm Magdalena Villegas," she said. "You can call me Magda. That's Totoy. We're from the agency. You're here for a job, yes? Come on, girl, it's all right."

Marivic began to walk with her. The three of them passed quickly through the terminal, out onto the boulevard, to a dark Toyota van parked at the curb. Totoy put the bag in the back, opened the doors, and slid behind the wheel. Magdalena got in up front, and Marivic found herself alone in the backseat.

Totoy started the engine and pulled out into the boulevard. He glanced back in the mirror. He was looking straight at her, Marivic realized, as if checking her. She caught something in his eyes that she didn't like.

Magdalena turned in her seat, looking back at Marivic.

"You must be hungry," she said. She held out a white paper bag. *"Siopao,"* she said. Steamed pork buns. "We picked them up just for you."

Marivic took the bag and opened it. Two plump buns, still warm. The scent of dough and sweet meat rose from the bag. Marivic realized that, yes, she was very hungry. She took one of the buns and tried to pass the bag back.

"No, that's for you," Magda said. She opened a small insulated cooler between the front seats and gave Marivic a chilled orange drink in a carton. Marivic quickly ate the second *siopao* and drained the drink.

"Is that better?" Magda said.

Marivic nodded. She did feel better. She was relaxing now. Traffic was light, and they were cruising along the boulevard. Manila was clipping past the window, and Marivic knew that she should be getting her first good look at the city, but for some reason it didn't seem to matter at this moment.

Tomorrow, she thought, and she leaned back against the seat.

They continued to drive through the city. Marivic wondered whether Totoy even knew where he was going. The route seemed aimless. Marivic tried to focus, examine what was happening, but she was suddenly so weary that she could barely keep her eyes open. Her head seemed thick.

She was tired. So very tired. She lay back and closed her eyes.

She dozed.

She became aware of Magda and Totoy speaking to each other. The voices came to Marivic as if from the other end of a very large, empty room.

"She's awake," Totoy said.

"Not really."

"You didn't put enough in."

"I did."

"Bullshit, she ate two. She should be out like a stone."

A small corner of Marivic's mind was still awake. From the conversation up front, she understood that she had been drugged. Something in the food.

She fought to stay conscious, hold off the encroaching darkness. A very loud shriek bored into her awareness from somewhere nearby. She forced her eyes half open and saw that the van was on a road beside an airport, an area with maintenance hangars and large jetliners parked on the pavement.

The van was slowing. It stopped in a pool of excruciating bright light. They were at a checkpoint. Someone in a uniform was leaning out the open window of the guard station, examining a document that Totoy held out for inspection.

Marivic tried to shout, to scream. No sound came. She couldn't be sure that her mouth was even open. The guard bent and looked into the van. His face was just on the other side of the window, and he was looking directly at her. She tried to move, thrash, get his attention. But her body didn't respond. Looking at her through the window, the guard saw only a sleepy girl.

The guard handed the document to Totoy and waved him on. The van drove away, out of the light.

They were inside the gate, driving slowly down a row of planes. But not jetliners: these were smaller planes, with propellers. In the van's headlights, Marivic saw a man standing on the tarmac. A white man, a foreigner.

Totoy stopped and got out. Marivic heard the foreigner speaking a rough kind of English, an accent that she didn't know. The foreigner came around and opened the door beside Marivic's seat. He leaned in, shone a flashlight into her eyes, took her pulse.

He reached in, hooked his hands under her shoulders, and pulled her out. He stood her against the van, put an arm around her waist.

"Okay. Now we walk." Again the rough accent. "Not far; you can do it."

He urged her forward, the arm at her waist pushing her along. She managed to get one foot in front of the other for three or four wobbly steps, but then a leg crumpled and she collapsed. The foreigner caught her before she hit the pavement. He scooped her up and carried her in his arms.

He was taking her to a small plane unlike anything she had seen before, with a strange, ungainly shape. A door opened where the wing joined the fuselage. A second foreigner came out, took Marivic, and lifted her and dragged her into the cabin.

There were four seats, two and two. The second foreigner put her in one of the rear seats. He cinched a seat belt around her waist, then fastened several more Velcro straps: one at each upper arm, one at each wrist, one more that bound her ankles together. When he was done, he climbed up front, behind the control wheel.

The other foreigner climbed in and sat beside Marivic. He shone a small light into her eyes, examining the pupils, and held the tips of two fingers against her neck, taking her pulse.

The plane's engine whined, coughed, and caught. It made a racket that filled the small cabin.

In the seat beside Marivic, the foreigner opened a black leather satchel and removed an intravenous needle. He examined Marivic's left forearm, found a vein, inserted the needle. He hung an IV drip bag from a hook above the window, connecting it by tubing to the needle.

The plane was moving now, trundling along. Marivic knew that she was being taken away. She would be lost forever to her family. She thought of them in their little home in the village by the gulf. The image gave her a surge of energy, and she tried to rise out of the seat.

But it was hopeless. The straps held her secure.

She could feel the weariness overtaking her again, the effect of the drugs surging back, and this time she decided not to fight it. Sleep—even endless sleep, if it came to that—seemed preferable to the awful unknown that must be waiting for her at the end of this flight.

Her eyes closed, her head sagged forward. She

was completely unaware a few minutes later when the plane lifted off, rising into the humid air, banking over the water.

The guard waved them through, and Totoy and Magda drove back along the airport access road.

"Where's her phone?" Totoy said.

Magda hesitated before she answered: "She didn't have one."

"They always have a phone."

"Not this one."

"Bullshit. You forgot to look, didn't you?"

"You forgot too."

"It's not my job."

"Should we call them? They're probably still on the ground."

"No," Totoy said. "She isn't in any shape to make calls. But get yourself together. You fuck up the dose, you forget the phone. One of these days, carelessness will bite you in the ass."

Go to hell, she wanted to say. But she held it back. She didn't want to argue with him.

She had the bracelet. It was cupped in her right hand, out of Totoy's sight. He hadn't noticed it on the girl's wrist, and she wasn't going to make a point of it now. They had an agreement to split the money from any valuables, and he would just want a piece of the proceeds.

But there wouldn't be any proceeds from this one, because she wasn't going to sell it. Such a lovely piece on the arm of a teenage girl from the countryside—who would imagine such a thing? And with the correct initial "M," as if it had been made for her. This was Providence at work for sure, and she wasn't sharing it.

She held her hand casually at her side, between the seat and the passenger door, feeling the delicious smoothness of the herringbone and the gems.

She waited until Totoy reached the end of the access road, where it met city streets. Manila was an early-waking city, and traffic was picking up already. Totoy waited for an opening. As he concentrated on traffic, Magdalena opened her purse and pretended to search for something inside. When she knew that he wasn't looking, she dropped the bracelet in.

At that moment Totoy saw his spot. He mashed the accelerator and the van darted forward, and the van disappeared into the Monday-morning stream.

Hours later, Marivic awoke fitfully from her drug stupor. Several times she drifted up toward the light of awareness, then sank back into oblivion, before she finally opened her eyes and forced herself into the present.

She was alone in a small room—a cell, really—with four high walls of bare concrete block. Her clothes were gone: she was naked beneath a shapeless white hospital gown. A fan twirled overhead, hung from the rafters below a high ceiling of corrugated steel.

In the room was a small table and a chair, and the cot where she lay. On the table, a plastic cup and a plastic water pitcher, a plastic dish with a meal of rice and sardines. On the floor at the foot of the bed was a metal chamber pot.

No windows. One steel door with no knob, no handle. A single light fixture high on a wall, but no switch. Marivic rose from the cot and started toward the door, three steps away. But she was still woozy from the drugs. She lost her balance and lurched into the table. It banged hard against the wall.

Marivic steadied herself.

"Wilfredo, is that you?" called the voice of a young man, speaking Tagalog.

Marivic was startled. The voice seemed to come from nowhere.

The voice said, "Did you return, Fredo? Was it a trick? I'm so sorry."

Marivic looked up. The high walls were open at the top, a ventilation space about a foot high between the concrete block and the ceiling, covered by a wire-mesh grille. The voice was coming from the other side of the concrete wall.

"I'm not Wilfredo. I'm Marivic."

"Oh! You're new. Did you just get here? I heard a plane. Was that you?"

Marivic's last solid memory was sitting in the back of a van in Manila. But now she hazily recalled an aircraft engine's drone in her ears, and half-opening her eyes to glimpse an airplane's cockpit instruments. They were flying. Through the windscreen was the sea far below. The image seemed dreamlike, but she knew it was real.

"Yes," she said. "That was me. Who are you?"

"Me, I'm Junior. Junior Peralta. From Vigan City."

Marivic took the last couple of steps toward the door, moving slowly to keep from getting dizzy once more. She placed her palm against the cool steel and pushed. The door didn't budge.

"I am a prisoner," Marivic said, as much to herself as to the disembodied voice on the other side of the wall.

"Yes. Me too."

"Were you kidnapped from Manila?"

"Yes."

"Why are we here?" Marivic said.

"I don't know."

"Who are they?"

"I don't know. Foreigners, that's all. But it's not so bad. There's lots of food. And anyway, we'll be leaving soon."

"How do you know?"

"Wilfredo told me. He figured it out. Fredo is very intelligent."

"Who is Fredo?"

"He was in the place you're in now. We talked all the time. He was here for almost one month, and he paid attention. He said they were getting ready to let him out, and then this morning they took him away, so I guess he must have been right. He really did leave after all."

"What makes you think he left?" Marivic said.

"We're on an island," the voice said. "A small one. I didn't see it, but Wilfredo said he got a good look when they brought him here. He said it's small. You can probably walk around it in ten or fifteen minutes."

Another dreamlike image drifted up into Marivic's consciousness. She was being lifted out of a boat. . . . No, it was the airplane, a plane that floated boatlike on the water, tied up at a dock. She was put into a motorized cart, bright green and yellow, and then driven up a hill toward a clump of concrete buildings among some coconut trees.

That's where I am now, she thought.

And yes it seemed to be an island. Not a big one.

"Think about it," Junior said. "If Wilfredo is not here, where else can he be? He must have left."

Somewhere outside, an engine stuttered to life. It made a loud buzz that flowed in through the grille at the top of the outside wall and rattled around the concrete cell.

The plane, Marivic thought.

"The plane!" said Junior. "You see? Fredo must be leaving."

The buzz became louder and more insistent. It grew into a roar that reverberated off the concrete walls, reaching an angry pitch so loud that neither of them tried to talk.

Then it began to recede. Gradually the sound diminished. Marivic knew that the plane was flying away. She imagined it climbing into the sky, disappearing. It had brought her here, and now it was leaving.

The thought saddened her. She was lost. Truly.

———

Junior and Marivic chatted for hours that day, each talking to a blank concrete wall, never seeing each other's face. Junior was twenty-two years old, son of a fisherman, fourth in a family of eight. A poor family, he told Marivic. Junior didn't like fishing. He was saving to buy a taxi. Junior's story was the same as hers: a job offer from Optimo, a long bus ride, met at the terminal by the creepy *matrona* and the thug, the ride in a van, the offering of *siopao* . . .

"That's the last time I ever take *siopao* from a stranger," Junior said.

Before the end of that first day they had become friends. They talked about their homes and families, about school and neighbors. Marivic had never been to Vigan, but she could imagine the little house where Junior had grown up, and all the people who lived in it.

Around nightfall, a key turned in the lock. Two men entered. Foreigners. They were a ridiculous pair: one slight and wiry, the other massive, so large that he had to bend his head in order to get through the door. Their faces were impassive. They didn't make eye contact, didn't even seem to notice her. One carried a tray with a bowl of food and a full pitcher of water. The other carried a clean chamber pot.

Marivic tried to speak to them in English. She said, "Where am I? Why am I here?"

They didn't say a word. They briskly switched out the chamber pot and the water pitcher, put the plate of food on the table, and took away the dirty dish with the leftover scraps of sardines and rice.

"Talk to me!" Marivic said. "What's going on? Say *anything*."

They left and locked the door behind them without acknowledging her presence, without even once meeting her eyes. Moments later they went into Junior's room and performed the same small tasks. Marivic couldn't see what was happening, but she recognized the sounds, the scraping of the dishes, the *thunk* of an empty chamber pot on the floor.

"Don't waste your breath," Junior said when they were gone, his door locked shut. "They have nothing to say. Believe me, I've tried."

They ate in silence. Marivic ate until she was full, then pushed the plate away and sat on the cot.

A high-pitched trill drifted over the wall. It sounded at first like the call of a songbird. But Marivic knew that no bird sang the tune "My Heart Will Go On."

She said, "Junior! You have a flute? How?"

The song stopped.

He said, "No flute. It's me. I am a whistler."

"Just you? Can't be."

"Yes," he said. "It's me. Name a song. I know them all."

She thought for a moment. One of her favorite songs was a Tagalog ballad by Freddie Aguilar, the Filipino folksinger. "Anak" was the name of the song: "Child." It had a lilting melody that soared and dipped—almost impossible to whistle, she imagined. She decided to test him.

"'Anak,'" she said.

Seconds later, the first bar wafted in over the wall. Perfect tempo, perfect pitch.

She squealed with delight.

The melody stopped and he said, "Marivic, are you all right?"

"Yes, yes, don't stop!"

He picked up right where he had left off.

They passed the evening that way, Marivic throwing the names of songs over the wall, and Junior sending back a beautifully rendered melody. After a while the lights went out in the rooms. Junior and Marivic chatted for a while, until Junior got sleepy and said good night.

Then silence from the other side of the wall.

Marivic couldn't sleep. She lay awake in the darkness, watching the fan turn above her. She tried to imagine what lay beyond the walls. That afternoon she had noticed indirect sunlight coming in over the top of one wall. She knew that wall must face outside.

If she could somehow climb up, she might be able to peer over the top of the wall, through the wire-mesh grille that ran along the top.

Was it possible?

The walls were several feet higher than in an ordinary room. Standing on the chair wouldn't get her close. Even standing on the table wouldn't get her high enough. But the chair on the table . . .

She moved the table into the corner formed by the outside walls, then placed the chair on the table. She climbed up on the table, then carefully onto the chair, balancing against the wall as she stepped up. The top of the wall was now at forehead height. She placed both hands on the lip of the wall and stretched up on the tips of her toes.

Now she could just see over the top. Through the wire grille, she looked down on a moonlit hillside that fell down to the ocean. A path led from this building, through a stand of trees. About halfway down the hill was a broad clearing. The path skirted this clearing and ran down to a dock.

A white speedboat was tied up there, bobbing in the water. She could hear the wash of waves against rocks, the swish of palm fronds in the wind.

At first she didn't see anyone. The path down to the dock was clear, and she got a wild urge to escape. Only the grille stood between her and freedom. If she pushed it out, she could climb over the wall, run down to the boat, drive it far away.

She grasped the grille and shook it. The grille didn't move. She pulled and tugged at the grille. It didn't budge. She looked closer and saw that heavy screws secured the base of the grille to the top of the wall. It wasn't going anywhere.

The urge faded. *Crazy,* she thought. She didn't know how to operate a speedboat, and even if she could get it to work, she didn't know where she was, which way to go.

Then a tiny flare of red light got her attention,

about halfway down the hillside. The glare revealed the face of a man. He was striking a match, cupping it in his hands as he lit a cigarette. The match died, replaced by the glowing tip of the cigarette. Now she could make out his dark form seated under a palm tree, looking out over the water. A gun, a rifle, was cradled in his lap.

The armed man was facing out toward the ocean. He didn't seem worried about anyone escaping. He wanted to keep others out.

She realized that her calves were aching. Too long up on her toes. And she had seen enough. She stepped down from the chair, off the table, back down to the floor. She quietly moved the chair and table back where they belonged, and she lay in the bed, staring up for a long time at the fan turning overhead, until finally she fell asleep.

Several days passed uneventfully in the little cell. Marivic was puzzled. She knew that she must have been brought there for some reason, and although she dreaded it, she wanted to know what was supposed to happen next.

Nothing happened.

The days followed an unvarying routine. About an hour after sunrise, the lock turned in the steel door, and the two foreigners entered. They removed the dishes from the previous evening's meal, took out the chamber pot and the water pitcher, brought in fresh water and a clean chamber pot. They worked quickly and never spoke a word, in and out in less than a minute, and when they left her cell they went to Junior's and worked just as quickly and silently.

Around midday the lock turned again and the two men entered once more. A woman was with them this time. They stood and watched as the woman checked Marivic's pulse and blood pressure, listened to her lungs through a stethoscope, and took her temperature.

Marivic tried to speak to the woman in English, telling her "I'm not sick, I feel fine. Why are you doing this to me?" as she unwrapped the pressure cuff from around Marivic's arm. But the woman didn't answer. She just led Marivic out of the cell, down a short corridor to a shower stall. The woman stood outside while Marivic bathed Filipino style, dipping cool water out of a bucket. When Marivic was finished, the woman handed her a towel and a clean gown and took her back to the cell, where a meal was waiting on the table.

In the evening came the third visit of the day. This time it was just the two men, bringing food and water.

Junior Peralta in the next room got exactly the same treatment: the meals, the shower, the checkup. And the same oblivious attitude. "Like I'm not even there," Junior said.

Marivic didn't feel threatened. She felt ignored.

The three visits left gaps of long hours when she was alone in the cell. Long conversations with Junior helped to fill the time, and in the evenings he would amuse her by playing the human jukebox, whistling the tunes that she called out. But inevitably he was ready for sleep before she was, and she would be left awake in the silent darkness, unable to avoid her thoughts any longer.

She didn't want that. Thinking led in just two directions, one frustrating, the other painful. There were the questions about her situation: *Why was I brought here? What is this place? Who are these people? What happens next?* All good questions, but impossible to answer, so that when she pondered the possibilities she felt as if she were running blindly into the high concrete walls—again and again and again.

Then there were the thoughts of her family and the village, all that she had left behind when she stepped onto the bus that early morning beside the gulf. But these memories and visions were unbearably poignant, impossibly distant from the reality of the cell. She couldn't dwell on home; it hurt too much.

"Marivic! I'm leaving! It's my turn to go."

Junior was calling to her over the wall. It was the morning of Marivic's fifth day on the island, and she was eating breakfast. The silent man and woman had been in her cell already, the usual routine, and they had gone into Junior's cell after they left hers.

"Marivic, did you hear me? I'll be leaving in two days."

"Did they tell you that?"

"No, they didn't talk. Of course not. But they took some blood from my arm. Then they gave me an injection. That's it. They've started the treatment."

This was what Wilfredo had called it. The Goodbye Treatment. Fredo had been on the island for a month, in the cell that Marivic now occupied. During that time, two different inmates had come and gone in the adjoining cell. Each time there had been a break in the routine, a new pattern.

Day One: During their morning visit, before delivering the meal, one of the two foreigners would draw a blood sample and give an injection.

Day Two: An injection and blood sample in the morning, both repeated in the evening.

Day Three: Before dawn, one last injection. Then the men took you out the door. Gone, just that quickly.

That was The Goodbye Treatment. Now it was starting for Junior, and he was excited: "My God, finally. I'm so tired of this hole. I can't wait to get out."

"I'm glad," Marivic said. But she didn't sound convincing, and Junior caught the hesitant tone.

"Marivic, I don't mean it that way. I'll miss you. I'm just so tired of being here. You understand."

"I don't blame you for wanting to be gone."

"Don't worry, your turn will come soon."

But Marivic wasn't sure that she wanted her turn to come. Blood samples and injections—all just to leave the island? That and the daily medical exams, the concern about their health. What was that all about?

An instinctive suspicion nagged at her, just the way it had that early morning when she stepped off the bus and confronted the *matrona* and her thuggish companion. *Something's not quite right here,* she wanted to tell Junior. *Don't you see it too?*

But there was a difference, she thought. At the bus terminal, she could have acted on the instinct. Refused to go with the *matrona*. Turned and fled, if it came to that. Run like hell. She could have saved herself then. Not any longer. She couldn't help herself now, and she definitely couldn't help Junior.

"I'm happy for you," Marivic said.

"You don't sound happy."

"I am. Really."

"Good," said Junior from the other side of the wall. "Don't be jealous. You won't be here much longer, either, I'm sure of it."

The Goodbye Treatment continued for Junior, exactly on schedule. The second morning, an injection and a blood sample. The evening of the second day, again a blood sample and an injection. Junior and Marivic didn't talk much after that. Junior was going in a few hours. They both understood it.

Marivic lay in the cell and tried to make sense of it all. Junior was going. But where? For what purpose? Why now instead of yesterday or tomorrow? Why were they even here at all? All this—the plane and the boat and the buildings and the guards—did all this exist just to provide a way station between Manila and some ultimate destination for a few unfortunate captives?

It didn't make sense.

As she lay in the darkness, she thought about the

glimpse of the island that she had gotten that first night as she peeked over the wall, through the wire grille. She remembered the path that ran past her cell wall, down the hill, to the dock.

Whether by boat or by floating plane, the dock seemed to be the point of entry and departure. This meant that Junior, when he left, would be on that path soon. *If* he was leaving.

She spoke in the darkness: "Junior? Are you awake?"

"Yes, Marivic, I am awake."

"When you leave the island, you'll walk past this building. Past my cell. You'll know it: the concrete block wall. It's the last building before you go down the hill to the dock."

"If you say so."

"When you pass by, I want you to let me know that you're there. Don't say anything. Just whistle 'Anak.' Make it loud so I'm sure to hear it. Will you remember that?"

"Sure, I'll do that," he said.

"Please don't forget. It's important."

"Like a last good-bye. Until we meet again."

"Something like that," she said.

They came for him before dawn. The light went on in his room and she heard his door opening, the low voices, getting him up.

He said, "Good-bye, Marivic. Don't worry, I remember. 'Anak.'"

From outside the building, somewhere in the sky, she heard a noise. It sounded at first like the snapping of a flag in a hard wind. It grew louder. A white light briefly swept through the grille above the wall.

She knew from the sound that it was a helicopter, coming in to land.

"You see, Marivic?" Junior shouted. She could tell that he was out of the room now, in the short hallway outside the cells. "That's for me. They've come for me."

The helicopter's beating grew louder and lower, until it was no longer dropping. The noise began to subside. It was on the ground.

Marivic moved the table to the corner of the room and placed the chair on the table, its back against the wall. She climbed up and looked over the top.

The helicopter had landed in the flat clearing about halfway down the hill. Floodlights bathed the area.

She wondered if they had really come for Junior. Was it possible?

A door opened on the helicopter as the blades did a last slow turn to a stop. From the shadows outside the floodlights came a man pushing a wheelchair. He helped someone down from the helicopter, into the chair, and he began to push the chair up the path. Who was this? Was some new occupant being brought in to fill the cell that Junior had left?

As they got closer, she saw that the figure in the chair was a white man, plump and jowly. She ducked her head down so that she wouldn't be noticed, and when she looked up again the chair was gone, out of sight. He didn't come into the cell, and she knew that they must have brought him back into the unseen buildings.

For the next ten or fifteen minutes she waited for Junior to come by, whistling "Anak" as he passed, on his way down to the helicopter. But Junior didn't appear. Down in the clearing, someone was refueling the helicopter from a cylindrical tank that sat on pipe-stand legs at the edge of the clearing. After a while he removed the nozzle from the helicopter and wound the hose back on a reel beside the tank, and he climbed into the helicopter and shut the door.

Still no Junior.

The helicopter whined; the blades began to turn. The helicopter lifted off with a clatter, airborne and climbing. When it was gone, the lights went out in the clearing.

The hillside was dark and still.

Marivic climbed down, took the chair from the table, and returned the table to where it belonged.

She stayed awake, stretched out on the cot, listening. She waited to hear "Anak" floating over the wall, telling her that all was well and that the prisoners in these cells really did leave the island.

Daybreak: no "Anak." In the morning, the two attendants came in as usual, then left. As the day wore on, a couple of times she heard low voices outside, and she hurried to climb up and look over the top of the wall, thinking that maybe Junior was being escorted down to the boat and that he was so excited to leave that he had forgotten his promise. But each time it was just foreigners on the path, faces and bodies that were now becoming familiar.

By midday she was sure that something was wrong. A small island, a few buildings. Where was Junior, if not here?

In the afternoon she heard another pair of voices outside. Two men, foreigners, speaking their foreign language. She didn't understand the words, but she recognized the tone. They were complaining.

She climbed up to look. It was the two men who tended to her cell every day, the mismatched pair. They were walking down the hill. They carried large white buckets, one in each hand, four in all. The buckets were deep and were covered with lids. They seemed to be heavy. The giant handled them easily, but the little guy was working hard and yapping loudly.

She watched as they hauled the buckets down the hill to the dock. They put the buckets down, not far from where the speedboat was tied up.

The two men began to talk between themselves, some kind of discussion. Then the small man pried the lid from one of the buckets, picked it up, and carried it to the end of the dock. He upended it and dumped out whatever was inside, spilling it into the sea.

An angry shout came from somewhere up the hill, just out of Marivic's sight. The men on the dock stopped and looked up toward the sound.

Now the shouting man stepped into view, right

below Marivic. He gesticulated, pointing with a sweep of his left hand. *Around back!* he seemed to be saying.

The two men didn't argue. They just carried the three remaining buckets into the speedboat. The giant cast off the lines; the other got behind the wheel and started the motor.

From his sharp bark and the way the others had obeyed him, Marivic guessed that the man who stood below her must have some authority. Maybe he was in charge. He stood watching as the boat backed out and headed around the island, and he didn't move until the boat was out of sight.

Then he turned just long enough for Marivic to glimpse his face. It was the foreigner who had sat beside her in the plane. He walked back the way he had come.

She wished that he would stay. She had some questions for him

Where is Junior? she wanted to ask. *What have you done with him?*

But he was gone, and the boat was gone too. There was just the path and the hillside down to the empty dock.

She climbed down from the top of the wall and went back to her cot.

SEVEN

Favor was wrong about the Gulfstream 550. For a transpacific flight, the charter operator needed six hours' notice, not three. And since the plane was based in Oakland, Favor would save time by meeting it there instead of routing it to Lake Tahoe. He suggested that they drive down together, have a good dinner, and board the plane when it was ready.

Stickney and Mendonza needed the extra time to get their passports. Mendonza's wife sent his by courier to Oakland. Stickney's housekeeper, who had a key to his home, found his passport in his desk; her son agreed to bring it down to Oakland.

All this came together in less than twenty minutes as the four of them sat in the gazebo along the Tahoe shore. Arielle handled most of it, down to the dinner reservations and the catering details for the Gulfstream.

"One thing we ought to talk about," Mendonza said. "I was wondering what you want to do about logistics in Manila. Maybe we ought to have somebody on the ground handling arrangements."

"You think we need that?" Favor said. "I figure we book suites at a kick-ass hotel, the hotel sends a limo to meet us at the airport, after that we play it by ear."

"It could get complicated," Mendonza said. "I need to get to Leyte right away. See the mother, get the story. We all ought to have cell phones. A couple of cars with drivers would be nice. We could do all that ourselves, but it'd be easier to have somebody else hassling the details."

"You're right. Yeah, let's do it," Favor said. "You have somebody in mind?"

"How about Edwin Santos?" Mendonza said, and in unison Arielle and Stickney yelled, "No Problem Eddie!"

They all remembered Santos. Bravo One Nine had once spent several weeks on assignment in Manila, and Santos was the team's local contact and logistical source—a critical asset. He boasted that he could supply whatever they needed: weapons, documents, electronics, vehicles.

"No problem!" he would crow.

It wasn't an empty claim. What he promised, Santos had always delivered.

And not just tangibles. Santos also dealt in access and knowledge. His contacts seemed endless. He moved among politicians and gangsters, bishops and pimps, Red guerrillas and right-wing vigilantes, brokering services and esoteric transactions. Edwin Santos was incredibly useful.

"Is Eddie still around?" Favor asked. "I wouldn't know where to find him."

"He's around. I used him last year," Mendonza said. "I handled security for a client on an Asian tour. Eddie took care of the crap at the Manila end. You know, the endless little wrinkles that bog you down. Crap came up, I handed it off to Eddie, he made it disappear."

Arielle said, "That's Eddie."

Favor turned to Winston Stickney. It was an automatic gesture from their years in the field. Stickney was the wise man, insightful and sober. Stick always seemed to know what to do.

He was having no part of it now, though. He held up his hands, shook his head.

"It's not my party, Ray. Do what you think is best."

Mendonza was looking at Favor, waiting for an answer.

"Sure," Favor said. "Call Eddie. Phones, cars, domestic flights."

Mendonza said, "What about paper?"

Paper meant forged passports and supporting documents. To a Bravo team, it was a staple. Paper was as basic as air.

"Why would we need paper?" Favor said. "To look for a girl gone lost? To scuba dive and lie on the beach?"

"Just asking," Mendonza said. "I guess it feels a little strange, the four of us going off somewhere without cover."

"We don't need cover," Favor said. "We're going to do a little good deed and then we're gonna have some fun. That's all. No cover, no paper. No fucking tradecraft, we're done with that shit."

He realized that his voice had risen. The others were looking at him. Staring.

Favor took a couple of seconds, composed himself. When he spoke again he made sure that he sounded calm.

"I just want to play it straight," he said. "Agreed?"

"Sure," Stickney said.

"Why not?" Arielle said.

"Whatever you think," Mendonza said.

"That's what I think," Favor said. "It's just a vacation, goddammit."

Arielle left them and went off to pack.

Her home was about fifteen minutes away, but she didn't have to go there. She had a bedroom at the converted lodge, a place to crash at the end of a long night of work. She kept clothes there, and an overnight bag that was always packed and ready to go. Favor often traveled on a few minutes' notice to inspect property, and usually he wanted Arielle with him.

When she got to the room, she spent a few minutes replacing winter clothes in the bag with some warm-weather pieces. Then she carried it to her office. She picked up a laptop computer—one of two that she kept in sync with the desktop machine—and she zipped it into a carrying case.

She opened a desk drawer and removed a piece of electronic equipment about the size and shape of a paperback book: a black case dotted with a row of LED lights. At a glance, it resembled the broadband modem found in many American homes. It was in fact a compact satellite antenna: when connected to the laptop, and properly aligned with a data satellite, it provided a reliable high-speed Internet connection virtually anywhere in the world.

Favor sometimes said that Arielle's job was to be the smartest person in a fifty-mile radius, major research universities not excepted. It was a joke with a large kernel of truth. When he researched a new business opportunity, Favor was full of questions, usually esoteric and difficult. And when he needed to know, he went to Arielle. She had a gift for learning. She read rapidly and retained almost everything, and above all she knew how to find the answers she didn't already know. The satellite antenna and her laptop allowed her to do it from anywhere.

She slid the antenna into a pocket of the laptop case.

On her way out, she paused at the top of the stairs. She asked herself: *What will Ray need?*

She answered: *Antibiotic ointment and dressings.* It was exactly the kind of thing he would neglect.

Looking after Ray Favor was not part of the job description. Yet she did it, probably more than was healthy for either of them. She didn't consider herself the nurturing type, and she was definitely not self-sacrificing. It came down to two reasons:

She cared for him.

He had nobody else to do it.

Their relationship was unique, as far as she could tell. They never married, but they knew each other far better and were far more intimate than most married couples. They had been lovers for the past dozen years, yet she had had others in her life, and Favor had had many women. They disdained sexual exclusivity and the jealousies that went with it, and they both resisted any infringement on their personal freedom. Still, they were mutually devoted.

Arielle thought that they had proved themselves to each other so often, in so many different ways, that they needed no formal commitment. They didn't need declarations of love. They didn't even need a name for what they had. They just *were*, and they always would be.

Arielle went to a supply room where Favor kept some first-aid supplies. She grabbed bandage squares and gauze, bandage tape and antibiotic ointment, and zipped it all into a pocket of her overnight bag.

When she got to the gazebo, Favor and the others were discussing which vehicle they should take and who would drive.

She said, "Slow down, hotshot. Let's take a look at those dressings."

"The dressings are fine," he said.

"Take off your shirt."

"You think I can't tell if the dressings are good? Think I haven't been banged up often enough to know when I need fresh bandages?"

"Ray," she said. "The shirt."

He opened the shirt.

The G550 had twelve seats, first two occupied by the two relief pilots. Halfway back in the cabin, four of the seats were grouped around a table. The four of them gathered there once the plane was airborne at cruising altitude.

They joked and laughed, drank champagne, and ate oysters and caviar before a meal of lobster bisque and tournedos Wellington.

By now the time was past midnight on the West Coast. They dimmed the cabin lights. Mendonza and Stickney went to the back of the cabin and were soon asleep, reclining in their seats.

Favor sat across the table from Arielle. She watched him fall asleep, his eyes gradually closing, his chest rising and falling in a measured rhythm.

His body suddenly tensed. He mumbled an extended guttural sound. It could have been words or just a tortured groan; she couldn't tell. His hands clenched the ends of the armrests.

She knew that he was dreaming. And from the anguished expression on his face, she thought it must be one of *those* dreams.

She was right: it was one of those dreams. Except Favor didn't think of them that way. True, they came while he slept, and they came on their own relentless schedule, even though he desperately willed them not to come. So in that way they were like dreams.

But dreams were supposed to be symbolic creations of the mind. These were real. Every moment came direct and unaltered from Favor's life, selected with brutal logic, assembled in such a way as to inflict maximum pain. They were a personal library of horror, episodes of his history that he had always tried to push aside. Long avoided in his waking hours, the memories came roaring back to him in sleep. But even as he slept, some part of his mind was always conscious when they played out. The memories seemed to want this. They demanded his awareness. No matter how bad they were, he could not turn away.

The one that played for him now as he slept in the Gulfstream's cabin was the worst of the worst. It was so searing, and so shameful, that he had never told anyone. He was the only living person who remembered it, and he knew that he would take it to his grave.

It begins with the voice of his mother, summoning him to attention.

Oh, Raymond, she says, a sad sigh that pierces him through the heart. He is eight years old, in the living room of their little bungalow on the back side of his grandparents' ranch. He's looking into her eyes. Dark eyes, red rimmed and glistening with tears. She's a beautiful woman. Long black hair and glowing pink skin and ripened-cherry lips. At eight, he doesn't comprehend her this way. But thirty-six years later, as he dozes in the seat, the alert part of his mind sees her as she was, the way others must have seen her. A beauty.

Oh, Raymond. Her tone is beseeching. He doesn't know what she wants, and this scares him, because it is the most important thing he has ever done or ever will do, and he has to get it right.

Tell me what you want, the eight-year-old boy wants to say. But he can't speak.

Tell me, the sleeping adult says across the distance of decades.

Pull the fucking trigger, says his father. It's a few days earlier, a summer evening. The boy is holding a .22 rifle, crouching with his father beside a fallen log in a forest. (The sleepborne memories do this sometimes, bouncing back and forth in time and place, but never at random. There is always a point.) The boy squints down the barrel. He has handled guns for more than a year: his father insisted on it. First it was paper targets and tin cans, now live game for the first time. Ten or fifteen paces away, a chipmunk squats on a flat rock, facing the fallen log, nose twitching. The rifle has a notched sight at the top of the receiver and a thin blade sight at the end of the barrel, and the boy has lined them up with the plump patch of fur at the chipmunk's throat.

Shoot, his father hisses into the boy's ear. His finger is at the trigger, touching the cool curve of steel. The animal's small head fills his vision. Black eyes, dancing whiskers, and the perfect alignment of notch and blade and fur. His finger doesn't move. Refuses to move. With a woodsman's stealth, the father snakes his arm along the boy's back and reaches around his neck. He takes the boy's ear between thumb and forefinger, and he pinches, nails digging into his son's flesh.

I said shoot, boy.

The boy doesn't flinch. This would be a mistake. As he watches the scene play out in his head, the adult Ray Favor knows that the father is a classic bully, insecure and unhappy and frightened, who slinks from the strong and turns his self-loathing outward to heap upon the weak. The eight-year-old understands none of this. He knows only that his father is an asshole.

The edges of the fingernails dig deeper into the boy's ear, breaking skin. The boy's vision becomes liquid, blurred. He blinks to clear it, and finds notch and blade still aligned with paunchy fur.

Pull the trigger, pussy.

The boy squeezes. The gun cracks. The chipmunk flips back and out of sight.

The father hops up, steps over the log, and walks to the rock. He bends down, picks up the limp body of the chipmunk, turns it over like a farmer inspecting a clod of dirt. He motions to the boy—*Come here*—and the eight-year-old Raymond Favor leans his rifle against the fallen log and stands and walks toward him. His father is holding the carcass out, displaying it.

Lookit here. You did that.

The boy forces himself to look. He sees that the animal has been gutted. The bullet entered beneath its throat and traveled the length of its body, ripping open the underbelly and tearing out the viscera. The body is a pelt, though the head is intact, the small black eyes vacant.

Zipped it right open. Not bad for a little puke.

The boy begins to sob. He doesn't know why.

Even the adult Ray Favor can't say why, exactly. It's the screeching pain at his ear, it's the humiliation, it's the dead black eyes, it's an asshole for a father.

The father. His face curdles at the sight of the tears. He bellows: *This? You cry for this? This is a rodent! This is a turd! This is nothing!* He grabs the boy behind the head, shoves the carcass into his face. The bloody underside. Rubs it into his face. The father's outrage builds. Spittle flies from his mouth as he shouts. *This is nothing! Nothing!* He cuffs the boy, a hard backhand swipe that knocks him to the ground.

The father bends. Unties one of the boy's sneakers. Pulls out the lace. Pushes one end into the mouth of the carcass, threads it out through an eye socket. He ties it around the boy's neck.

Wear this 'til I tell you to quit. You'll learn.

Now the boy is in bed, saying his prayers. He feels a caress at his cheek. His mother's hand. She's touching the spot where the father struck him. The bruise is mostly faded. She bends to kiss him. It's a supreme act of motherly love, because he stinks of death. The chipmunk is rotting on the shoestring around his neck, the odor overpowering in the summer heat.

The father won't allow him to remove it.

Now his mother stands over the boy. Stares down in pity. Her face becomes resolute. She reaches down, unties the shoestring, pulls it away.

This is defiance. It means trouble. She knows it; the boy knows it.

She leaves the room with the string and its stinking pendant.

The boy waits for upheaval. It happens in a hurry.

It starts with shouts—his father's. Then an anguished scream—his mother's. The boy listens. He tenses in his bed, but he doesn't panic. He has heard this before, too often, and as bad as it sounds, somehow everything has always come out right. No broken bones, sometimes even an awkward lull for a few days before the next outburst.

More shouts. The scuffling sounds of struggle. A heavy thump, a crash—this is *not* usual—and then a long scream of terror that he has never heard before.

The boy bolts out of bed and runs to the living room. He stops at the entryway, arrested by what he sees.

His father is holding a shotgun. It's a twelve-gauge Remington, and the boy knows that it is always loaded with buckshot. And now it's pointed at his mother.

Both of them, father and mother, turn to look at the boy when he appears. She is sprawled on the floor. The father stands astride her waist, holding the shotgun low, its muzzle inches from her face.

Just inside the entryway, where the boy stands, is a small table with a lamp. There is a single drawer in the table.

Inside the drawer of the lamp table is a Colt .45 pistol. The boy has never fired it, but he knows how it works. He knows all about the pistol. He knows that his father keeps a round chambered, hammer cocked, safety on. The father has taught him these things the way other fathers teach their boys to throw a baseball.

The boy opens the drawer and picks up the pistol, holding it with both hands, and he raises it. Notch and blade align with his father's chest.

A sneering grin spreads across the father's face. He turns toward the boy but keeps the shotgun trained on the mother's face, holding it pistol-like at her head.

This is rich, he says. *This is just too perfect.*

Without disturbing his aim, the boy crooks the thumb of his right hand, pushing the safety off.

Go ahead, says the father to the son. *I want to see this.*

The boy looks at his mother. Meets the dark beautiful eyes, full of love.

Oh, Raymond, she says, a sorrowful sigh.

He searches her face, trying to understand. What does she mean? What does she want?

Oh, Raymond, put the gun down—is that it?

Oh, Raymond, I'm so sorry you had to see this.

Oh, Raymond, you'll only make it worse.

Oh, Raymond, please protect me.

It could be any of these. Or more.

The boy wants to know how he should react, what he's supposed to do. It's the biggest moment of his life. He has to be sure, he has to get it right.

Pull the fucking trigger, his father says. The boy hesitates. His gaze jumps from his mother's eyes to the target at the end of his gun sights. Back to his mother's eyes, where he searches once more for a cue. Nothing there: she's purely terrified, the shot-gun's muzzle inches from her face.

His father shoots. The shotgun roars. The beautiful face is instantly transformed to bloody pulp.

The father jacks a fresh round as he swings the gun toward his son.

The boy pulls the fucking trigger. The pistol bucks, the father falls.

The boy puts down the pistol and goes to the phone and calls his grandparents at the main ranch house a couple of miles away.

The grandparents are good people. They will persuade the sheriff, a friend, to call it a murder-suicide. They will raise the boy, they will love him. But they will never look at him quite the way they did before.

While he waits for his grandparents to come, the boy takes a seat in a chair near his mother's body. He angles the chair so he doesn't have to see her face. He sits and looks down at the father. That doesn't bother him a bit. The father is on his back, looking up at the ceiling, his eyes unblinking. There's a hole in the front of his shirt, dead center through the shirt pocket on his left side. Heart shot. Already blood is darkening the front of the shirt and pooling beneath the body.

The boy sits there and stares at what he's done. And a thought comes to him that will return a thousand times more in the years that follow.

What's in him is in me, he tells himself.

What's in him is in me.

What's in him is in me.

———

Arielle wondered whether she should wake him. But before she could decide, a wracked shudder passed through his body, and he snapped awake. She looked away so that he wouldn't know she'd been staring at him, but he caught her anyway.

"What?" he said. "Hey, it's nothing, I'm fine. You worry too much."

HARVEST DAY

–5

Eight

It was morning in Manila, 7:10 a.m., when the call from Alex Mendonza came in to the cell phone of Edwin Santos. The phone was, in fact, one of three that Santos carried at all times.

Each represented a niche in his life, a certain level of significance.

The first phone he used for communicating with the employees and managers of the seven businesses around Manila that he owned and supervised. He ran a taxi and car service; a bakery; a ready-to-wear manufacturing company; a travel agency; two restaurants; and a beer garden. This was the busiest phone, and the one he was most likely to ignore if he was otherwise occupied: the internal workings of the businesses were important, but they could usually wait. And he paid others to deal with emergencies.

The second phone was dedicated to the customers and potential customers and suppliers of his businesses. It represented cash in hand, and he would always leave the first phone to answer the second.

The third phone carried the fewest phone numbers but the most important. They included his few close friends, his attorney and accountant, and his less conventional business contacts, representing discreet understandings, unwritten but mortally binding agreements, and an intricate balance sheet of obligations and payments in kind.

His twenty-year-old daughter, Anabeth, had a dedicated ring tone on each phone. He would drop any of them to pick up her call.

The call from Mendonza came over the third phone as Santos was finishing breakfast with Anabeth in their apartment on President Quirino Avenue in Manila. The phones were lined up on a side table, each plugged into a charger. A meal with Anabeth came along too seldom, so he had turned off the ringers on the first two phones but not the third—never the third.

He reached for it, recognized the number. Anabeth threw him a look of reproach, and for a moment Santos considered putting the phone aside. But Mendonza had paid well a year earlier, and Santos had once enjoyed working with the four Americans. He was never sure exactly what they were doing, but he knew it wasn't ordinary. They had expected tact and discretion and loyalty; he liked that, and he liked high stakes, and now he hoped that this call might bring him more of the same.

He put up an apologetic hand to his daughter and took the phone into another room.

They exchanged pleasantries before Mendonza said, "Eddie, we're coming into Manila late tonight. We can use your help, if you're free."

" 'We'? All four?"

"The gang's all here."

"Wonderful," Santos said. "I'm always available for you."

"We'll need four phones and a couple of cars with good drivers. Tickets on an early flight to Tacloban for Alex Mendonza and Raymond Favor."

Santos said, "Using your true name? And who is Raymond Favor?"

"You knew him as Jules. Real names all the way this time."

"No paper? No safe house?"

Mendonza laughed and said, "None of that. We don't need it. We're on the straight."

Santos felt vaguely cheated. It was not so much the money as the camaraderie, the shared experience. He said, "I see. This is business or pleasure?"

"A lot of pleasure, I hope, but we have a small chore to take care of first."

"I'll be glad to help any way I can," Santos said, trying to sound sincere. But he didn't feel much enthusiasm anymore. Four phones, a couple of cars, and plane tickets? Anybody could do that.

Mendonza told him that they would arrive at the general aviation terminal after midnight; he would call later with a more specific time.

"It'll be great to see you again," Mendonza said.

"Yes, thanks. You, too, of course," Santos said. He clicked off, and went into the dining room. Anabeth was gone from her chair.

He said, "Beth? Where are you? I'm done."

She came in from her room, carrying a book bag.

She attended Assumption College, one of the nation's most exclusive schools, a Catholic women's university. It was a school for the daughters of Manila's elite, and Santos qualified neither by birth nor bankroll.

But she was a very good student, and in her senior year the brother of a certain Mother Superior in the order had required a certain intervention to avoid a public scandal. Eddie Santos had been happy to use his connections, and his daughter's application was accepted shortly after.

He said, "Come, finish breakfast. I'm sorry I left. It was nothing."

"That's okay. I should be going anyway," she said. She pecked him on the cheek and started for the door.

He said, "How are you fixed for cash? Can you use a little money?"

That stopped her and brought her back. He took some cash from his pocket, decided not to count it, and pressed it into her hand.

Anabeth counted it, though.

"Thanks," she said, and she turned and left.

He watched her walk out the door.

Unusual among Filipinos, Santos had little social life or extended family. Anabeth was his family. After her mother died, when Anabeth was three, Santos had thrown himself into work. A devoted *yaya*—a babysitter—had raised her until she was sixteen. Santos was devoted to her, but now that she was grown, he realized that he had missed much of her growing up, and that the lost time could never be re-claimed. She seemed to leave his presence much too easily these days.

Now another morning gone. Damn.

He picked up the phones from the table, dropped all three into his pockets, and he followed his daughter out the door.

Santos was waiting for them when the four Americans cleared customs and immigration around 4:45 a.m. He had been awake all night, after working all day.

"Welcome back to the Philippines," he said, and shook their hands in turn as Mendonza gave their true names.

This didn't seem right. He felt uneasy, as if they had just disrobed in front of him. But it didn't matter, he thought: apparently he wouldn't be seeing much of them anyway.

He gave them the four telephones, along with tickets and boarding passes for Favor and Mendonza on the first flight to Tacloban, departing in about an hour from a domestic terminal on the other side of the airport property. Santos had brought two cars to the airport, one with a driver named Elvis Vega. Favor and Mendonza went with Vega to their flight, and Santos put Arielle and Stickney into his own car and drove them to their hotel.

They had reservations at one of the four-star monoliths in Makati, the city's international business district. Santos insisted on helping them to check in.

He took their passports to the front desk and waited while the clerk made photocopies.

Santos brought Arielle and Stickney their key cards and check-in portfolios.

Arielle asked if he wanted to come up with them, and he did. They had spectacular suites, each occupying one corner of the top floor, at least triple the size of his own apartment.

They ordered breakfast from room service. Arielle asked Santos if he would stay and eat.

"Thank you, no," he said. "I should be leaving."

The truth was, he felt like a tour guide. There was nothing wrong with that—he had once been a tour guide, and a damn good one—but it wasn't what he had hoped for now.

Arielle said, "I have something for you." She gave him a Bank of America cash envelope.

Santos opened it discreetly and saw a slim stack of bills. They were U.S. hundred-dollar bills, new ones. Santos guessed about twenty bills in the stack.

It was far too much, and Santos was ready to tell her so. But he looked at the suites, and he thought about the private jet and about how they were operating so openly, not even really operating.

They were tourists, he decided. This made him a tour guide after all. And tour guides always know what to do with an overindulgent client.

"Thank you," he said, and pocketed the money.

NINE

Favor followed Mendonza onto the stairway that the ground crew rolled out. Directly ahead, across an asphalt apron, was the trim white terminal building of the airport at Tacloban. Beyond the terminal he saw the sharp ridges of tree-clad hills. Clouds were breaking up against the hilltops, leftovers of a predawn shower that made the foliage glisten dark green in the light of the rising sun.

The airfield lay the full length of a narrow peninsula that jutted into Leyte Gulf. Tacloban lay near the far end of the peninsula, across a narrow bay, with the sand-colored steeple of a cathedral rising above the city's low skyline.

Favor and Mendonza walked down the stairway. They had no baggage except what they had carried on, and they went straight to the sole rental-car counter in the small terminal.

Soon they were driving away from the airport, Mendonza behind the wheel. He followed a road that skirted the south end of Tacloban, an area of small homes and modest businesses. Mendonza had spent most of his childhood in the Philippines, and Favor thought he seemed happy and relaxed. A couple of miles from the airport, they turned south along the coastal highway, putting the city behind them. The settlements became more sparse, grouping into small clusters a mile or more apart, tucked between the hills and the shore.

Mendonza was driving with a map and a portable GPS receiver. He slowed and turned off onto a strip of broken pavement that climbed a couple of hundred yards into the village.

About forty homes and huts, standing three and four deep, surrounded a concrete courtyard. The dwellings were all small and plain, seemingly built with whatever the owners had at hand or could afford to buy: nipa and corrugated metal, plywood and panels of woven coconut fronds, bamboo and concrete blocks. Men and teenage boys were playing basketball at each end of the courtyard while small children laughed and ran among them.

Mendonza got out and asked for Lorna Valencia's home.

"That's my mommy!" said one of the children, a girl of about ten, and she led Mendonza and Favor through the maze of dwellings, some so close together that they left only a shoulder's width to pass. Most had small bare yards with chickens and penned pigs and goats.

The Valencia home was outside the main cluster of houses, at the edge of the forest: a small stucco cottage with a thatched roof. Lorna was outside, sweeping fallen leaves from the apron of packed clay that surrounded the house. She stopped and watched them as they approached. Her lower lip trembled as they stood before her.

"Alex?" she said. "Alex Mendonza, is this you?"

"Yes, it's me," Mendonza said. "And this is my friend and former coworker, Mr. Raymond Favor. We've come to help."

At that moment, Ronnie Valencia was seated among more than a dozen strangers packed into the rear of a vehicle in a clot of morning rush traffic in Manila. He was wedged on a padded bench between two teenage girls wearing identical plaid skirts and white blouses, school uniforms. The girls were chatting to each other, speaking across him as if he didn't exist. But Ronnie was painfully aware of them. Their thighs pressed against his thighs. Their hips rode against his hips. Ronnie's heart was pounding. He had never been so close to a girl in his life, much less two at the same time. A grandmotherly woman faced him from the opposite side, staring at him through wire-rim glasses, a look of harsh appraisal. He wore *sinilas*—rubber sandals—and pants that he had outgrown several years and several inches earlier, and a T-shirt with the faded emblem of his high school. Ronnie knew that his shabby clothes made him look exactly like a country bumpkin overwhelmed in a big city, which he was. The vehicle accelerated suddenly, throwing Ronnie and the two girls even closer together, and the grandmother scowled.

The vehicle was a jeepney, the country's most popular form of public transport. In appearance it is the bastard child of a station wagon and a farm truck. The universal design has two long bench seats fixed lengthwise on an elongated rear compartment. Originally built from the stretched chassis of World War II jeeps, the jeepney is uniquely Filipino, reflecting three of the nation's fundamental social traits: indifference to hardship, practical ingenuity, and an eagerness to surrender personal space.

In Manila, thousands of jeepneys circulated along a complex system of routes that Ronnie was now navigating for the first time. When he first arrived in the city, he had gone to the home of a family friend from San Felipe. The friend lived in the far southern suburbs of Metro Manila. He had given Ronnie a space to sleep and had drawn a map with a bewildering list of jeepney connections that would carry Ronnie to his destination.

Ronnie was heading for the Optimo headquarters. The address was on Amorsolo Street, in the Malate district of Manila. His next stop was the intersection of Taft and Buendia avenues, and he had asked the driver to call it out. But Ronnie wasn't sure that the driver would remember, and he was trying to watch the street signs. The map was in a side pocket of his pants. Ronnie wanted to take it out and check it, but that would require sliding his hand down against the hip of the girl on that side. Unthinkable.

Manila was impossible: big and loud and abrupt and dirty and fast moving. Of course he had always heard this from those who had been there and returned, but now the words seemed laughably inadequate.

The jeepney shot ahead for about half a block and then braked hard at an intersection. The driver yelled at Ronnie without looking back. "Buendia-Taft. Your stop, boondock boy."

The two girls giggled at that, and even the grand-mother broke into a grin. Ronnie's face burned as he got up from the bench. He worked his way down the narrow aisle, through a thicket of legs and knees, to the exit at the back. He grasped a steel hanger bar and swung down to the pavement. As soon as he let go of the bar, the jeepney pulled away, enveloping him in a cloud of blue exhaust smoke. He stepped onto the crowded sidewalk, out of the path of an onrushing bus.

He took out the map, studied it, trying to orient himself. He was at the intersection of Buendia and Taft avenues. The instructions said that he should cross Taft. But the signals weren't working. Taft Avenue was a coursing river of traffic, three lanes in each direction. Somehow pedestrians were picking their way through, finding imperceptible gaps in the headlong flow.

The dash across the avenue seemed suicidal. Ronnie thought of how he had long wished to come to Manila, the adventure it would be. Now he wanted to be anywhere but here—anywhere but this sidewalk, with the instructions in his hand that said CROSS TAFT AVE.

Then he reminded himself that he was here for a purpose. This was for Marivic. He was going to clear up this Optimo bullshit.

He moved up to the edge of the sidewalk. He scanned the oncoming stream of vehicles, judging speed and distance, and at the first blink of an opening he stepped out into the street.

"You don't remember me," an old man said to Mendonza. "But I remember you." The man was no more than five feet tall, wispy thin. Mendonza was almost a foot taller, thick necked and burly. But the old man reached out and touched his cheek and fondly tousled his hair as if he were a child.

Apparently Mendonza had visited San Felipe with his mother when he was six years old. He didn't remember it, but it seemed to be a vivid memory for everyone in the village who was alive at that time, and they had come out to see him now. More than an hour after they had arrived in the village, Favor and Mendonza hadn't yet spoken to Lorna Valencia about her missing daughter. The first visitors had appeared before Lorna finished boiling water for coffee, and soon there were so many that Lorna moved them all outside. She put out chairs for Favor and Mendonza under the shade of a big tree, and the villagers gathered around them.

They were friendly with Favor, and curious, but he knew that they mostly cared about Mendonza. They fawned over him, they cooed over the snapshots of his wife and children that he took from his wallet to show around. And one after the other they all approached him to speak about his childhood visit and to discuss their mutual lineage. Nearly everyone in the village was related to everyone else. Mendonza, by being distantly related to one of them through his mother, was in fact related to them all. As far as they were concerned, he was a child of San Felipe, and this was a homecoming.

Favor wondered how it must feel, that sense of belonging.

He got up after a while and went into the house. Lorna Valencia kept a neat home. It sat at the edge of a jungle and was surrounded by bare earth, but the furniture was spotless and the floors gleamed. Favor went over to a wall in the front room that was covered in family photographs. The photos were mounted on wood plaques and preserved under clear-coat varnish. Two children, a girl and a boy, dominated the collection. They appeared in various ages, usually together, toddlers through teenagers, with the younger children gradually appearing in the more recent photos.

Favor turned when he sensed movement at the door. It was Lorna, carrying glasses on a tray. She put down the tray and joined him at the wall.

"This is my family," she said. She pointed to one of the photos, a man standing on the deck of a ship. "My late husband, chief mate on a freighter. Not so many photographs of him. He was gone so much."

"And the missing girl?"

"Marivic is her name. Here. With Ronnie. My two firstborn."

"Twins?"

"Yes, twins. They've always been very close."

The most recent photo showed them as near adults, standing at the doorway of the cottage. She was shy and pretty. Her brother was darker, sun bronzed, almost a head taller.

Lorna said, "They're trying to tell me that she ran off. I don't believe it. She wouldn't do that."

"I'd like to hear about it," Favor said.

"Good," she said. "Do you want to do it now?"

"That's why we're here."

She went out and got Mendonza, and the three of them sat at her dining table while the curious villagers looked in through an open window.

"This is how it started," she said, and pushed the Optimo newspaper ad across the table to them, handling it with a look of distaste. She told them about Marivic's visit to the office in Tacloban, and then the phone call from Manila, and the bus ticket, and the text messages on her son's phone, including the last one: *arrived*.

"Are you sure about that?" Favor asked. The message was on Ronnie's phone, now with him.

"He showed it to me the day before he left," Lorna said. "I saw it with my own eyes."

She told them about her own visit to the Optimo office in Tacloban, the dismissive woman in the office there, the discouraging reaction of the PNP sergeant, and finally Ronnie's dash to Manila.

"He isn't usually hotheaded," she said, "but he loves his sister very much. Now Manila has taken away both of my firstborn."

"We'll have at least one of them back here in a

hurry," Favor said. He wrote two phone numbers on the back of a business card, his new cell number and Mendonza's, and gave her the card.

He said, "Tell him to call us. We have friends in Manila. They'll take care of him tonight and send him home on the first plane tomorrow."

"Oh, thank God," she said. "And about Marivic?"

"No promises," Mendonza said. "But we'll do all we can."

Mendonza asked her for photos of Marivic. She told him that the only pictures were those on the wall.

Mendonza always traveled with a good digital camera, a tool of his business. He removed it from his shoulder bag and took several close-up shots of the two most recent photos that Lorna pointed out to him.

Lorna stood by Favor at the table and they both watched Mendonza. He was intent, carefully framing his shots and checking the results on the LCD screen, reshooting them until he got what he wanted.

"Alex's mother told me that he is a resourceful man," she said. "Very determined."

"Yes he is," Favor said.

"I think you are also," she said. "More than that. I sense that you're a hard man. I think you could be dangerous. No offense, but this is the impression I get."

"I'm a nice guy, I really am," Favor said. "But I have my moments."

"I'm glad to hear it," she said. "I need all the help I can get."

Mendonza shot another photo, then lowered the camera.

"I'm done," he said. "We should be leaving."

"So soon?" said Lorna Valencia

"We have work to do," Mendonza said.

She walked out with them to the taxi. Everybody else followed, dozens of them, an amazing procession out to the courtyard. It was empty when they got there. Favor, looking around, realized that the basketball players and the laughing children had gone to Lorna's home and were in the crowd that had trooped out behind them.

The good-byes took at least ten minutes. The villagers swarmed around Mendonza and Favor. Some spoke; others only reached out to grasp their hands or simply to touch them.

"We'll be back, we'll return, yes we'll try to come back with Marivic," Mendonza murmured as they edged back to the car. Finally Mendonza got in behind the wheel and tugged Favor inside through the open passenger door. He started the car and drove down the path to the highway.

Favor looked back through the rear window. They were all waving good-bye as the car trundled down the broken pavement. The gray-haired old ones, the very youngest—all of them—stood waving and watching until the taxi turned onto the highway.

"You have to excuse them," Mendonza said. "They don't get a lot of excitement out here."

"I didn't mind," Favor said. He could still feel their hands on him, the gentle but insistent way they reached out for him, wanting that moment of contact.

He sat back and looked out at the gulf and the steep forested hillsides and at the road that ran between them. The sun was high and hot. He thought about sitting with Mendonza and Ari and Stickney in the gazebo beside Lake Tahoe. How he had talked about doing a little good deed, as though it were a trivial obligation before they got on with the important business of pleasure seeking.

It was just hours in the past, but that evening felt distant and unreal. Something had changed. He could feel it. Partly it was the dislocation of having traveled halfway around the world between sunset and sunrise, but there was more. That evening at the lake, he hadn't yet met Lorna Valencia or seen her spotless floors in the little cottage at the edge of the jungle. He hadn't looked at Marivic's picture, carefully preserved under a coat of varnish. He hadn't been to San Felipe.

He said, "How are you feeling, Al? Tired?"

"No," Mendonza said. "I'm feeling all right."

"Good," Favor said. "Then let's get to work. I want to bring that girl home."

Moments before he disappeared into the back of the taxi, the American named Raymond seemed to scan the faces of the crowd around him. He was looking for Lorna. He had something important to tell her. As soon as he found her, he leaned toward her and said quietly but firmly, "Don't forget, like we talked about, call your son and have him contact me or Alex."

"So that your friends in Manila can look after him."

"I also want him to stay clear of Optimo. Be sure you tell him that."

"You believe there is danger?" she said.

She was watching his face when he answered. She noticed the slightest catch in his voice, an almost imperceptible hesitation before he spoke.

"There's no reason for him to be involved. That's why we're here," Favor said.

"I will tell him," Lorna said, and Favor nodded as he ducked into the car.

Something about Favor unsettled her. Under any other circumstances, she would fear him. Yet, as she watched the car drive away with him looking over his shoulder as he departed, she knew that he wished her well and that his advice was not to be disregarded.

She took out her phone and called her son.

TEN

When he left the last jeepney, Ronnie walked half a block up Amorsolo Street to the address where Optimo was supposed to be. He expected an office building. He found, instead, a gaudy nightclub, warehouse sized, with a three-story facade of dark reflective panels.

He looked up and down the block. Along one side of Amorsolo was a series of small shops and a travel agent and a Jollibee fast-food restaurant. On the other side of the street—the side where Optimo was supposed to be—there was only the nightclub and a residential compound behind a high wall, surely the home of a very rich family. A walkway ran between the side of the nightclub and the barrier wall of the residence.

Ronnie walked two blocks in each direction along Amorsolo Street. He couldn't find Optimo. He crossed to the other side of the street and again walked two blocks in each direction. No Optimo. His route brought him back to the double front door of the nightclub. The door was closed, locked. The neon sign was dormant, red and orange neon tubes against the shiny copper-toned panels of the facade. The tubes formed the outline of licking flames that surrounded the name of the club: *Impierno*.

The locked front door was completely unpromising. Optimo couldn't be here. He wandered along the sidewalk on Amorsolo until he reached the corner of the building. He stopped and stood looking back at it, perplexed.

Nearby, an old woman was selling newspapers and magazines. She sat against the corner of the wall that surrounded the compound, her stock spread out on the sidewalk in front of her. Someone stopped, picked out a newspaper from a stack, handed her a fifty-peso bill. She made change from a cigar box and dropped it into the customer's waiting hand. Her expression didn't change. She looked as if she had been sitting there forever.

Ronnie walked over to her, stood over her. She ignored him. Someone picked up a paper and gave her a few coins; she tossed them into the cigar box.

Ronnie said, "Ma'am, excuse me, I'm trying to find Optimo."

She stared out across the street, face blank.

Ronnie said: "Do you know Optimo?"

She lifted her right arm and made a go-away motion without looking up.

Then Ronnie realized that she was not brushing him off. She was pointing. Her bony fingers were gesturing down the walkway that ran between the residence and the Impierno building. For the first time, he noticed a door in the side of the building.

Ronnie went up the walkway, to the door. It was easy to miss, set flush into the side of the building. A discreet placard on the door read:

Impierno Talent Management
Optimo Employment Agency

He was standing at the door when his phone chirped. He checked the screen and saw his mother's number. Reflexively his thumb went to the TALK button . . .

. . . and paused, hovering a fraction of an inch above the button.

He knew what waited for him on the other side of that button click. His mother would be angry. She would scold him for remaining in Manila. She would chew his ass good. And when the chewing ended, the pleading would begin. Begging him to return. Weeping at his absence.

God, the weeping was worst of all.

The phone continued to sound in his hand. Ronnie stared at it for a few more seconds, and then did something he had never done before—never expected to do.

He slid his thumb over the keypad and pressed the button that read END.

He felt guilty when he did it. He also felt guilty about the lie he would have to tell later: *Sorry, Mother, I didn't hear it. Manila is so noisy.*

He promised himself that he would call her back right away, as soon as he had some answers from Optimo. This was why he had come, to confront them face-to-face. Now he was literally on the threshold, and he couldn't let anyone stop him.

Not even his mother.

He put the phone in his pocket and opened the door.

"Where did she get off the bus?" Mendonza asked Favor. They were in the car, headed away from San Felipe, north toward Tacloban. "Was she still on it when it got to Manila? Or did she take off somewhere between here and there?"

"She went to Manila. Why wouldn't she?" Favor said. "She wanted the job. Nice money. She was excited."

"Maybe she's a spur-of-the-moment runaway. She's on the bus, she decides she doesn't want the job, but she's too ashamed to go home."

"I don't think so," Favor said. "I asked a lot of people this morning; I couldn't find one who believed that she would run away and disappear for a week. Nobody. It was 'Not Marivic, never in a million years.' They might all be wrong, but I doubt it. I think she rode that bus all the way to Manila, just the way she was supposed to."

"I agree," Mendonza said. "I just wanted to hear you say it."

"So, what happened in Manila after she sent that text to her brother? The agency claims she never got off the bus. Maybe they missed her. Or maybe whoever was supposed to meet her didn't get there in time and doesn't want to admit it. Either way, she ends up at the terminal with no place to go."

"That's very possible."

"But then what?" Favor said. "She would let

someone know, right? Stranded at the terminal, she would call somebody."

"Maybe her phone was busted. Or she lost it."

"I'll buy that. But I don't buy that she would go four or five days without finding a way to let Mom know she's okay."

"No," Mendonza said.

"Unless something kept her from calling. She had an accident. Or she gets snatched by some random creep."

"She was carrying a residence certificate and birth certificate for her passport. If there was an accident, her mother would've been notified," Mendonza said. "The random predator, I don't think so. Manila's a rough town in a lot of ways, and there's sure plenty of chances for a young woman to get into trouble. But the psycho killer, the Ted Bundy kind that picks a stranger out of a crowd and snuffs her out, that's something you just don't see in this country."

"So we're saying that she did ride the bus all the way to Manila."

"Correct."

"But she didn't get lost or stranded at the terminal, because by now she would've checked in at home."

"Correct."

"But you see where this leaves us," Favor said. "If she took the bus all the way to Manila, and didn't get stranded . . ."

"Then somebody from the agency met her after all."

"Exactly."

"And now they deny it?" Mendonza said. "And they won't let her call home?"

"I know it seems unlikely," Favor said. "But that's where you end up, if you think it all the way through."

Mendonza looked up the highway, considering this. They were passing a village tucked in between the highway and shoreline. It seemed to be about the size of San Felipe, with the same mix of huts and tiny thatched cottages and makeshift shanties.

Mendonza said, "Something's been bugging me about the whole setup. Marivic getting that job offer. It seems like such a long shot."

Favor shifted in his seat, looking at Mendonza, catching the tone of worry in his voice.

"You see this place?" Mendonza said. He was motioning out toward the seafront village. "How many like it did we pass on the way down?"

"At least ten," Favor said.

"Uh-huh. That's on one stretch of road. Now think of all the other villages just like this on all the other roads. And in every one, I guarantee, you'll find girls just like Marivic, stuck in a dead end, praying for a job abroad."

Directly ahead, a jeepney pulled out onto the highway from the village. Mendonza smoothly flicked the car into the oncoming lane to avoid it, then back into the northbound lane when he was clear. The jeepney was fully loaded, and nearly two dozen pairs of eyes turned to watch as the car swept past.

Mendonza continued as if nothing had happened.

He said, "Half this country wants to work abroad, just because the money's that much better. You've got MDs leaving to become nurses in the States. Masters in electrical engineering are begging for the chance to install light fixtures in Saudi Arabia.

"But here Marivic puts in a job app—no experience, not even a high school diploma—and two days later she gets a call: 'Come to Manila, you're going abroad to work.' Why her? What made her special? What did Optimo see in her? That's what I want to know."

Ronnie opened the door in the side wall of the building that housed the Impierno nightclub. He stepped across the threshold, expecting to see, maybe, a dance floor and a stage, tables and chairs, a bar.

Instead, he found himself at the bottom of a stairwell, looking up at a long flight of stairs. He began to climb the steps. He was alone, his footfalls echoing off the narrow walls. For a moment Ronnie felt like an interloper going someplace he had not been invited and where he wouldn't be welcome. But he told himself that he didn't need an invitation to be here. Marivic's disappearance was his permission.

At the top of the stairs was a landing and a door at the far end, dark glass in a metal frame, solid and heavy when he pushed it open. He stepped into an office. It was a large open space with ten or so cubicles and at least as many young women, some at their work spaces, others at file cabinets and a printer and photocopier.

Ronnie guessed that all this sat above the night-club, an extra floor that you would never imagine as you looked at it from the street.

"Can I help you?"

He turned to face a woman who stood at the nearest cubicle, looking at him.

"Yes. I want to talk to somebody about my sister."

"Your sister works in this office?"

"No. She came to Manila for a job. Optimo brought her here. But now they say she wasn't on the bus. That's a lie."

"Oh, she's a job applicant. You should contact the local office, in that case. We're the business office; we don't deal directly with applicants."

Her tone was dismissive. Ronnie didn't like that. And, like everyone else in Manila, she seemed to be staring at his clothes, her eyes measuring him as she spoke. He was getting tired of it.

"She isn't an applicant," Ronnie said. "She came to Manila, Optimo brought her to Manila. Marivic Valencia is her name. Now she has disappeared, and I want to know where she is."

"I don't know what you're talking about."

"Who is in charge here? I am sick of this goddamn bullshit! I want to speak to your goddamn boss."

Heads were turning all around the office. For Filipinos, an angry voice in public was a major so-cial taboo. Ronnie heard the words in his head as if someone else had spoken them.

"I'm sorry," she said. "That isn't possible."

"I want to speak to the fucking boss! *Now!*"

The young woman was stunned. Her mouth moved as if to speak, but it only dropped open, without a sound, until she recovered enough to say: "One moment, sir."

She scurried away, toward the back of the office, where she rapped at a door. A woman stepped out. Older, well dressed, with a stern face that grew harder as she listened to the young woman. *Matrona,* Ronnie thought. A fearsome *matrona*, as most *matronas* are. She shot him a sharp look, drilling him from across the room, and she crooked a finger—just once—commanding him.

He felt his anger draining away as he crossed the room. He couldn't help it. Her eyes were locked on him as he approached, deflating him.

Before he could speak, she said, "What are you doing, disrupting my place of business? Your manners are terrible. Is this how you were raised?"

He found himself stammering: "Ma'am, it's about my sister, ma'am. Marivic Valencia is her name. She came to Manila on a bus. We know that she arrived. But we have heard nothing more from her; it's one week now. Oh, ma'am, my mother is so worried."

"I recall the name," she said. "Your mother or someone was in the Tacloban office, inquiring."

"My mother, yes."

"And she got an answer, did she not?"

"Yes, but, ma'am—"

"The answer is the same. You came all the way here from Leyte, disturbing my office, just to hear it again? Fine. I'll say it one more time. The girl took the ticket and expense money, but she wasn't on the bus when it arrived. I should be upset about that, because she breached her contract; but as a gesture of maternal sympathy for your mother, I won't pursue it."

"Thank you, but—"

"And before you doubt that account, you should know that I am one hundred percent certain that your sister was not on the bus when it arrived at the terminal. Do you know how I can be so sure? *Because I was there!* Yes. I myself went to the terminal that night. Three o'clock in the morning. Just because I wanted to be certain that the girl saw a friendly face when she stepped off the bus.

"So to say that she was on the bus when it arrived in Manila is to say that I am a liar. I hope you're not calling me a liar. Now go. You have your answer for a second time, the final time. I hope you won't force me to have you thrown out. Your mother would be ashamed, I'm sure."

She turned and started back through the door.

"I'm sorry to say it, ma'am, but I do know that my sister arrived in Manila. I have proof."

She stopped, paused, turned slowly back to Ronnie.

She said, "Proof? How is this possible?"

"Because she told me," he said. He dug out the cell phone from his pocket, paged down through the stored text messages, and found the last one from Marivic:

arrived

He raised the phone to show her, turning the screen outward, holding it out at the end of his outstretched arm. She took the phone from him to see it closer.

"That's her phone number," Ronnie said. "You see the date and the time."

At first he didn't notice her wrist, what she wore there. He was focused on her face, watching her expression as she squinted at the screen. But as she pushed the phone back at him, Ronnie caught the flash of gold at her wrist. It was a bracelet. Herringbone gold. A circle of diamonds. Red rubies that formed the letter "M."

He roared with rage.

Five Russians, including Ilya Andropov, lived in the compound on Amorsolo Street. At the moment that Ronnie spotted his sister's bracelet on the *matrona*'s wrist, one was sleeping in his quarters and the other four were in the big front room that served as the ops room and informal lounge. Andropov was at a table, discussing business with Totoy Ribera. Two others were playing cards through a curtain of cigarette smoke.

Anatoly Markov, the last of the group, was working his regular shift at the bank of video screens showing the feeds from sixteen surveillance cameras throughout the compound and the building next door. Markov was forty-eight years old, squat, and burly. He was sitting back in a swivel chair, feet propped up on the desk in front of him, when he spotted unusual movement on the camera that covered the offices above Impierno.

It was the hag, Magdalena. She was on her back, arms and legs thrashing. A man had pinned her down and appeared to be choking the life out of her.

"Boss, trouble next door," Markov said. Andropov stood up and came over, with Ribera following.

"Totoy, handle this," Andropov said.

Ribera was already headed for the door. He knew this was his job. The division of labor in this deal was clear-cut. The operation belonged to the Russians; they called the shots but remained inside the compound as much as possible. Any tasks outside the walls were performed by locals: Totoy and Magda and the crew of Filipinos who worked beneath them, doing jobs that were never explained. Totoy alone was granted access to the residence, but he got only glimpses of what happened in there. He knew even less about what happened to the drugged young men and women he and Magda took out of the bus terminals. He didn't even bother to think about it. The money was good—in fact, it was spectacular by his standards—and he had long lost any inhibitions about playing his part in the eternal process by which the strong culled the weak from the herd of humanity.

He went out a side door to a steel gate in the high white wall. A Filipino guard sat on a stool beside the gate, a shotgun propped on his knees. When he got closer, Totoy saw that the guard was nodding off. Totoy pulled out the pin that fastened the gate latch.

He slapped the guard in his face, a hard smack that woke him right away, and said, "Close it behind me, and get your head out your ass."

Totoy went out the gate, across the walkway to the side door of the Impierno building. He climbed the steps two at a time, pushed open the glass front door. He found the office workers shrieking as they stood in a frantic circle near a half-open door at the back of the room. Totoy shoved his way through and found Magdalena still on her back, still thrashing, face going purple, as a provincial farmer type, practically a boy, held her neck in his hands.

The country boy was in Magda's face, snarling.

"You're a lying whore!" he shouted.

One hundred percent correct, Totoy thought. He drew back his right leg and unleashed a kick to the boy's ribs. The force of it knocked him off Magda and sent him thumping hard against the doorframe.

Magda gasped, the boy groaned. Totoy bent close to Magda's mouth, to make sure she was actually breathing. When he heard the hissing intake of breath, he turned to the boy, picked him up by the T-shirt, and dragged him through the half-open door and into the hallway beyond.

It was a short hall with the entrances to two private offices. One was his; the other was Magda's. Totoy dragged the boy into his own dark office, dropped him onto a chair.

"Stay," he said, but the boy lunged at him as soon as Totoy stepped back, so he punched the kid hard, doubling him up.

"Stay," Totoy said again, and went out to where Magda was now sitting up. He helped her to her feet, started to lead her to the back. She stopped and made a motion toward the floor behind her. Totoy spotted the cell phone and reached down, scooped it up. To the young women who were watching all this, he said, "It's all over now, girls. Back to work."

He closed the door behind them and said to Magda, "What did you do to piss him off?"

She cleared her throat and found that she could speak.

"He's the brother of the Valencia girl. From last week. He says he's sure that she arrived in Manila. She sent a text."

She gestured to the phone. Totoy read the message, saw the date and time.

"That's it? That's why he went off?"

She raised her arm to show the bracelet.

"Christ," he said. He thought about it for a few moments, the implications. Greedy little thief, the trouble she had caused. But he decided that it wasn't so bad if it was handled right.

"I'll take care of this," he said. "You get things back to normal out there. Tell them the kid's a nutcase. They'll believe it."

Totoy returned to his office. The boy was doubled over on the chair, clutching his sides, quietly retching. Totoy put the cell phone on his desk. He pushed the boy up, straightening his back against the chair.

The boy continued to retch.

"It'll stop in a minute," Totoy said. "That's what

happens if you're not expecting a gut punch. You don't fight much, I can tell."

The retching did stop. The first words out of the boy were: "As soon as I get out of here, I'm going straight to the police."

"You don't have to wait," Totoy said. "You want to make a complaint, we can get started anytime."

He went around to his desk, opened the top drawer, took out a slim black ID wallet. He opened it to reveal the engraved seal of the Philippine National Police.

Name: RIBERA, Placido Antonio
Rank: Captain

"But maybe first we should discuss your assault on a fine lady three times your age, in front of a dozen witnesses, including myself."

"My sister is gone, and the old bitch knows what happened to her."

"A fine way to talk about the woman I love. I've been courting her for years, since her husband died."

"She's wearing my sister's bracelet. Diamonds and rubies and the letter 'M' for 'Marivic.'"

"The letter 'M' for 'Magdalena.' I should know, because I bought it for her."

"The text," he said. He pointed to his phone on the desk.

"That? She says that she arrived, the lady says she never saw her. But there's no contradiction. How many passengers on a Philtranco bus? Eighty? One hundred? They missed each other in the crowd, that's all."

Totoy picked up the phone. It was an older model, but he knew the commands.

"Besides . . ." he said. He deleted the message, holding the phone so the boy could see the word disappear. "Do you understand?" he said. "You're pushing against the tide. Keep pushing and you'll drown. Or you can go home and wait for your sister to return. Maybe she does, maybe not. Life goes on. You think you feel bad now, but believe me, it can get much worse."

Totoy watched the boy, looking to see how he would react. *Could go either way,* he thought.

The phone sounded in his hand.

A text.

Stay away from Optimo.
There is danger.

Totoy showed it to the boy.

"My mother," the boy said.

"Why would she think there's danger at Optimo?"

"She just doesn't want me getting into trouble."

Again the phone sounded. Another text. This time Totoy didn't show it to the boy.

Call me now.
Help is on the way.

"All right, I understand," the boy said. "I'll go home and take care of my mom."

He started to get up. Totoy pushed him back down into the chair.

"Maybe not," Totoy said.

Favor and Mendonza stood at a street corner in Tacloban, in front of the building where the local Optimo branch had its address. It was a modest commercial neighborhood at the edge of downtown. Favor could see a car repair shop, a small clothing store, a pension house, an outdoor food stall where customers carried their food away in plastic bags.

Nothing fancy. Not even close.

"A small office, a woman alone," Mendonza said, repeating Lorna Valencia's description of the office. "We need to impress her, but it would be easy to overdo it."

"Firm but not hostile," Favor said. "Not *overtly* hostile."

"I think you ought to talk to her," Mendonza said. "She might react to me like I'm a homeboy, just because I've got that look. But you're straight-up *americano*, and that'll impress her for sure."

"If you say so," Favor said.

They went into the building, up the creaking stairs with the flaking paint on the walls. Halfway up, they met a man coming down: midthirties, a local. Favor stood aside to let him pass and noticed a gauze pad on the inside of his left forearm, held in place by a piece of surgical tape. The man nodded a greeting and kept going; Favor and Mendonza climbed the second flight and stepped into the office.

Four in the room, Favor noted. Three in chairs, the clerk behind her desk. All four looked up and stared as Favor and Mendonza entered. Favor stood silently in front of the desk, staring down at the woman, while Mendonza went to the three in the chairs and asked them to wait outside.

"We'd like a few moments of your time," Favor said to the woman. "It's important, and we need your full attention."

The three scurried out. Mendonza closed the door behind them, then stood beside Favor with his arms folded.

"What is your name?" Favor said.

"I don't believe that I have any business with you," she answered.

Mendonza spoke in Tagalog. He said, "Pay attention to him, auntie. You don't want to play games with this one."

She looked from Mendonza to Favor.

"I am Lisabet Bambanao," she said. "And you?"

"We are friends of the Valencia family," Favor said. "Marivic Valencia was in this office recently."

"I know nothing about it," the woman said.

"You don't know Marivic Valencia? You gave her a bus ticket to Manila and some expense money. That was just a few days ago."

"Of course I remember that, but I don't know what happened to her."

"What can you tell me about her?"

"There's nothing to tell."

"Nothing special about her?"

"Just a girl, that's all."

"How many applications do you process per week in this office?"

"About two hundred and fifty, most weeks."

"And how many of those are offered jobs?"

"I don't know. I just take the applications and send them on. I don't know what happens after that."

"No? You don't issue bus tickets and expense money to all who have been offered a job?"

"Not routinely."

"How many bus tickets do you issue, an average week?"

"I don't know—" she said, before cutting herself off. She could see where he had led her, but it was too late. He knew.

"You issued one to Marivic. Why?"

"Instructions from Manila."

"This office has been open how long?"

"About seven months."

"And in all that time, how many other applicants got the same treatment as Marivic?"

"I can't say any more. Please go now. I know nothing about any of this. I take applications and send them on, that's all."

"Was Marivic unusually qualified? Gifted? Exceptional in some way?"

The woman shook her head. No. No. No. Not so much answering him as trying to refuse him.

She said, "Please. I have no part in this."

"What was special about Marivic? What made her different?"

"Nothing," she said. "Nothing that I could see. Please go now. *Please.*"

Favor got up from the chair and walked out, with Mendonza following. On their way down, they met a young woman, college age, headed up. She was holding a clipboard with an application form. On the inside of her left forearm, visible to Favor as he stepped aside, was a gauze pad held in place by a piece of surgical tape.

Favor said, "Miss? Excuse me? Your arm, did you hurt it?"

She paused.

She said, "Not at all, sir. It's from the examination. The physical exam, the doctor takes a blood sample."

"You were required to take a physical?"

She said, "All applicants are required, sir."

They watched her go up the stairs and into the Optimo office.

Among several offices at the bottom floor, Favor found one with a hand-lettered sign, CLINIC, taped to the door. He opened it, peeked in, found a nurse in a small waiting room.

He said, "I woke up this morning with a sore throat and a headache. I think I'm running a fever. Can I get an appointment this afternoon?"

The nurse looked up and said, "I'm very sorry, this is a private facility."

"Associated with the agency upstairs?"

"That's correct."

He went out and joined Mendonza on the sidewalk.

"It's an Optimo clinic," he said. "I don't see how that pays off."

"Sending people overseas, you want to make sure they're healthy," Mendonza said.

"Yeah, when they're actually ready to go," Favor said. "I get that. But most of these people will wait weeks or months for a job. By then you just have to do it all over again. I'm guessing most won't ever get that call. So why would they do the exams now?"

They walked along the front of the office building. Just above eye level was a row of windows. Favor knew that one or two of the windows must belong to the clinic.

He crossed the street to the pension house, with Mendonza following. MIRADOR PENSION said the sign above the front door. Inside looked like the film noir set of a cheap hotel. The desk clerk appeared stunned to see them, even more surprised when Favor said that he wanted to see a room. Second floor, street side.

The clerk plucked a couple of keys off a peg-board and led them up to the second floor. He told Favor that the street-facing rooms were six hundred pesos a night—about twelve dollars—but the rooms at the back were larger and quieter, just one hundred pesos more.

"American style," he said. "Much nicer."

"I prefer the street side," Favor said. "I'm on a limited budget."

The room had a dank and musty smell. One small bed, an ancient armchair. Favor went to the single window, parted the drapes, and looked out into the street.

"Perfect," he said.

"It is?" the clerk said.

"Exactly what I want," Favor said. He stripped some bills from a wad of cash, gave it to the clerk, and said, "My friend will be down in a while to check us in."

The clerk walked out and shut the door behind him.

"Remind me why we're here," Mendonza said.

Favor pushed the drapes open a few more inches. Across the narrow street was the building they had just left. From here he could see two windows that opened onto the clinic. The windows were set above sidewalk eye level, but from up here they allowed a perfect angle down into the clinic.

"I like the view," he said.

For about an hour after the two men walked out of the office, Lisabet Bambanao resumed her usual routine, acting as if nothing unusual had happened. She continued to handle applications while interacting with the applicants as little as possible. When she received completed applications, she fed them through a document scanner, checked to be sure that the files had been saved to the appropriate directory on her computer, and then filed the paper originals in a cabinet beside her desk.

Outwardly, she continued to function just as she always had, six days a week, eight a.m. to six p.m., during the seven months since Optimo had hired her to open its office in Tacloban. But while she clicked through the tasks as smoothly as ever, a part of her mind was fully occupied with a debate about how she ought to react to the visit by the two strangers.

There should have been no question. When she was hired, she was given a numbered list of directives that described and governed her tasks. Most of it was minutiae:

11. Verify that all pages are correctly oriented before placing documents in the auto feed tray.

But a few were sweeping, and ominous.

23. The business of the Agency is confidential. Do not discuss your work with anyone.
24. Report any remarkable occurrence at once.

That was plain enough. The visit was remarkable—and disturbing—and as soon as the two men left, Lisabet knew that she ought to call the Manila office and tell them what had happened.

But she hesitated.

The American's interrogation had been unnerving, partly because she had asked herself some of the same questions. *What was different about Marivic Valencia? Why did she get the special treatment?* It was as if he had looked into her mind and read her doubts.

But not completely. The American apparently didn't know about Danilo Magcapasag. That was a month after the office opened. It was the same story as Marivic: a seemingly ordinary applicant who was quickly summoned to Manila with a bus ticket and expense money from petty cash.

And the same outcome: the disappearance, the distraught family demanding answers, the denial from Manila.

The first time, Lisabet had seen no reason to doubt the denial. But now the story was playing itself out again.

This was why she hesitated. Something seemed wrong here, and she wasn't sure that she wanted to be a part of it.

Her indecision lasted until she went into her purse, looking for lipstick. Her eye fell on an envelope stuck near the top. It was a tuition envelope for her youngest daughter at a technical college in Tacloban. The school cost 5,500 pesos per quarter, and Lisabet kept the envelope in her purse as a reminder. Whenever she was tempted by an extravagance—a pair of shoes, maybe, or a magazine—she would see the envelope and put the money there instead. The payment was due in a week and a half, and Lisabet was still 1,400 pesos short, but she knew that she would make it on time. She had a payday between now and then.

Now the envelope told her what she had to do. She knew almost nothing about Optimo or those behind it, and she felt no loyalty to the company or the people. But without those paydays . . .

She reached for the phone.

ELEVEN

Who told you to come here?" said Totoy Ribera. "Who put you up to it?"

"Nobody," said the boy. "It was my idea."

They were still in Totoy's office. The boy, who said his name was Ronnie, was seated in the chair while Totoy stood beside his desk, looming over him.

"You did all this on your own?" Totoy said. "Jumped on a bus and came all the way from Leyte just to ask a few questions here?"

"Yes."

"Bullshit, I don't believe you."

"It's true. I had to sneak out of the house."

In one ear, Totoy heard Magda's voice coming through his Bluetooth earpiece: "Ilya wants you to ask what made him believe that we have his sister. And move over, you're blocking the camera. Ilya wants to see his face."

Magdalena and Andropov were in the operations room at the residence, taking in a feed from a surveillance camera in Totoy's office, with Magda relaying instructions through the earpiece. The boy didn't know this.

He also didn't realize that he was making a case for his own life.

Totoy sidled to the other end of the desk, moving out of the camera's view.

"On what suspicion?" he said.

"The text message from Marivic."

"You were going on nothing more than a one-word text on your phone?"

"That's enough. I knew that Marivic arrived on the bus and Optimo said that she didn't. So I knew that you were lying. I was right too. The old bitch has her bracelet. She knows what happened to my sister."

Shut up, you're digging your own grave, Totoy wanted to tell him.

He knew that Ronnie would leave this office one of two ways. Andropov could decide that the boy was acting alone and posed no threat, that his story would not be believed no matter how passionately he told it. In that case, Ronnie would be allowed to walk out and disappear into the world, unaware of how close he had come to the end of his life.

Or Andropov could decide that the boy needed more persuasive interrogation than Totoy could do here in the office with the staff just a wall away. In that case, Ronnie would be taken out to the compound. And that would be the end. Having seen the compound and the Russians, he would know too much. He could never be allowed to leave alive.

Totoy didn't especially care either way, but some distant part of him was actually rooting for the kid. He was a gutsy little fucker.

Magda, in his ear, said: "Ask about the second text."

Totoy said, "What did your mother mean, 'Help is on the way'?"

"I don't know," Ronnie said. "It doesn't make any sense to me."

In his earpiece, Totoy heard a sound that he recognized as the ring tone on Magda's cell. He heard her voice as she answered the call.

A hell of a way to conduct an interrogation, he thought.

To Ronnie he said, "Who is coming to help you?"

"Nobody is helping us. That's why I came here."

Magda was chattering in his earpiece. Not to him—to somebody on the cell. Loud, displeased.

Totoy said, "Why would your mother say something like that if it's not true?"

"She probably wanted to keep me out of trouble, keep me from coming here. I don't know."

Now Andropov and Magda were talking back and forth in the earpiece. Totoy couldn't make out the words, but it was loud and insistent, so distracting that he couldn't continue. He stood and looked down at the boy and waited for the racket to die down in his earpiece.

"A call from Tacloban: two men were asking about Marivic this morning," Magda said. She was talking directly to Totoy this time. "A Fil-Am and an American. Tough guys. What does he know about that?"

Totoy said, "Who are the men asking about your sister in Tacloban today at the Optimo office? A Filipino-American and an *americano.*"

"I don't know any Fil-Ams. And I don't know any *'canos.*"

Totoy said, "Claiming to be friends of the family, threatening our representative there." He was repeating Magda's words in his ear now, word for word. "A mestizo built like a tank, an American with eyes like ice."

"I never heard of them before," Ronnie said. "You're making this up."

The boy wasn't defiant anymore. He was scared. His voice was unsteady, and his lower lip trembled.

"No," Totoy said. "This is for real."

The boy said nothing. The earpiece was quiet, too, for a moment. Then Andropov spoke. His voice was hard, but somewhere underneath there was a note of worry. He said, "Who the fuck are these men?"

Totoy moved around to the side of the chair, so that he was directly over Ronnie. He leaned in close, getting right in Ronnie's face—blocking the camera, he knew, but to hell with it—and he snarled, *"Who the fuck are these men?"*

Then he stood aside to let Andropov watch the response.

"Sir, truly, I have no idea."

The kid was telling the truth. Totoy was sure of it. He had been doing this for twenty-five years, putting the squeeze on assholes with something to hide, and he had learned to detect the rare golden nugget of truth buried in the endless shitpile of deception.

Now it was up to Andropov.

Totoy waited.

Andropov said, "I want him over here."

And that was it. The question was how to get him out, past the office staff, who believed that they were working for a legitimate employment agency. It was almost midday: lunch hour. Totoy got the idea of having Magda take them all out for lunch, a special treat from Optimo. Nobody turned that down. The office cleared out in a hurry.

Two of the Filipino guards came over from the compound. Ronnie still didn't know what was happening. He was sitting in the chair in Totoy's office, waiting.

He tried to bolt when he saw the guards, but he couldn't get past them. They threw him to the floor. One of them had brought a tranquilizer in a syringe. The kid fought hard when he saw the needle, but Totoy knelt on his arm, pinning it down, while he found a vein and stuck it in.

The boy started to fade right away.

They wanted to take him out while he could still walk, so they brought him to his feet and led him through the deserted office, one guard holding him up by each arm. He was stumbling, nearly dead-weight, too far gone to resist. They got him down the stairs and crossed the walkway to the gate in the wall of the residence compound. They were practically dragging him now, and if anyone had seen them, the scene would have looked like exactly what it was: two thugs strong-arming a kid from the country.

But this was bustling Manila. Nobody noticed; nobody cared. They hustled the kid across the walkway and through the opening in the wall, Totoy shut the gate behind them, and it was done.

TWELVE

Favor told Mendonza that he wanted to wait for the last plane of the day from Tacloban to Manila. It left at 7:35 p.m., which gave them a few hours to watch the building across the street from the pension house. The path from the moment of Marivic's disappearance, traced backward in time, lay through the building. Therefore it was worthy of observation.

Patient and unobtrusive observation was a callback to their Bravo years. To go convincingly undercover, you learned to quietly absorb a place and a situation. Watch and listen . . . just be there.

While Mendonza left to buy the plane tickets, Favor stationed himself in a chair at the window with Mendonza's camera and a telephoto lens. He watched young men and women entering the building, then coming out about an hour later with the gauze patch under a piece of tape. About four an hour, he guessed.

He had a good view down into the two first-floor windows. One showed a partial view down into the clinic's waiting room. It showed a chair that was sometimes occupied, sometimes not. The other gave him an angle down into a room that Favor thought might be a storage area.

Through the powerful lens, Favor saw boxes of bandages and tape and latex gloves and tongue depressors. On a white counter along one side of the room, Favor could make out a rack with small vials, clear glass or plastic, sealed with a stopper. About every quarter of an hour, a middle-aged Filipino man in a lab coat—the doctor, Favor guessed—would enter the room and stand at the counter to fill one of the vials with dark liquid from a syringe. Favor knew this must be the blood draw from an examination, taken from another applicant. The doctor would seal the vial, write out a label, wrap the label around the vial, and place it in a small refrigerator under the counter. A couple of minutes later, one more young man or woman would leave the building: exam completed, application submitted.

This routine continued throughout the day, unvarying, into the afternoon. Mendonza returned after a while with a roasted chicken and rice and some San Miguel beer and soft drinks. Favor kept watching the building while he ate. When Mendonza stretched out on the bed to nap, Favor stayed by the window, sipping from a bottle of beer, patiently watching.

In the late afternoon, the light softened and shadows lengthened. The people of Tacloban began heading home. Traffic picked up in the street below, mostly jeepneys and three-wheel motorcycles with rudimentary covered passenger seats. In Tacloban, they were sometimes called trikes, sometimes sidecars.

At 5:55, the nurse from the clinic left the building

and flagged down an empty trike. She folded herself into the passenger compartment and the trike buzzed off, skittering through traffic like a rasping water bug.

At 6:05, Lisabet Bambanao walked out of the front door and out to the sidewalk. She waved at a jeepney; it pulled across traffic to stop in front of her, and she climbed into the back.

A few minutes later, Mendonza woke and looked out the window. He checked his watch. The airport was about four miles away, ten or fifteen minutes. He told Favor that they ought to leave by quarter to seven, give themselves plenty of time to make the 7:35 flight.

"Sure," Favor said. He was watching the second window across the street, the storage room. The doctor was at the white counter, but he wasn't doing the usual routine of filling a vial this time. Instead he was reaching into the refrigerator and taking out a rack with a couple dozen filled vials, blood specimens.

He took a box from under the counter. The box was plain, cream-colored, no printing. He placed the rack with the filled vials into the box.

"You hear from Lorna's boy, Ronnie?" Mendonza asked.

"No," Favor said. "I thought he must've called you while you were out." Favor was still watching through the telephoto lens on the camera, which was zoomed in all the way to get a good look at the box and the vials. The box seemed to have thick walls, maybe Styrofoam, some kind of padding.

"No, he didn't call me," Mendonza said.

The doctor reached into the refrigerator for another rack of vials—sealed specimens—and placed it into the box. He took a plastic bag from the freezer compartment—ice cubes, Favor saw—and placed the bag on top of the vials, and closed the box.

"He should've called by now," Mendonza said.

"Call Lorna and see what's up," Favor said.

The doctor had a roll of red packing tape. He was laying a wide strip of it across the top seam of the box. Sealing the package.

"Damn, he's leaving with it," Favor said.

Mendonza had his phone in hand when Favor turned from the window.

Favor said, "Al, hang loose, I have to follow this package."

Favor hurried from the room. He ran down the hall, bounded down the stairs, hurried through the lobby.

Favor stepped out, then withdrew back inside. He didn't want the doctor to notice him. Favor waited until the doctor had turned up the street, a few steps along the sidewalk, the package under his arm. Then Favor started out the door and up the street, tracking the doctor on the opposite sidewalk with the streaming lanes of traffic between them.

It was a brief pursuit. After half a block, the doctor stopped at a Kia sedan parked at the curb. Favor ducked into the entrance of a bakeshop and watched. The doctor pulled keys from his pocket, opened the passenger-side door, placed the package in the foot well of the passenger seat, shut the door.

He walked around to the other side, opened the door, got behind the wheel.

The headlights came on; the backup lamps glowed.

Favor stepped out from the doorway. The car backed up a few feet as the driver turned the wheel, ready to pull out. Favor looked out into oncoming traffic and tried to spot an empty taxi headed his way.

The doctor found an opening and swung out into traffic. Favor watched the Kia blend into traffic as it accelerated away, down the street.

As Favor watched the Kia disappear, a trike whipped into a sudden 180-degree turn, cutting through traffic, stopping inches from Favor. The driver was a small man in shorts and T-shirt. He stood up on the foot pegs, looking at Favor over the passenger awning, and said, "Hey, Joe. Need a ride?"

The Kia was out of sight now, gone.

"Hey, Joe" was an archaic phrase. In World War II it was Filipinos' universal greeting to American GIs, and then for a few decades it was applied to all foreigners. But it was now long out of use, an old man's phrase. When Favor looked closer in the dim evening light, he saw that the driver really was an old man. Thin gray hair, a near-toothless grin.

"How about it, Joe. You need trike?"

Not anymore, Favor was about to answer. Then he realized what he had just seen, the amazing move, the agile way the driver had cut across traffic. Favor knew he could use this guy.

"Not tonight," Favor said. "Tomorrow. You know Tacloban?"

"Tacloban is my home, Joe. All my life."

"What is your name?" Favor asked.

"I am Romeo Mandaligan."

"My name is Ray," Favor said. "I'm in the Mirador, over there. You come around in the afternoon, I'll tell you what I need."

"Sure, whatever you say, Joe."

Favor dug in his pocket, came up with some bills: Philippine currency, a five-hundred-peso note at the top. He stripped it off and walked around the front of the trike and gave it to the driver. The typical trike fare in a provincial city was ten or twenty pesos, and Romeo Mandaligan accepted the five hundred with something like reverence.

He said, "For what?"

"So you know I'm serious," Favor said. "Come around tomorrow, I have a one-thousand-peso job for you."

Romeo Mandaligan slid the bill carefully into the front pocket of his shirt.

He said, "Ray, you can count on me."

Mendonza was on the phone with Lorna Valencia when Favor returned to the room.

Mendonza said, "Ray's here now, let me talk to him. Send me that text. Don't you worry, I'm sure he's all right."

He clicked off and said to Favor: "Lorna tried all day to get Ronnie, phone calls and texts, no luck.

But about an hour ago she gets a text from him—"
Mendonza's phone cut him off. He looked down and
found a text, and showed it to Favor.

> *No problem Optimo*
> *coming home soon*
> *bttry low see you later luv u*

"She says it doesn't sound like him," Mendonza
said. "I don't know what that means, but she has a
bad feeling." He checked the time and said, "We have
a little time; we can grab a bite on the way to the
airport."

"I'm not leaving," Favor said. "I want to be here
this time tomorrow."

"All right," Mendonza said. "There's a nice resort
hotel on the north side of town. We'll get a couple of
rooms there, come back here tomorrow afternoon."

"I'd rather stay where I am."

"Here?" Mendonza said.

"Right now that building across the street is the
most interesting place in Tacloban. By far. But you go
ahead. I'll catch you in the morning."

"No way, cowboy," Mendonza said. "You're staying, I'm staying."

Mendonza did persuade Favor to go out for a
meal, a seafood restaurant a couple of blocks away.
Afterward, Favor went back to the room while Mendonza stopped at an Internet café to send the photo
of Marivic and Ronnie to Arielle in Manila.

Then he returned to the room.

Mendonza wondered what the sleeping arrangements would be: just one small bed. He thought they might need a second room. But when Mendonza returned to the room, Favor was back in the armchair, and he stayed there while they talked for a couple of hours, with Mendonza perched at the side of the bed. Then they both got sleepy.

Favor just stretched out his legs and lounged back in the chair, and that was the last sight Mendonza saw before he nodded off: Favor still in the ratty armchair, still facing out the window toward the building across the street.

The drugs wore off sometime around nightfall. When Ronnie came around, Markov and Totoy Ribera were comparing methods for squeezing information out of reluctant prisoners.

It was a professional discussion that drew on long years of experience, going back to when they were both young men. Markov's initiation had come as a junior KGB officer in the waning years of the Soviet Union. Totoy Ribera had trained by questioning suspected Reds during the latter years of the Ferdinand Marcos era.

Ilya Andropov was standing nearby, listening, and was the first to notice that Ronnie was conscious again.

Ronnie was on the floor, hog-tied.

Andropov stood over him and bent down low, getting in Ronnie's face.

He said, "Okay. Now listen. This is very important. The big Fil-Am and the American. Who are they?"

"I don't know."

"Why do they care about your sister?"

"I don't know."

"Why are they bothering my office in Tacloban?"

"I don't know."

Andropov reached back and brought out a hand towel, terry cloth. He quickly wound the towel, rope-like, and tried to gag Ronnie with it. Ronnie fought it, keeping his teeth clenched, but Markov came over and pinched his nostrils shut, and this forced Ronnie to open his mouth.

Then Andropov pushed the towel into Ronnie's mouth, and tied it tight behind his neck.

Markov said, "How long do we go?"

"Until I believe him," Andropov said.

HARVEST DAY
−4

THIRTEEN

This is it?" Stickney said.

"This is the address," said Elvis Vega.

They were stopped in the street in front of Impierno, Stickney in the front seat of a Nissan sedan, one of the rides that Edwin Santos had arranged. The driver was Elvis Vega. He was about forty. When they chatted earlier he had told Stickney that he was a lifelong *manileño*, had been driving in the city for twenty years.

The car was spotless, and Elvis had carved through morning traffic with professional ease. Stickney decided that the guy knew what he was doing. Yet, here they were in front of a place called Impierno.

"This is a nightclub," Stickney said.

"Correct. Impierno is well known for its bold shows." Stickney recognized the phrase from his last time in Manila. "Bold" meant "nude."

While they were speaking, a parking space opened up in front of Impierno, and Elvis slipped the sedan in against the curb. He said, "Come. We will investigate."

They got out and stood on the sidewalk. Stickney tried the front door of Impierno: locked. He walked with Elvis toward the middle of the block, across the walkway between the nightclub and the high concrete wall next door, to where the old woman was sitting among stacks of newspapers and magazines.

"I will ask," Elvis said, and he bent and spoke a few words to the woman.

She rolled her eyes and spoke a couple of words that Stickney didn't recognize.

She lifted her arm and motioned into the walkway, an impatient swipe of her hand.

"Back here?" Stickney said. Now he saw the door at the side of the building.

"I think so."

Elvis walked with him until Stickney read the sign on the door.

"This is it," Stickney said. "I probably won't be long."

"No matter. I will be waiting."

Elvis was turning away when Stickney said, "The old woman? That look she gave you? What was that all about?"

"She was being rude."

"What did she say?"

"It was Tagalog," Elvis said. "*Isa pa*. It means 'One more.' But she was being sarcastic. Like 'Great, another one.' I think she's sick of being asked."

Andropov called to tell Magda that a stranger, a foreigner, was on his way up the stairs.

They must have been watching close, she thought, to pick him up so quickly on the monitors.

The Russians seemed to be spooked about this Marivic matter. Totoy had told her so over dinner the evening before. He said that they didn't understand the fuss. Why would a couple of Americans—scary ones—take an interest in an insignificant province girl?

"The Russians don't like unanswered questions," Totoy had said. "It makes them nervous."

Now another foreigner was showing up, and Andropov was practically coming apart.

"Get up to the front and intercept him," he was saying in her earpiece. "If it's about the girl, take him into your room. Don't let him question the staff. String him along. See how much he knows."

She was already out of her office, turning toward the door. *Calm down,* she wanted to tell Andropov.

Although it would depend on what they were hiding down on the island, she thought. Maybe they had good reason to be nervous.

The foreigner entered from the landing at the top of the stairs. About forty-five or fifty, dark-skinned, black hair flecked with gray. He wore a loose Hawaiian-style floral-print shirt that marked him as a tourist for sure.

Magda stepped between him and the woman at the front desk who usually handled any stray visitors.

"I wonder if someone can help me," he began. A quiet voice with a soft accent that sounded vaguely British. "I wanted to ask about a girl. Actually, it would be a boy as well."

He was taking a snapshot from the front pocket,

ready to hold it out to her. She needed just a glance—not even that—to know who he was talking about.

She took the snapshot from him and smoothly reached for his elbow, moving him along as she said, "Yes, yes, of course. Why don't we go into my office? It's much more comfortable."

Markov hauled Ronnie into the ops room, sat him in a swivel chair in front of a monitor.

"Who is he?" Markov said.

The boy squinted.

"I can't see," he said.

The boy's face was swollen and bruised, his lips split. His eyes were nearly shut.

"Don't screw with me," Markov said.

Ronnie leaned close to the monitor.

"No, it's too small. I really can't see."

It was one of the small monitors, maybe six inches across. Markov patched the feed into one of the bigger screens, off to the side of the console. He grabbed the boy by the shoulders and shoved his face toward it.

"Still too small?"

"No. I can see now."

"And?"

"I don't know him," the boy said. "Please don't hit me. But it's true. I've never seen him before; I have no idea."

Andropov was standing at the console, listening to the conversation in Magda's office.

"He has a photo of you and your sister," Andropov said. "Where did that come from?"

"I don't know how he got it."

"Must be a real mystery," Markov says.

"Yes, it is," the boy said. "It's a mystery."

Markov hit him across the face, a backhand blow that knocked the boy off the chair, down to the floor. He lay there, curled up, arms crossed over his face.

The two Russians turned away from him. They were watching the visitor's image on the monitor, listening to his voice, understated and polite.

"I'm just a friend of the family," he was saying. "The mother is distraught, you can imagine. I want to help any way I can."

He spoke so quietly that the mics in Magda's office almost didn't pick it up. Markov had to crank the volume all the way up just to make out the words.

"I don't know about the two in Tacloban," Markov said. "But this one's nothing. Totoy will know how to deal with this pussy."

Andropov watched the monitor for a few seconds, and nodded.

"Yes," he said. "This one's for Totoy."

She was lying. Stickney knew it from the start.

First it was the picture, the way she had almost jumped at it when he brought it out, snatching it out of his hand before she had even taken a good look. Then, here in the office, she had passed it back to him—still having taken no more than a glance—and said, "I've heard her name, but I've never seen her."

"We run a legitimate business," she was saying. "We send approximately fifty workers abroad every week, to jobs they would never find on their own. Manila is just a stopover for them. We try to take care of them while they're here, but of course we can't be responsible for every one."

"Of course. And the boy—"

"I've never seen either of them."

"That's a shame," Stickney said.

"But if I think of anything, I'll be in touch. Your phone . . ."

"No phone. I'm just a visitor, you know."

"Staying at which hotel?"

"I'm not sure. I moved out of my first one this morning, and my travel agent is booking another for me."

"How long will you be in Manila?"

"It's indefinite," Stickney said.

"Perhaps you'll have a chance to enjoy our nightlife. My club is popular. Come by some night."

She took a business card from a holder on her desk, jotted on the back, and passed it over to him. The card was bright red, stamped IMPIERNO in gold lettering. *Full Compliments,* she had written on the back, above her signature.

She said, "Show that to the manager, you'll be well taken care of. We have many beautiful performers." She gave a dry laugh. "Marivic isn't one of them, I promise. But you're welcome to see for yourself."

Stickney got up to leave, and she quickly rose to follow. She stuck close, interposing herself between him and the office workers. She held the door open for him and then stood at the landing and watched him all the way to the bottom of the stairs.

She was still standing there, watching, as Stickney opened the door and went outside.

Elvis Vega was standing beside the Nissan when Stickney got to the sidewalk on Amorsolo Street. Vega went to open the passenger door for him, but Stickney stopped and turned toward the old woman with the newspapers. She ignored him as he stood there, and Stickney hunched down, putting himself at her level.

He said, "I know it's a waste of your time, people bothering you when all you want to do is sell papers. But I need your help for a moment. It won't take long, and it's very important."

She turned her head and looked at him, eye to eye, for the first time.

"It's all right," she said.

Stickney showed her the snapshot.

"Have you seen this boy?"

She gave it a long look.

"Yesterday. He was standing where you are now. He asked for the same place you asked."

"You mean Optimo."

"Yes."

"And then?"

"He went back there. The same place you went. I didn't see him after that."

"Thank you very much," Stickney said.

He stood up and started to walk toward Elvis Vega.

Two cars, both sedans with tinted windows, pulled up fast and parked in the street in front of him. Doors swung open; three men got out and came toward Stickney—one straight at him, the other two swinging around to cut him off, left and right, as he stood on the sidewalk. One of them wore a loose white over-the-waist dress shirt, short-sleeved, a style Filipinos call *polo barong*. Stickney caught the blue steel muzzle of an automatic pistol below the hem of the shirt, poking through the tip of a holster.

One of them flipped open an ID wallet for half a second to show a badge and ID.

He said, "Philippine National Police. Come with me, please."

They hustled him to the first car. After a quick, professional pat-down, they levered him into the backseat and closed the door behind him.

The car moved out, down Amorsolo Street.

Across from Stickney on the backseat was a man in his late forties. Acne scars. Impassive half-hooded eyes. His thick lips seemed poised to snarl. Stickney thought that assholes didn't necessarily look the part. But when they did, the effect was something to behold.

"You have your passport, I hope," said the man with the pockmarked face.

Stickney took it from the pocket of his trousers and handed it over.

He paged through it, found the entry stamp.

"You work fast. You've been here less than a day

and a half, already you're in the kind of trouble that can wreck your life."

"I've done nothing wrong," Stickney said.

"What you've done is immaterial. What you *could* have done—that's what matters. We're a friendly nation, but certain offenses by visitors can't be overlooked. Pedophilia, that's twenty years hard. Drug smuggling, that's death. You understand?"

He reached into Stickney's shirt pocket for the photo that he must have known was there. He took it, held it, flicked a corner.

"How are you acquainted with these teenagers?"

"I'm not," Stickney said. "I never met them."

"I see. But you have their photograph. And you've been harassing citizens—upstanding individuals—allegedly on their behalf. I'm sorry, this is not credible. Most tourists, the day after they arrive, they're sitting on a beach."

"That was my plan after I cleared up a couple of questions."

"You should have gone there directly."

He handed the passport back with his right hand. Stickney took the passport. As Stickney reached back to put it in his pocket, the left hand of the scar-faced man swung in a short, sharp arc toward Stickney's midsection. He was holding a sap, leather-bound and about six inches long.

Stickney saw it but couldn't block it. The corner of the sap caught him mid-chest, around diaphragm level. An instant later Stickney was on the floor of the car, his arms wrapped around his torso, with the sensation that his guts would spill out if he didn't hold them back.

The man leaned close and spoke softly into Stickney's ear.

"You're out of your element. You and your friends. Yes, I know about your two friends in Tacloban. This is not your business, and no good can come of pursuing it. You have a chance now to leave the Philippines. You should go while you can. Otherwise, I promise, you'll regret that you didn't take my advice."

Stickney caught movement at the periphery of his vision. He turned his head to see the man with the pitted face swinging the sap again—not hard, just another well-placed tap at the base of the skull.

He was out before his face hit the floor.

Elvis Vega watched as the three men hustled Stickney off the sidewalk. It happened too quickly for Vega to help. He was about to shout, maybe try to distract them, but when he saw the wallet flip open, the badge gleaming, he knew that it would have been a mistake.

Still, he felt obligated. When the two cars drove off down Amorsolo Street, carrying Stickney away, Elvis Vega got into the Nissan and started to follow. While he drove, he called Edwin Santos on his cell phone: *Eddie should know about this,* he thought.

Eddie's number rang and rang.

At first three other vehicles separated the Nissan from the two sedans Vega was pursuing. But within the next couple of blocks, the other cars turned off, and Vega found himself behind the second of the two police vehicles.

For a couple of blocks Vega drove close to the cops, trying to see what was happening with Stickney.

But he realized that he was driving too close, seemingly too interested, when one of the police in the car ahead turned in his seat and threw him a look of casual menace.

Vega slowed and dropped away and turned off at the next intersection.

Sorry, he thought. *But better you than me.*

When Stickney regained consciousness, he was at the side of a road, a back street. The smell of rotting garbage was strong, and he saw that he was sprawled beside a pile of trash. He wondered how long he had been out. Long enough to attract about a dozen curious young children, who stood across the road, staring.

Stickney sat up and took inventory. The passport was in his shirt pocket. Wallet, gone. Cell phone, gone. He had no money. Not a dollar, not a peso or a centavo.

His pockets were empty. He tried to remember what else he had been carrying. It came to him in a couple of seconds.

Hotel key card.

Gone.

The hotel name had been on the back of the card. So they would know where he had been staying. They could find Arielle.

He got up, walked toward the children. They looked ready to scatter as he approached.

"I need a phone," he said. "Anybody? Please?"

The tallest, a boy about twelve or thirteen, spoke up first. He was a skinny kid holding a basketball that was nearly worn smooth, and he wore an over-size singlet that said PUREFOODS HOT DOGS. He took an old Nokia from his shorts and held it out. "Text only, okay?" the boy said.

"Sure," Stickney said.

He took the phone, and paged to the text-messaging screen. It asked for a number. Ari should be told, he thought. Ari first.

Ari's number . . .

Old training taught that if it mattered, you committed it to memory. He had used Ari's number exactly once, when he had keyed it into his own phone's contacts list.

He closed his eyes and summoned it.

With about eighty percent confidence.

He tapped out a message:

Blown. Bail now. Rspnd asap. Stick

He handed the phone back to the boy, and said, "Can you wait for a minute? I might get an answer."

"Okay," the boy said.

Stickney felt dizzy. He sat with his back against a power pole. His head was roaring.

The boy stood nearby and said, "You from the States?"

"Yes," Stickney said.

"Do you know LeBron James?"

"No, but I've seen him play."

"Lebron is the best."

"How about Kobe?" Stickney said.

"Kobe rocks, but LeBron is the man."

Stickney sat and waited for the phone to ring. His head hurt, his elbows and one cheek were scraped and sore. He guessed that he had been dumped hard from the car.

He felt old and silly. He was unprepared for all this. For the past ten years he had been living a placid existence among the redwoods in Mendocino, absorbed in his sculpture and writing, among people whom he knew and trusted. It was a contemplative life without peril or jeopardy. After his Bravo service he had needed peace—had craved it—but the years of tranquillity had left him unprepared for the way the world really behaves.

The boy stood beside Stickney for a couple of minutes. No call yet from Arielle. Stickney thought, *Shit, probably screwed up the number.*

The boy said, "Sir, I have to go."

"All right," Stickney said. "Thank you."

The boy went off down the street, bouncing the basketball. He got about one hundred yards away, then stopped, held the ball and turned. He ran back to Stickney.

The phone was in his hand. He offered it to Stickney.

"It's for you," he said.

———

Arielle was in the suite when she got the text. She put on her shoes, zipped the laptop into the case, slung it over her shoulder, and picked up her purse. She was out the door within twenty seconds.

She started for the elevator, then thought, *No. The stairs.* When you bail, you look for alternatives, the unexpected. She couldn't get a cell signal in the stairs, though. She went all the way down, past the lobby level, into the basement. The stairs ended at a utility hall, and she walked past several housekeeping carts to an exit that opened onto a street behind the hotel.

She walked to the corner, flagged a taxi, and tapped in a callback to the phone that had sent the text.

At that moment, Totoy Ribera and one of his lieutenants were in the lobby with the hotel manager, who told them that Stickney had checked in with an American woman and that they occupied separate suites. Totoy demanded keys to the suites and copies of their passports. It was a brief conversation: Totoy got everything he wanted.

In the taxi, Arielle listened to Stickney's description of what had happened at the Optimo office and then in the backseat of the black sedan, then passed the phone up to the taxi driver so that the boy with Stickney could give him the address.

Then she called Mendonza in Tacloban. He was

with Favor in the pension house. She told them what she had learned from Stickney. "This puts things in a whole new light," she said. "Stick thinks we should talk it over, and I agree, but first we need to get in off the street. Do you know someplace that's under the radar and won't ask questions?"

She heard a soft laugh from Mendonza.

"Oh yeah, I know a place," he said. "I know a couple hundred places. You're going to love this."

The Philippines is one of the most devout nations on earth. It is a country where the Roman Catholic Church often has the last word in public policy debates, where many ferry voyages begin with the recitation of the rosary on the public address system, where millions of faithful line the roads on Good Friday to watch processions and gruesome Passion reenactments.

Paradoxically—or not—it is also a nation where the word "motel" has a specific, lurid meaning. "Motel" is not a budget lodging choice or an overnight stop for families on a driving vacation. In the Philippines, a motel is a discreet, short-term accommodation for sexual assignations, usually the illicit kind. No identification is required at check-in, because there is no check-in. Charges are by the hour, with payment in cash.

Anonymous, accessible—and with twenty-four-hour room-service menus—motels in the Philippines are an ideal impromptu hideout. And Manila has dozens.

There were five motels within half a mile of where Arielle picked up Stickney. The taxi driver, of course, knew them all. Arielle asked him to stop first at a drugstore, where she picked up some first-aid supplies. The motel was a windowless two-story building. They drove in through a portal off the street, into a dimly lit indoor courtyard where individual garage doors lined the walls. An attendant stepped forward to open the door as the taxi stopped. He whisked them up to a deluxe room on the second floor. The room had a circular bed under a mirrored ceiling, condoms on the nightstand, porn on a flat-screen television.

Arielle cleaned Stickney's cuts and abrasions, put a cold pack on the bump at the back of his head, and checked his pupils for dilation. He looked okay so far.

Then she called Favor. She put the phone on speaker, and Favor did the same, with Mendonza beside him in the pension room in Tacloban.

Mendonza said, "Stick, if I get this right, both kids have definitely been taken against their will, and Optimo is involved."

"No question," Stickney said.

"And Optimo is wired into the PNP, or they've got enough juice that they can pretend to be PNP without getting in trouble. Either way, that makes them dangerous."

"I agree with that too," Stickney said.

Mendonza said, "Then we need to reevaluate. This is more than any of you signed on for back at

Tahoe, and as of this moment I'm voiding any commitments that were made then."

Arielle spoke up: "Are you out, Al?"

"No," Mendonza said. "I've looked these people in the eye. I can't walk away now."

She said: "Ray?"

"I'm in," Favor said.

She looked at Stickney. His turn.

"I'll help any way I can," he said. "But I don't know what it's worth. I was half a beat slow every time it mattered today. It was pathetic."

"We're all out of practice," Favor said. "I had us going in like we were taking a ride at Disney World."

Arielle said, "So we have to tighten up. Do this right. The way we know how. Operational standards all the way. I should call Eddie Santos and put him to work. We need a safe house, paper, weapons . . . we need everything. You agree, Ray? This is all on your dime."

"Agreed," Favor said. "We should have done it that way going in."

"We didn't know then," she said. "But we know now."

"You talk like you're in, Ari," Mendonza said.

"Yes, I'm in," she said. "Of course I'm in."

"One more thing you all should know," Stickney said, "I'm not going to kill anybody. I'll do what I can to help the kids, but I won't take a life. I decided ten years ago that I had killed for the last time. I didn't expect that it would ever come up again, but it was a good choice, and I'm not going back on it. Can everybody live with that?"

They all said yes.

As Mendonza clicked off the call, he recalled the conversation in the gazebo beside Lake Tahoe: Stickney talking karma, Favor confessing his unease about One Nine and what they had done in their years together. He thought about Arielle telling them, "Something is up with Ray."

Mendonza said, "How about that from Stick? He's gone pacifist or something."

"I'm not surprised," Favor said. "I can see how a guy could get there."

"Really?" Mendonza said. "You getting there too, Ray?"

Mendonza looked at Favor. He tried to make it a casual glance, but he wanted to see Favor's reaction.

Favor was looking down at his hands. Staring at them. Mendonza glanced down at the hands as well, wondering what had caught Favor's attention. But they were just hands, held palms up.

Favor's face was pensive and hard. He clenched the hands slowly, then opened them. Still gazing down.

The things those hands have done, Mendonza thought. *The things they could do.*

Favor lowered his hands to his side, like holstering weapons, and he looked at Mendonza and answered the question.

"No," Favor said. "I guess I'm not."

FOURTEEN

Totoy Ribera walked into the ops room at the residential compound, to where Ilya Andropov was seated. He put four sheets of paper on the desk: copies of the check-in records from the hotel, with photocopies of the two passports.

BOUCHARD, Arielle
STICKNEY, Winston

"They're registered in adjacent suites," Totoy said. "Very expensive, eighteen hundred a night. That's dollars, not pesos. We went through their things. They didn't have much, nothing of interest. Both suites are in the woman's name, paid for on an American Express card in her name, and she has two more reserved for tonight."

"The two from Tacloban," Andropov said.

"Probably. I left word at the hotel to inform me if those parties check in."

"They shouldn't be checking in," Andropov said. "They should be leaving, correct?"

"That was the message," Totoy said.

Andropov called to Markov.

"Bring the boy in," he said.

Markov went out and came back dragging Ronnie with the help of another Russian.

Andropov put the photocopy of the woman's passport in his face, giving him a good look at the photo.

"Know her?" Andropov said.

Ronnie shook his head wearily. "No."

Markov said, "Little bastard, you haven't had enough? I guess we go at it again."

"No," Andropov said. "You don't have to do that."

Markov seemed puzzled.

"I believe him," Andropov said.

"You do?" Markov said.

"Look at him. Look at that shirt. Those trousers. Does he really look like he has anything in common with the kind of people who pay seven thousand U.S. dollars per night for hotel rooms? I don't know who these Americans are or why they care, but I'm sure they have no personal connection with this sorry specimen."

Markov, dropping into Russian, said, "What should we do with him?"

Andropov answered in Russian: "Take care of him tonight."

Markov nodded and started to take Ronnie from the room.

Andropov stopped him. "Have Leonid do a blood draw first."

Markov gave a derisive snort.

"What?" he said. "You expect to strike gold twice in the same family?"

"Let me tell you about gold mining, hunting for nuggets," Andropov said. "You spend a lot of time and money just to get in the right place to do it. If you go to all that trouble, you're a stupid fuck if you don't turn over all the stones."

He saw that Markov still didn't understand.

"Just do it," he said.

He turned to Totoy Ribera.

"Find the Americans," he said.

"It isn't that easy," Totoy said. "This is a city of twenty million people, with thousands of foreign visitors at any time."

"I want to know where they are. I want to know what they're doing," Andropov said.

Totoy thought that finding the four might have been easier if Andropov hadn't overplayed his hand with the soft-spoken visitor named Winston Stickney. Totoy had suggested a discreet tail. Andropov had insisted on the rough stuff.

"Muscle up on him a little," Andropov had ordered.

And Andropov was unquestionably the boss.

Now Totoy began to ask himself how he might find four Americans in one of the largest and most chaotic cities on the planet.

He went to the video monitors, where one of the Russians sat staring blankly.

"This morning," Totoy said. "Around the time the American arrived and I took him for a ride. What do you have on the sidewalk outside?"

One of the views was from a camera above the

front door of Impierno. Another looked up the walkway to the sidewalk. The operator began to rewind both cameras, jumping back in time, first rewinding in large chunks, then slowing the rate.

Then it was there, at the top of one view: Winston Stickney speaking with the old woman on the sidewalk.

"Back more," Totoy said, and the view loped backward in time until it caught Stickney and another man speaking on the sidewalk, then standing in front of the front door of Impierno, then leaving a car—a Nissan sedan—that was backing into a parking space as it arrived.

A car, not a taxi. He had a driver.

"Stop. Slowly forward."

Totoy was watching the Impierno camera, the rear bumper of the car, looking for the license plate as it backed in toward the curb.

A group of pedestrians cut off the view just before the plate became visible. By the time they moved out of the way, the car was parallel to the curb, the plate unreadable.

"Okay, forward again."

It all began to unfold in the proper sequence now, the American and his driver getting out together, looking around, the American going into Optimo and coming back out again, speaking to the woman, standing, and being hustled off the sidewalk, into the car.

The camera above the front door caught the driver watching this, hesitating, then going around and getting behind the wheel, backing up, turning out, into the street . . .

"Stop," Totoy said. "Forward by frames."

And there it was, caught in a single frame, the license plate. Totoy leaned in close to the monitor screen. Three digits, three letters.

Totoy reached for a piece of paper.

FIFTEEN

Favor was watching from the front window when the old trike driver named Romeo Mandaligan pulled up to the hotel precisely at four p.m. Favor went down and folded himself into the cramped passenger seat, hunching under the low canopy, and they rode a block and a half down the street to where the doctor's Kia was parked.

"Do you know this car?" Favor asked.

"I have seen it around here. I don't know the owner, and I don't know where it belongs."

"Good," Favor said. He had wanted to make sure that the old man wasn't somehow connected to the doctor and the Kia. Tacloban seemed just small enough.

"Let me tell you what I need. In about two hours, somebody's going to get into that car and drive away, and I want to follow it, see where it goes. Can you do that?"

"Can you tell me why?"

"I can tell you that we're helping a nice lady who has lost two children."

"Oh, terrible! And is the driver of this car involved?"

"I believe that he is."

"This is like the movies? You want to follow the driver and see what he is up to?"

"That's the idea."

"I can follow him. But will he be suspicious if one trike follows him everywhere? It is not better to use two? Then we can alternate staying behind him. It will not be so obvious."

A rolling tail. The old guy was thinking like a pro.

"Do you know another good driver?" Favor said.

"My son Erming is as good as me. I'll arrange it with him. Don't worry, Ray, we will follow the son of a bitch like fleas on a dog."

"Have you ever done this before?" Favor asked.

A gap-toothed grin spread across the old man's face.

He said, "No, but I have always wanted to try."

Two hours later, Mendonza was up in the second-floor room at the Mirador pension, looking through his camera's viewfinder. The telescopic zoom was pointed down into the first-floor office of the clinic across the street.

At twelve minutes past six, Mendonza watched as the doctor removed a rack of blood samples from the refrigerator in the clinic's back room and placed the rack into a cream-colored packing box. Mendonza dialed Favor's cell phone. They were using new SIM cards, on the assumption that the original numbers had been compromised. He snapped off several photos and said, "Ray, you were right. He's doing it again."

A second vial went into the box. Then an ice pack. The doctor closed the carton, sealed it with red packing tape, and took the carton off the counter, and carried it out of sight.

About half a minute later, the doctor stepped out from the front door of the office building.

Mendonza said, "Here he is," and then, a moment later, "Shit, Ray—no box."

Favor was sitting in Romeo Mandaligan's sidecar, parked opposite the Kia, while Erming Mandaligan waited on his own trike, half a block away.

"Where's the carton?" Favor said into the phone.

"I don't know," Mendonza answered. "Can't see it. Still in the clinic, I assume."

Favor poked his head out from the sidecar's enclosure and looked down the street, toward the office building. Nightfall comes suddenly in the tropics, and twilight was now quickly fading to darkness. But Favor spotted the doctor coming up the sidewalk toward the Kia. He seemed to be walking casually. His hands were empty.

"You going with him?" Mendonza asked.

"No. We follow the blood, not the man. Keep watching that front door."

A couple of times, as the doctor approached the car, he glanced back over his shoulder. Favor realized that he was looking to see if he was being followed.

"He's nervous," Favor said. "Someone knows we've been poking around; they probably told him to be careful."

The doctor approached the car, stepped around to the driver's-side door. Romeo revved the trike's engine. Favor tapped him on the leg and said, "No. Not yet."

Romeo shook his head at his son across the street.

The doctor slid in behind the wheel, the Kia's headlights came on, the car moved into traffic. It turned right at the next intersection and swung out of sight.

"Wait," Favor said to Mendonza on the phone and to Romeo on the motorcycle seat beside him. But he was saying it almost as much to himself.

Minutes passed. Five minutes. The lights went dark in the clinic. Seven minutes.

"Romeo, let's wait over here," Favor said, pointing down the street toward the pension and the clinic.

Romeo blipped the gas and turned the front wheel.

From the pension's second-floor window, Mendonza had a partial view of the trike, a block and a half away. He could no longer make out the details in the fading twilight, but he knew where it was parked; and when the headlamp swung out into traffic, he knew that this was Favor and the driver, now on the move, coming his way.

He looked back to the office building, where a woman was leaving, stepping out into the sidewalk. The clinic nurse. A bulky shopping bag hung from her right hand.

The blue Kia appeared from around the corner and stopped abruptly in front of the building, where the nurse stood on the sidewalk.

Mendonza said, "Ray, it's going down, this has to be it."

The doctor, behind the wheel, leaned over and opened the passenger door. The nurse passed the shopping bag into the car, then stepped back empty-handed and closed the door.

The Kia moved away from the curb, fast.

"Ray, on the move," Mendonza said.

Romeo Mandaligan was approaching the intersection as the Kia, headed in the opposite direction, turned right.

Romeo pointed at the turning sedan and said, "Ray, that's it?"

"That's it," Favor said. The words had barely cleared his throat when the trike shot forward, swinging into the opposite lane. A pair of headlights filled Favor's vision through the sidecar's windscreen. Romeo levered the handlebars left and the trike instantly pivoted and darted out of the path of the onrushing traffic, down the uncongested cross street where the Kia had disappeared.

They were about one hundred feet behind the car. Favor looked back and saw another trike swing in off the main street and accelerate behind them. They went three blocks this way, the Kia with the two trikes following, until the Kia turned left without signaling. Romeo continued straight ahead, but the second trike swung in behind the sedan.

Favor knew that that must be Erming Mandaligan picking up the tail, but he couldn't be sure. Every sidecar in Tacloban seemed identical to the next. But this was an advantage, he thought: the driver of the Kia wouldn't be able to recognize the two trikes as they swapped positions behind him.

Romeo turned left at the next intersection and accelerated up the street parallel to the Kia. It was a residential neighborhood, with no streetlights. The trike's headlight punched weakly into a low-hanging pall of smoke from cooking fires. The pavement was broken, and the unsprung third wheel of the sidecar slammed down hard in a long pothole. Favor could feel the shock up through his spine.

Favor, looking left, spotted the Kia as they flew through an intersection. They were now abreast of the car and gaining. One block later, Romeo zipped left and then turned in behind the Kia again as Erming's trike dropped off.

It was a perfect handoff. Favor knew that the driver would never catch the tail now.

Traffic was picking up again as they drove through a busier part of the city. The Kia slowed as it came up on a truck, and Romeo too backed off, slowing enough to let a car and a jeepney pass. The Kia was still visible, easily within contact.

The road headed south along the waterfront. They were leaving the city. The brake lights blazed on the Kia as it turned left onto a wide two-lane.

Favor recognized the road. He had seen it before, a day and a half earlier.

Romeo Mandaligan leaned in close and, over wind and the rapping of the engine, said, "I believe he is going for the airport."

The call with Mendonza was still open. Mendonza said, "Ray? What's that?"

Favor said, "Airport, Al. Better haul. I think we're out of here."

The package went out by airfreight aboard Philippine Airlines. The doctor brought it into the terminal. Favor didn't follow him in—he thought that he would be conspicuous in the little place—but Romeo went in to watch, and after the doctor returned empty-handed and drove away, Romeo came back out and reported to Favor that the man had handed the package to an attendant at the PAL counter.

So it was airfreight, and it had to be the evening flight to Manila, the only remaining PAL flight of the day.

Romeo Mandaligan said, "I did good, huh?"

"You sure as hell did," Favor said.

While Mendonza bought tickets at the counter, Favor went to a nearby window that looked out onto an open shed where several baggage carts were parked. A short conveyor belt ran into the shed from the PAL ticket counter, and two baggage handlers plucked baggage off the belt and loaded it onto the carts. An open bulb hung from the ceiling of the shed, and the cream-colored package with the red tape stood out in the light.

Favor took out his phone and called Arielle.

He explained what they were doing, following a carton with vials of blood. He asked her and Stickney to bring two cars to the PAL domestic terminal.

They were going to follow the carton to its final destination.

He described the carton and said, "Find the pickup area for PAL air freight and wait for us there. I want somebody watching that package as soon as it shows up. Al and I should be off the plane before the cargo is offloaded, but you never know."

She said, "Cream color, red tape, about a foot and a half on each side."

"Correct. I don't know who will pick it up, but Stick needs to stay with the cars, out of sight. He has definitely been burned."

She said, "I'm probably burned too, if they have the passport photocopies."

"I know," Favor said. "But I want an eyeball on the package, and you aren't burned the way Stick is burned. You can do this. Be discreet, mix with the crowd. You remember the drill."

"Dimly," she said with a small laugh.

"I wouldn't ask if it didn't matter. I believe the path back to those two kids starts with that blood."

"Eyes on the box. You've got it," she said.

When he spoke with Arielle, Favor kept watching the package as it sat on the cart in the PAL baggage shed. He watched the package as Mendonza returned with boarding passes for seats near the front exit. He watched the package while he ate food that Mendonza brought from a snack bar in the terminal.

A loudspeaker announced first call for boarding of the PAL flight. But the cart with the cream-colored box still sat in the baggage shed, and Favor stayed by the window and kept it in sight until a handler hitched the cart to a small tractor and pulled it out to the waiting plane.

Then Favor left the window and went through the gate. He walked out across the asphalt apron and stood at the bottom of the ramp as the baggage handlers loaded the carton into the belly of the plane, then he walked up the ramp and took his seat beside Mendonza.

The plane touched down a few minutes late, a little after 8:30 p.m. Favor turned on his phone while the plane was still rolling and called Arielle when the jetway ramp rolled up to the door.

She said, "I'm at PAL air freight. It's near the baggage claim, straight across the concourse from your gate. Get over here as soon as you can. There's something you need to see."

"As soon as we're out. It shouldn't be long."

"You did say cream-colored carton, right? Red packing tape, about eighteen inches on a side?"

The passengers on the plane were standing. A flight attendant was opening the hatch, swinging the door open. Favor looked out the window and saw that a baggage tug was wheeling under the fuselage.

"Right," Favor said. "But the cargo is still in the hold. We'll be there before the package shows up."

"Just get over here," she said.

Favor and Mendonza were among the first half dozen passengers off the plane and through the gate. From halfway across the concourse, Favor spotted Arielle. She was seated near a baggage carousel, reading a magazine. Or seeming to read.

He stopped about twenty paces short of where she sat. It was ingrained training. She gave no sign that she had seen him, but she took a phone out of her purse, tapped a speed-dial number.

In a few seconds the call came in on his own phone.

He turned away from her. She was looking away from him. To a casual observer they were strangers who both happened to be using phones, in a place where almost everyone was using a phone.

She said, "Second shelf from the top, left side."

Various packages and crates lined the shelves along the back wall of the office. A PAL logo on the glass partly blocked the view, but at second glance he spotted the familiar cream carton and red packing tape.

This wasn't right, he thought. The carton he had chased through the streets of Tacloban couldn't be off the plane already.

Then he realized that it was not one box.

"Three?" he said.

"How about that?" Arielle said. "It was two just a little while ago. They must've put another one up there when I was waiting for you. I guess we can say three and counting."

Favor watched as a fourth carton—probably from the Tacloban flight—went onto the shelf beside the others. He realized that the cartons were arriving on flights from other cities around the Philippines. This had to be the daily collection of blood samples from other Optimo offices.

He wanted to keep the cartons in sight, so he could track them to their final destination. But the terminal was clearing out. Unlike the international terminal, this one shut down for several hours a night. There were no more outbound flights until the morning, and just a few still to arrive. Favor knew that as the place emptied, he would be increasingly conspicuous, a foreigner hanging around with no apparent purpose. Arielle and Stickney would be just as visible. Even Mendonza didn't really fit in.

He walked outside and studied the layout.

The terminal had one passenger exit, a set of doors that opened onto a taxi stand and a loading zone. To one side was a freight dock, large enough to accommodate a single truck. Across the street, a parking area. From the spot, one car could watch the passenger exit and the freight dock.

Favor called Mendonza and Arielle and asked them to join him in the parking lot across from the terminal. Stickney was there already, and they all sat together in one of the two cars that Stickney and Arielle had brought.

Favor said, "We can't hang around in there watching the cartons, but we don't have to. We can watch from here to see when they come out. It'll either be through this front door or the loading dock. And it'll go down soon. This terminal will be closing after the last flight is in."

"How do you know it won't be tomorrow?" Mendonza asked.

"It's blood," Favor said, "and somebody went to a lot of trouble to collect it. I don't know why they want it, but I can't believe that they'll let it sit overnight, even if it's on ice."

"You don't need all four of us to watch," Stickney said.

"Correct," Favor said. "I thought I'd leave you and Al with one car here. Ari and I will park out on the street, where the terminal traffic exits. You let us know what we're looking for, we'll latch onto them there. Give them about half a minute, then you hustle up behind us."

"We really ought to have three vehicles," Mendonza said. "This looks like a daily routine, right? Wait a day, we can have that third car, do it right."

"No," Favor said. "I feel like I already gave away a day yesterday. I don't want to give away any more. Two vehicles is what we've got, so we make it happen with two."

He looked around at them, checking their faces. He was looking for hesitation, disagreement.

He saw that they were all with them.

"Then we're on," he said.

He got into the second car with Arielle and drove out of the parking lot, past the terminal, down the one-way terminal. He found a parking space on the street where the terminal road exited into city traffic.

He pulled in and parked, and waited for the call from Mendonza and Stickney that would ID their target for the tail. Cars and jeepneys surged past his window, moving fast. Favor knew that darkness would help mask the tail, but he would have to hustle to stay with the target. Mendonza in the second car might not be able to catch up. Then it would be just him, hanging with the target while trying to stay unnoticed.

He realized that Arielle was looking at him. She had turned partway toward him and was taking him in, studying him. Smiling.

She said, "Ray, you're looking good."

"I appreciate that, but we probably ought to wait until we get to a room."

"I didn't say you looked edible. Although you do. I said you look good."

"What's that supposed to mean?"

"Solid. Squared away. On the beam," she said. *"Good."*

"Why wouldn't I be?" he said.

Stickney and Mendonza sat waiting in their car, Mendonza behind the wheel. The parking area was thinning out, and foot traffic through the front doors was light.

A red Honda CR-V pulled up and parked at the curb in front of the terminal. Mendonza watched the new arrival, but there was no movement, and about half a minute later a dark blue Toyota van stopped short of the pickup zone, reversed, and backed up to the loading dock.

Mendonza said, "This may be it."

A side door opened on the van, and the overhead light briefly illuminated the driver and a passenger, both young men, as the passenger got out and walked around to the back.

At the periphery of his vision, Mendonza caught movement at the red Honda in front of the terminal—someone stepping out onto the sidewalk—but he disregarded it and focused on the blue van at the loading dock.

A door opened at the dock. Someone pushed out a freight dolly. Stacked on the dolly were five cream-colored cartons sealed with red tape.

Mendonza had his camera out, shooting with the telephoto lens. He said, "Call Ray. Dark blue Toyota van, driver and passenger, coming his way."

"No," Stickney said. "Let that one go."

"Let it go? Stick, they're putting the cartons in the van."

He looked over at Stickney and saw him bent low at the waist. Stickney was hiding behind the front dash.

"Ray'll be burned if he follows the van," Stickney said. "Guy that just got out of the red Honda, standing on the sidewalk—I think he's running cover for the shipment. Tell Ray to follow him. He'll go where the shipment goes."

Mendonza saw him now: a stocky Filipino standing at the entrance of the terminal.

"Close-cropped hair, late forties, white shirt worn untucked?"

"That's him," Stickney said.

The man was appraising the situation, alert. For a moment he looked straight at the car where Mendonza was sitting, checking him out, before he clocked over somewhere else.

Mendonza had put the camera in his lap. He raised it now and fired off several frames, getting a couple of good shots as the man stood beneath a light at the entrance.

Stickney was still bent down, trying to stay out of sight.

Mendonza said, "I think you're right. Good read, Stick. How did you know?"

"I met him this morning," Stickney said.

Most of the time, Totoy Ribera left his drones to handle the daily cargo run from the airport, and most of the time the Russians were fine with that. Not tonight, though. Tonight Andropov had insisted that Totoy go along for the pickup.

The Russians were nervous, Totoy thought. It was because of the unknown Americans poking around, even though they hadn't actually done anything more than ask a few questions.

At first Totoy thought that the Russians were

overreacting. This was the first little bump in the road since this deal first came together seven months earlier, and it didn't seem like much of a threat.

But Totoy was aware that he had one big disadvantage: he didn't know what the Russians were hiding at the other end of the seaplane ride from Manila. The Russians knew, though, and Totoy told himself that if they were uneasy, maybe he should be too.

So when Andropov told him to accompany the pickup crew to the airport and back, Totoy didn't argue. And he didn't just go along for the ride, either. He took a separate car so he could shadow the pickup on the return trip. While the van was loaded, he parked the red Honda at the terminal concourse. He got out and scanned the scene, looking for some disturbance, some subtle hint of jeopardy.

He noticed the car in a front row of the parking lot. One occupant, a driver, sitting in the dark. Totoy couldn't make out details, but he saw that it was a man. A big man.

Toto thought about the description from the Optimo office manager in Tacloban. *A big Fil-Am. Very very big.*

Totoy considered whether he ought to go over to the car, check out the big guy.

To Totoy's left, at the loading dock, his boys were pushing the last of the cartons into the van, shutting the door. They were getting ready to leave. Totoy knew that crossing the road and checking out the car in the parking lot would take at least two or three minutes, maybe more. He could order the boys in the van to wait, but he didn't like the idea. He wanted that shipment on the move.

But there was an easier way to check: just watch the car, see how the driver reacted when the van left the terminal. If the car remained behind, then Totoy could assume that the big driver was harmless. But if the car pulled out of the lot and followed the van, then Totoy would know that the Americans had somehow discovered the nightly delivery, and that the big Fil-Am was trying to track the shipment to its destination.

That can be dealt with, Totoy thought.

The van was moving, wheeling away from the loading dock. It passed Totoy and continued down the terminal road to the exit.

The car with the big man inside didn't move.

Totoy waited. He counted out half a minute, and still the car didn't move. By now the van was at the exit, turning into the city streets. Totoy climbed into the Honda and pulled out from the curb at the terminal. He looked back in his rearview mirror and saw that the car with the big man at the wheel still hadn't moved.

In the clear, Totoy thought. He put the car and the big man out of mind as he accelerated along the terminal road. The van was now turning into the street, entering traffic. When Totoy pulled into the street, he was about half a block behind the van.

That was just right for his purposes. He was checking for a tail, watching the vehicles between him and the van, how they moved and behaved.

He saw nothing unusual.

The direct route from the airport to the residence was just a couple of miles, usually no more than ten or fifteen minutes, but Totoy had told the van driver to make a couple of sudden turns, and he hung back to see how the other vehicles reacted. After the second detour, the set of vehicles between him and the van was completely different from those at the beginning of the trip, so he was sure they were unobserved.

At that point Totoy pulled in close behind the van as it crossed Amorsolo Street and turned down the alley that ran behind the Impierno building and the residence.

They stopped at the back entrance of the residence, a black-painted gate of solid steel that the guards opened and swung in. Totoy followed the van in, and the gate closed behind them.

Done, and not a ripple of trouble. Maybe the Russians really were paranoid after all.

Favor followed the Honda as far as the alley behind the residence. He swung around the block and came back the other way, and when he passed the alley again the two vehicles were pulling through the open gate. Mendonza and Stickney were behind Favor's car, and they, too, got a glimpse of the Honda following the van inside.

They all had plenty to talk about. Mendonza suggested dinner, and they gathered at a restaurant called Aristocrat, on the curving boulevard that ran along the bay front, where they got a private room and talked over all that had happened and what they would do next.

Two missing teenagers, shipments of blood samples, and all of it going to a block on Amorsolo Street, a place so touchy that Winston Stickney had been assaulted just for going near it.

They had finished dinner and were still talking when Eddie Santos called Arielle to tell her that he had found a hideout. She gave the phone to Mendonza so that he could get directions.

"Where are we going?" Mendonza asked.

"Bear in mind, I was working on short notice," Santos said.

"Where, Eddie?"

"North side of the Pasig River."

"How far north?"

"Oh, it's close in, don't worry about that."

"Eddie—where?"

"It is in Tondo."

Mendonza muted the phone. He turned to the others. He said, "My friends, life just got very real."

SIXTEEN

With more than four hundred thousand residents in an area of about one and a half square miles, the Tondo district of Manila is among the most densely populated places on earth. It is the home of Manila's main slaughterhouse and its docks, a place of freight depots and tenements and off-kilter utility poles that bristle with illegal electrical connections, daringly installed. It is a place where gray water stands in the crevices of broken sidewalks. Tondo is the birthplace of pickpockets and revolutionaries and whores and anonymous saints. It is rich in heart and humanity and history, but rousingly poor by almost every other standard.

Tondo was also the childhood home of Edwin Santos. He operated many of his businesses there, and when he learned from Arielle Bouchard that she and the others required secure emergency lodging, he immediately thought of Tondo. In all the Philippines, it was probably the last place anyone would look for four wealthy Americans.

Arielle didn't say why they needed safe haven, but obviously they were in some difficulty, not of the kind that could be fixed with the infusion of money. Trouble wasn't something he would have wished for them, but since it had happened, he did feel a small thrill knowing that he was being depended upon by serious people acting seriously.

The place he had in mind for them was hardly luxurious, but it was as discreet and secure as any place they could hope to find. Thirteen years earlier, the four Americans would have recognized it for the gem that it was.

Now Santos would find out just how much they had changed.

Mendonza followed Santos's directions to one of Tondo's dark side streets. They found him waiting outside a bleak, bare structure with barred windows and a steel roll-up door as big and wide as a truck.

When he saw them, Santos reached down and lifted the door, running it up on tracks until they could drive in and park.

It was a bodega, a storehouse, with stacks of cartons and crates, and walls full of steel shelves. But Santos had brought in cots, about half a dozen box fans, and a water cooler, a refrigerator, and a microwave oven. In one corner was a toilet and a native-style shower: a bucket and dipper that filled from a spigot in the wall.

When they were in, he rolled the door down and locked it. He turned to watch their faces as they got out and looked around.

He said, "It's clean, and you'll have plenty of room. I guarantee that you won't be disturbed. You can keep your cars off the street, out of sight. There is room for two vehicles in here."

Arielle said, "I'll need Internet access somehow. I don't think I can find the satellite from here."

"No problem," Santos said. "Behind this back wall is an Internet café. I made arrangements; they ran a line in. Here, see?"

He pointed to where an Ethernet cable lay coiled on the floor beside a steel table.

Arielle opened her laptop on the table and powered it up. She plugged in the cable.

"Good," she said. "But is it secure?"

"The owner of the café guarantees that it's secure." He flashed a quick smile. "That would be me."

Stickney looked around, nodded approval.

Mendonza grinned. Santos thought he seemed amused by the idea, enjoying it.

Santos looked at Favor.

"It's perfect," Favor said.

Santos showed them around. The roll-up door was opened by key from outside—he gave them two keys—and was manually locked from inside. The second entrance was at the rear, a steel-sheathed door with a security peephole and a buzzer. The steel looked thick enough to stop a pistol round. The windows were barred from the outside, boarded over on the inside. Mendonza thought this wasn't the first time the place had been used for something more than storing dry goods.

Santos began describing the neighborhood—a bakery, the shops, a fruit and vegetable market, a small restaurant—while Arielle got the memory card from Mendonza's camera. She copied the files to the laptop and opened an image viewer to organize them.

Mendonza stood behind her chair as she clicked through the images. She stopped to study the photo of Totoy Ribera, standing under the light at the concourse of the domestic airport.

Santos was a few feet away, talking to Favor and Stickney. He had a view of the screen and occasionally glanced down at it as the images clicked by.

He suddenly stopped and said, "Excuse me, it's none of my business, but that photo—"

"Yes?" Favor said.

"I shouldn't say anything. I suppose you're already aware of who you're dealing with."

"You know this man?" Favor said.

"I know *of* him. His name is Antonio Ribera. Totoy Ribera. He is a captain of the PNP. The PNP has a certain reputation, that's no secret. And to me, it's mostly undeserved. These guys aren't paid well, they have families to feed, so I don't blame them for maybe doing a little monkey business where they can. But mostly they're good cops. They care; they want to do what's right. Most of them."

"But Ribera?" Favor said.

"Totoy Ribera is different," Santos said. "He's no better than a gangster. He has a crew that answers only to him. He uses the badge for his own purposes. I don't know all that he is involved in, but I hear stories. And I can guarantee that if he's in it, it's dirty."

They were all looking at Santos now.

He said, "I won't ask why you're here or what is going on. But I know that you didn't expect trouble at first, and now you must be in trouble to need a place like this. So I think you should know, if you're in trouble with the man in that photo, you're really in trouble."

Ronnie lay tied and gagged on the floor of Ilya Andropov's office at the compound in Manila. He had been there since early afternoon. He was parched: the cloth gag had long soaked up all the moisture from his mouth. And after hours of needing a toilet, fighting his bowels, he had finally given up and soiled his pants.

He had never so been miserable.

His thirst was overwhelming. He loathed his captors and was terrified to be in their presence. Yet he desperately needed water.

He wormed his way around the floor until he was close to the door. He kicked the door as hard as he could, slamming his heels into the panel.

Andropov opened the door. He had to push Ronnie aside to get in, and he stopped before he took his second step over the threshold.

"Fuck my mother, he's shit all over himself," Andropov yelled. "Toly, get in here."

Ronnie continued to kick and grunt, trying to speak.

Anatoly Markov came into the room.

"Find out what he wants," Andropov said.

"Yes, boss," Markov said, and stood over the boy to loosen the gag.

Their faces nearly touched. Ronnie's stomach clenched with the thought of the hours of pain that Markov had inflicted on him. A sudden surge of anger came over him. On impulse, without a thought, he snapped his head forward and butted Markov directly in the face, forehead to nose.

Markov grunted, rocked back, clapped a hand to his face. Blood gushed through his fingers and he roared in Russian. Ronnie didn't understand the words, but he saw the fury in Markov's face; and when Markov grabbed him by the throat, Ronnie knew exactly what was happening. He felt thumbs pressing deep into his throat, and he knew that Markov was about to kill him.

"Stop," Andropov said. Markov eased his grip.

Ronnie saw that one of the lab techs had come over and was speaking to Andropov.

"Let me have the little fucker," Markov said to Andropov. Blood was dripping from his nose onto Ronnie's chest. "Please."

"Clean him up good," Andropov said to Markov. "Get a little food in him, and make sure that you replenish his fluids."

"Clean him up before I kill him?" Markov said.

"You aren't going to kill him," Andropov said. "You're going to get him ready to fly."

"You got a hit?"

"Right across the board."

"No shit. A big client?"

"The biggest," said Ilya Andropov.

———

It was after midnight, and the former members of Bravo One Nine were stretched out in their cots, which were scattered around the floor of the bodega, tucked behind crates and stacks of boxes.

In the darkness, Favor said, "Ari. You awake?"

"Yes," she said. "Thinking."

"Me too," he said. "I'm thinking how everything leads to that one block on Amorsolo Street. Marivic's application must've been sent to that office. Her blood went next door. Ronnie goes to the office looking for Marivic, and he isn't seen again."

He sat up at the edge of the bed, and she sat up too, facing him.

"Where did the kids go?" he said. "And what's the story with that blood? What are they doing with it there in the house?"

"We'd probably have some answers if we could get into their network," Arielle said.

"You think they have a network?"

She said, "Most likely. Stick says they have a busy office up there above the nightclub. He saw a lot of security cameras. They're probably IP cameras, being remotely monitored. Could be from anywhere, but my guess it's there in the villa next door. Being as close as they are, they've probably got a little intranet put together, either wireless or Ethernet. My bet would be on Ethernet. It's more secure. If you somehow had access to one of the machines on the net . . ."

"You mean hacking?"

"Hacking in from outside, no. They would have

to be egregiously dumb. But if you could get physical access to a network machine, that's different. Then you'd be on the other side of the firewall. You could do almost anything at that point."

A light came on. It was Stickney. He walked over and sat between them.

He said, "The office would be the place to do it. Not that it would be easy. But if you could get in, you'd know right where the machines are. The house, who knows?"

Favor said, "I wonder where the nightclub fits."

"The woman at Optimo, the owner, seemed ready to have me visit," Stickney said. "Take that for what it's worth, but it could be legitimate."

"What kind of club is it?"

Mendonza answered from his cot in the shadows: "It's called a KTV. Think of it as a high-dollar strip club, Manila-style. The girls come out individually and dance. No brass pole, though. If you see one you like, you pay to take her into a private room. The rooms, believe it or not, are set up with video karaoke players—KTV, right?—and the idea is that when you shut the door, the girl is going to pick up a microphone and entertain you with 'Don't Cry For Me, Argentina.' I don't think a lot of singing happens back there, though."

He got up and came walking over, joining the others.

"A lot of the KTV places also have fishbowl massage parlors: the attendants are sitting behind a big glass window," he said. "The massage parlors are as much about massage as the KTV rooms are about singing.

"Impierno is one of the big-expense-account places for the local businessmen. It's been around for a while, a lot longer than Optimo, which makes me think that it isn't part of whatever is happening here."

"They do share a building," Favor said.

"And the same woman owns them," Stickney said.

"Allegedly," Mendonza said. "Unless she's fronting for one or both."

"If we got into the network, we'd know for sure," Arielle said. "We'd probably know everything if we stay on long enough."

"How would that work?" Favor asked. "You'd have to get into the office and use one of their machines? That sounds ambitious. Also dangerous."

"You would only need access long enough to release a worm into the system," she explained. "A few seconds would do it. Write the worm so that it immediately opens up a connection to this machine. I can sit here or anywhere on the Net and start going through the directories and pulling down anything that looks good. It would be just as if I were sitting there in the office."

"How long could you do that?" Mendonza asked.

"Until they figured out what was happening and shut it down."

Favor said, "How much time would you need to whip one of those together?"

"Maybe half a day."

"And then any idiot could put it onto one of their machines? An idiot such as myself?"

"The program would self-install from a USB flash drive. The worm will do the rest. Idiotproof."

"That's reassuring," Favor said. To Mendonza he said, "Any foreigners go in there, you think?"

"Japanese and Koreans love KTVs. Not so many Westerners, but you wouldn't be a rarity, if that's what you're asking."

"How long would a KTV stay open?"

"Until things get quiet. Three or four in the morning, anyway. Manila's a night town."

"Plenty of time," Favor said.

"You're going out tonight?" Stickney said.

"That's right. Al, you can't come. We were seen together in Tacloban. Somebody might make the connection. Stick, you've been burned: you can't go anywhere near the place. Ari, you can't come because this is Boy's Town, and you'd draw way too much attention. So it's just me."

"Doing recon?" Arielle asked.

"That's right. I want to look around that building, so I'll start where the door is open. That's Impierno. It's a dirty job, but . . . well, you know what they say. . . ."

SEVENTEEN

Before he parked at Impierno, Favor drove around the block twice, slowing each time as he drove down Amorsolo Street. He looked at the high concrete wall around the residence and paused where he could see the walkway between the two buildings, the unobtrusive door at the side of Impierno. He knew from Stickney that this was the only known entrance to the Optimo headquarters.

The second time, he pulled up and parked at Impierno's front door, by a valet parking stand.

By day the Impierno building seemed awkward and purposeless. After dark, it was transformed. The copper-colored facade panels shimmered from hidden footlights, and the big neon sign blazed in ripe and wicked shapes. It looked like the throbbing palace of flesh that it was.

A red-coated parking valet took Favor's car key. A doorman with a coat of gold lamé greeted him and admitted him inside. Favor entered a small lobby with gleaming black walls and a floor of polished marble. A greeter in a white dinner jacket stood before two sets of stairs, one ascending at his left, the other descending at his right.

"Floor show, sir, or massage?"

"I think the show, for starters," Favor said. The greeter smiled as if Favor had just made the wisest of all possible choices, and stepped to one side, indicating the ascending stairs. At the top of the steps, Favor looked down onto a shallow amphitheater, with tiers of tables and banquettes—several dozen—surrounding a narrow stage that protruded halfway onto the floor.

The floor manager was a woman in her late thirties, white blouse and a dark pencil skirt and bolero jacket. She took Favor to a table near the back of the room and lit the candle. Seconds later, a waiter came over to take Favor's order: whiskey neat.

Favor looked around.

The room was dim, dark enough that he couldn't see the faces of most of the customers unless they leaned in close to the tabletop candles. Twin spotlights, high up at the back of the room, sent down shafts that cut through the darkness and met at a single point onstage.

Where the shafts of light intersected, a young woman—very young, Favor thought, no more than nineteen or twenty—was slowly, dramatically, stripping off a chartreuse gown, to the accompaniment of an overwrought American power ballad from the eighties. He couldn't remember the name.

To his left, along the back wall of the room, were about ten large glass windows, each with a door beside it. Favor guessed that these were the private rooms. On some, the doors were closed and red velvet curtains were drawn. Occupied.

As the song reached its last few bars, the gown fell to the floor and the young woman stepped out of it and walked to the edge of the stage. She stood there for two or three seconds before the stage went dark. Favor could just make out her outline as she gathered the gown and hurried off.

A couple of minutes later, another young woman came out, another gown. While this one danced, the other came out from behind the stage. The floor manager led her to one of the private rooms, where someone shut the door and drew the curtains.

Favor watched for a few minutes, then paid his check and got up to leave. He walked around the back of the club toward the private rooms, went in one, and looked around. Plush couches, pile carpet.

He walked out to the lobby.

"Okay, now the massage," he said, and again the greeter smiled and nodded as if Favor had just made a choice even wiser than before.

Favor walked down the polished marble stairs to a reception desk. Beside the desk was the big fishbowl display window that Mendonza had described. At least three dozen women, dressed in short white sleeveless dresses, sat on tiered benches behind the glass.

The receptionist asked Favor to choose a room. She pointed to a large placard on the wall, showing different room types and their prices.

Favor told her that he was a newcomer. Could he please look at some of the rooms?

She said, "Why don't you choose a girl? Let her show you around."

Favor knew he was supposed to go to the fish-bowl and examine the women. He was no prude, but something about this bothered him. *Fishbowl.* He had eaten at seafood restaurants in Hong Kong where you pick your meal from a live tank and watch it taken off to be prepared. This was uncomfortably similar, selecting a woman for sex like choosing a grouper to be grilled.

But he had to get back into those rooms, and he didn't want to draw any more attention to himself. He took one step over to the glass, glanced in. The women were wearing number tags pinned to their bodice.

He said, "Sixty-three." It was the first number he saw. The receptionist spoke into a microphone at the desk and called out the number, and a pretty young woman climbed off one of the benches and came out from around the side.

"Give this gentleman a tour," the receptionist said, and the young woman led him through a set of doors to a hall.

She was about twenty-five, slim and pretty. Her name was Patricia, she said: she pronounced it *PuhTREESia.* She showed him into one room and another in turn, all those that weren't in use.

Favor glanced around each room. He knew exactly what he was looking for. As they moved down the hall he tried to imagine the layout of the place, where they stood in reference to the club floor above.

He pointed to a room down the hall.

"Can we look at that one?" he asked.

A flicker of hesitation passed over Patricia's face, as if she sensed that something beyond the ordinary was happening here. *Smart,* Favor thought. He knew that most men, given the chance to be alone in a room with Patricia, wouldn't be too picky about the room. But she seemed to dismiss it, and took Favor down the hall and into the room.

It was the biggest and most lavish so far, a large room in a jungle motif, faux leopard-skin wall coverings and potted plants, with a glass wall at one end that looked onto a large shower and whirlpool bath.

Favor looked around and saw what he needed.

"Sir, this is the Ultimate VIP Safari Suite. It's our most exclusive room. You wish to see another?"

"No," Favor said, "this is good."

"The price is three thousand. If you wish, you can give me the money. I'll take it to the front. You can disrobe, wait for me in the shower. I will bathe you; it's part of the service."

"It's all right," Favor said. "I don't need the service tonight. I just wanted to look at the rooms. But thank you."

He left her in the room as he walked out to the front, past the desk.

The receptionist seemed startled to see him leaving.

"It's all right, I'll be back soon," Favor said. "You can count on it."

Favor brought the car around to the front of the bodega, the roll-up steel door. He got out, unlocked the door, pulled it up.

The others were still awake, sitting on their cots. Favor drove the car in, and Stickney came over to pull the door down and lock it.

They all gathered around the table.

Favor said to Stickney, "Just to be sure I have this straight. The only way up to the Optimo offices is through that door on the north side of the Impierno building."

"Correct," Stickney said.

"It's through that door, up a long staircase, right?"

"Under video surveillance the whole time," Stickney said.

"Okay. Then there's just a glass door and you're in the offices."

"Thick glass. It looks solid," Stickney said.

"That's all right. I think we can do this."

"Do what, Ray?" Arielle asked.

"Get into the office. Get onto one of those machines. Plant your worm. I know a way."

HARVEST DAY
–3

EIGHTEEN

Eddie Santos rose early in his apartment. He checked his phone—the one that really mattered—and found a text message from the man whom he was now learning to call Ray Favor.

Pls call me asap any hour

Favor's voice was breathy. He told Santos that he was in the middle of a morning run. But Favor quickly gathered himself and rattled off a list of items that he needed from Santos.

"Is that possible?" Favor asked. "I know the chemicals might be a reach on short notice."

"No, the chemicals are easy. I have a source. I'll bring them after lunchtime. Some of the other items might take a little longer. Maybe tomorrow morning."

"That's fine," Favor said. "Now, what are the chances of getting passports and weapons?"

"Passports? Come on, Ray, you're in Manila. It's like asking for a pastry in Vienna."

"Okay. Just make sure they're good pastries. Use the old identities, if you remember them."

"I remember."

"Weapons, a couple of handguns at least. But I'm sure Al would love to get his hands on an M10 or an Uzi."

"On short notice, the best I can do is a couple of Colt .45s. Things have tightened up here. It's not the way it used to be."

"We'll take what we can get."

Santos had something to say. He wasn't sure he should mention it; he didn't want Favor to think he was wheedling for information. He didn't know—he didn't *need* to know.

But as he reviewed the list in his head, making sure that it was safely cached in his memory, Santos knew he had to say it: "You guys are operating again."

"Yeah. I guess we are," Favor said.

Santos had assigned Elvis Vega to keep the Americans fed. Shortly before eight a.m., Vega delivered a basket of fresh fruit and brewed coffee and the bread rolls that Filipinos call *pandesal*.

A couple of minutes later, as they were eating, Arielle said, "I was lying awake last night thinking about this. We may be able to get a fix on where Marivic and Ronnie went after they disappeared. At least part of the way."

"Get a fix?" Mendonza said. "Like tracking with GPS?"

"Almost that accurate," Arielle said. "Both of these kids were carrying highly sophisticated tracking devices."

She waited to see who would get it first.

"Cell phones," Stickney said after a couple of seconds.

"Cell phones. Of *course*," Favor said. "Cell phones talk to towers."

"Exactly," Arielle said. "A cell phone continually identifies itself to all the stations in its vicinity. The stations, the towers, send that information to the system, and the system keeps track of it. If I want to talk to Al, I don't need to know where he is."

"The system already knows," Favor said.

"Yes," Arielle continued. "I send the call in, the system recognizes the number, does a quick search of its records, and says, 'Okay, he's in Tacloban,' his phone is logged in with towers seven eighty-eight and seven eighty-nine—whatever—and it picks one of those towers and sends the call through to that location.

"If you're in motion, moving in and out of range of different stations, things really get busy. Your phone goes into overdrive, making sure to stay in contact. It looks for new stations coming into range, and it announces itself to each one: 'Hey, here I am.' At the same time, it's going 'Sayonara' to the ones you're leaving. Even when these kids went missing to the world, the cell system knew where their phones were."

"To what accuracy?" Stickney said.

"Depends. The more towers you're working with, the more accurate you would be. In an area dense with stations, you could probably locate a phone to within a hundred yards or so, just by looking at which combination of stations it's talking to at any given time. Rural areas, with fewer towers, not so much. But probably closer than you'd think."

"Which is fine," Mendonza said, "unless the phones are turned off. Then they're lost."

"You'd think so, but that's not the case," Arielle said. "Even when a phone is turned off, it still interacts with the nearby towers for as long as there's power from the battery. The only way to break the link is to remove the battery. Otherwise, it stays in contact with the network, checking in. And all these transactions are being logged. A record exists somewhere."

"And how do we get it?" Favor said.

"We ask."

Totoy Ribera was stuck in an impossible snarl of midday traffic in Quiapo, the old downtown area of historic Manila. The sidewalks were jammed with carts and vendors selling cheap handicrafts, religious statues and charms, fruit, bootleg software, and DVDs. Totoy was looking for an address about two blocks away, but at the moment it might have been two hundred miles, for all the progress he was making.

He was looking for the owner of the car that had brought the American visitor to Optimo. The registration showed that it was owned by a corporation, Tres Agilas, Inc.—Three Eagles—with an address in the Paco neighborhood of Manila. Fair enough.

But the Paco address was a neighborhood restaurant where nobody knew anything about a Nissan sedan.

Totoy had then learned that Tres Agilas was itself owned by several corporations with addresses scattered around metropolitan Manila. One of those was here in Quiapo, two blocks away, and Totoy was pretty sure that when he reached the address he would find another place where nobody knew anything about Tres Agilas or a Nissan sedan for hire.

Andropov was still paranoid about the four curious Americans, although they hadn't reappeared in more than twenty-four hours. Not in Tacloban, not in Manila. Winston Stickney and Arielle Bouchard hadn't returned to their $1,800 luxury suites, and Totoy was sure that they wouldn't be back. They had either gone to ground or had heeded the warning and left the country.

In the first case, they would be much harder to find; if they had left, he could waste an infinite number of hours in fruitless searching.

Yet he didn't want to stop looking. Not now. He was getting the sense that someone had gone to a lot of trouble here, creating layers of opacity, as if to avoid scrutiny.

This made him all the more anxious to peel back the layers. Someone who didn't want to be scrutinized was someone he should get to know better.

Up ahead, the welter of cars and people nudged forward for a few feet and then stopped again.

The man Totoy sought—the actual owner of the Nissan Sentra—was less than three blocks away, stuck in the same traffic. And he was bound for the bodega where the four Americans were ensconced. In the backseat of the vehicle was a plastic storage bin that contained the first part of Ray Favor's want list.

Eddie Santos had spent the morning out and around the city, gathering the items from Favor's list. He could have delegated it to others, but he knew he could do it more quickly than anyone, working his phones as he drove, making sure that the items he needed at each stop were ready and waiting for pickup.

And it wasn't just a matter of efficiency. He was enjoying this. He didn't know how Favor and the others were going to use the items on the list, but he would recognize it when it happened, and he knew he didn't have long to wait.

That, and the fact that Favor paid generously— outrageously—had Santos out on the streets.

A light turned green up ahead, and miraculously the three or four cars ahead of him moved into the intersection. He followed them through.

"I wish I could help," said Arturo Guzman. "But it's out of the question."

He was a technical superintendent of the cell service that both Marivic and Ronnie used. Arielle had managed to talk her way past several layers of employees and representatives and management—Filipinos were amazingly open and accessible, she thought—and now Arturo Guzman was the last barrier between her and the data that she wanted.

"Two lives are at stake," Arielle said.

"I'm sure that the cause is legitimate. But it's strictly against corporate policy. If we allowed everyone with a cause to rummage through our data, we would never get any work done."

The walls of Guzman's office were glass from waist height to the ceiling. The office was in the middle of a large open floor, and Guzman could look out over several dozen desks and consoles that were spread in all directions. Arielle smiled pleasantly and said, "But no one is standing in line behind me. And when I have what I need, I'll say good-bye with thanks, and I'll never bother you again. Please. Two numbers only, covering just the past ten days."

He said, "Ten days, with well over one billion individual records per day, even more if you include hits at our competitors' unique sites. And I'm sure that you do want that, correct?"

"The more data, the better."

"There—you see how difficult this would be?"

She said, "But the data does exist, correct?"

"In theory, yes. Sites retain their records for about fifteen days. But it's moot, because we access that data only on a large scale, to track traffic flows and patterns. The kind of granularity you're talking about, we just don't do."

"I see," she said. "I guess I had the wrong

impression. I mean, based on my experience in the States."

"How's that?"

"A couple of years ago I had occasion to make the same request of a cell provider in the U.S., and it seemed to be a trivial matter for them. But naturally their software would be highly sophisticated. It isn't fair to expect that a company in a developing country would have tools so powerful and robust."

Guzman recoiled. His face showed disbelief. Outrage.

"Robust?" he said. "From a U.S. cell company? Give me a break. My American counterparts are constantly griping about their kludgy software. Inadequate software infrastructure is the curse of the early adopter. By the time the Philippines was ready for cellular, we understood what was possible. We had a chance to do it right, and we did. *Robust? Powerful?* Please. My software tools will blow away anything that the fat cats in the U.S. are working with."

Arielle didn't say anything. She wanted to give it a chance to sink in, what he had just said.

After a couple of seconds, he got it. His face took on a wry expression.

Checkmate. And he knew it.

"Give me those numbers," he said. "Let me see what I can do."

Marivic Valencia stood on her precarious perch and watched two orderlies carry a limp passenger off the seaplane and load him into the green and yellow six-wheel utility vehicle they regularly used at the dock.

Marivic had noted the markings early on. The side panel said JOHN DEERE and on the back was the word GATOR. She had also learned to recognize the sound of its engine as it passed, and would move her chair and table against the wall and scramble up to see what was happening. She rarely learned much, but it was at least a break in the monotony of the day.

This time she hadn't needed the Gator to arouse her. She had jumped up when she heard the drone of the seaplane, its first visit to the island since the day she arrived. She thought it might be bringing a new prisoner to occupy the cell that Junior had left, and as she watched the scene on the dock, she was even more certain. It jibed perfectly with her drug-addled memory of her own arrival.

Now the Gator was working back up the hill, with one orderly driving while the other sat in back with the new arrival, holding him to keep him from falling out.

The Gator had a steel tube frame above the body. Sometimes an awning was stretched over the frame, sometimes not. Today the awning was pulled back, and she got a good view as the vehicle worked toward the building and then pulled up outside.

Oh, God.

The passenger was Ronnie.

NINETEEN

Favor said, "Stick, you got a minute?"

The three men were in the bodega, Favor and Stickney and Mendonza. Arielle was still out, and they were waiting for Edwin Santos.

Mendonza was asleep.

"Sure, Ray," Stickney said.

"What you were saying the other day, about not wanting to kill anybody . . ."

"If that's a problem, I'll bow out," Stickney said quickly.

"That's not it, Stick. I was just wondering how you came to get there."

"It's not a big revelation, Ray. I just have this idea that when I finally cash out, I want to be able to think that I've done more good than wrong. I figure I'm in the hole to life right now, and I want to even things out if I can."

"The karmic balance sheet," Favor said.

"For lack of a better term."

"I feel the same way," Favor said. "But I think I'm so far in the hole, I'll never get on the right side."

"Not necessarily," Stickney said. "Look for a chance to do the great act of good. Or strike down a great evil. You can turn things around in a hurry that way."

"And if that means hurting people?"

"I don't know, Ray. I draw the line there, but I can't tell you what to do. You're not me. You're not like anybody else I ever knew. Be yourself, but always look for a chance to do the right thing. That's the best I can say. It shouldn't lead you too far wrong."

A few minutes later, Favor told Stickney that he was going out for a while, that he would be back in an hour or less.

He walked out into the crowded sidewalks of Tondo. Three blocks south, two east. It brought him to a grimy storefront window. Inside the glass was a hand-lettered sign on a board:

KNIVES & CUTLERY
Galicano Esqueviel, Prop.

He had passed this place during his morning run, but the door had been locked. Inside was a small room, a single old display case. Favor saw nobody inside, but from out on the sidewalk he could hear the raspy squeal of steel against a grinding wheel.

This time the door opened. The squeal got louder. It was coming from a room behind the shop. A bell rang on the door when Favor entered and closed the door, but the squeal continued.

Favor looked through the glass top of the display case at the knives inside. It was a mixed bag: kitchen knives, a butcher's set of skinning and boning knives, a bowie-style with a bone handle. And off to one side, two balisongs: butterfly knives with split handles that would fold up to cover the blades. Or swing back to expose them.

The squeal stopped. Favor reached back for the door, opened it and shut it. The bell chimed, and in a few seconds a man came out from the back, pushing aside a grimy curtain that hung over a rear door. He was about Favor's age. He wore shorts and rubber sandals, and his face and naked torso were sweat drenched. He squinted at Favor through the smoke from a cigarette clamped in his mouth. Favor guessed that this must be Galicano Esqueviel, Prop.

He waited for Favor to speak.

"I'd like to see a knife," Favor said.

Sweat dropped off the end of the man's nose as he reached inside for the bowie.

"No, a balisong," Favor said.

The man put down the bowie and reached in and took out one of the balisongs and laid it on the glass. He watched through the curling cigarette smoke as Favor opened the knife with a shake of the wrist, one side of the split handle swinging back, the blade locking into position, switchblade quick.

Favor studied the knife blade. Like most balisongs, it was a single-edge, with a slightly dropped point and a flat back that tapered down to a fine edge. Clean, simple. Nice.

"Four hundred pesos," Esqueviel said. Eight dollars. "It's one thousand in the gift shop at the Shangri-La hotel. They take everything I send them."

"This is much too good for a tourist's souvenir," Favor said.

"I disagree. The way I see it, every man should have a chance to own a good knife. Even if he doesn't appreciate what he holds in his hand."

Favor folded the handle forward, back over the blade. He latched it and put it on the counter and said, "Thank you. That's very nice work."

He pushed it back across the counter.

Esqueviel stared at Favor. He said, "This knife isn't worth four hundred pesos?"

"It's worth much more than that. But it's not quite right for me."

Esqueviel took the cigarette from his mouth and balanced it on the edge of the counter. It took the veil of smoke away from his eyes, and he looked at Favor as if for the first time.

"What are your needs?" he said.

"I want a carry knife that I can hang my life on."

"You're not a collector?"

"I'm a user," Favor said.

"Thrust or slash?"

"Both."

"What are you carrying now?"

"I'm not. I used to carry a good knife, but I put it away some time ago. I wish I had it now. I'm far from home, though, and I think I might need it soon, but I can't get to it."

"What exactly are you looking for?"

"Something that will go in my pocket. A very sturdy balisong would be good. A blade of three or four inches. Double-edged or at least with a hollow-ground swage. A strong spine for sure."

"You plan on hitting bone?"

"I don't plan on it, but sometimes it happens."

Esqueviel said, "Okay, you're a user." He picked up the cigarette and gestured Favor to come along as he disappeared through the curtain at the rear.

Favor followed him into a small workshop. In the middle of the floor was a brick forge where chunks of charcoal were glowing red. Esqueviel stood on a wooden bench and reached up into an overhead shelf. He came down with a handful of soiled rag, and when he unfolded the rag he revealed a knife, a balisong, with a very dark, smooth handle.

He put the knife in Favor's outstretched right hand.

The knife had heft, Favor noticed. Heavier than the usual balisong.

"Ironwood?" Favor said.

"I had some laying around."

Favor opened the knife. The split sides revealed a wide dagger shape, the twin edges curving to a point. A raised spine added weight and strength.

Favor held the knife at arm's length. He turned it over in his fingers, studying the blade at different angles. It was perfectly symmetrical. The steel was bluish gray, burnished to a glow.

"What is your bar stock?" Favor said.

"The steel is from the leaf spring of a 1953 Dodge flatbed truck. My father bought the leafs when I was a boy. He made dozens of knives from it, and I have made dozens more. Now I'm down to my last two pieces."

"This is a fantastic piece of work."

"I make knives for meat markets and for housewives and for tourists," Esqueviel said. "Once in a while I make one for myself. I don't keep it forever. I'm no collector. I don't care for collectors. I just hang on to it until I'm ready to make another. Then I find a good place for the old one."

"I want this knife."

"I wouldn't know what it's worth."

"It's worth plenty. Name your price."

"You're from the States, huh?"

"Yes," Favor said.

"There's something you can do for me."

"Just say it."

"If this knife helps get you home, I want you to send me another set of leaf springs from a 1953 Dodge flatbed truck."

Favor admired the knife for a few more seconds. The fit. The balance. *Perfect.*

"I can do that," he said.

TWENTY

The door buzzer sounded in the bodega.

Favor went to the door, checked the peephole. Edwin Santos. Favor opened the door and Santos came in carrying the clamshell storage bin. He brought it to the table. Stickney opened the folding top and began removing items. A length of PVC pipe, about a foot and a half. Electric drill and bits. Soldering iron. Two gallon-size cans, labeled by hand.

Stickney looked at what was left inside, taking inventory.

He said, "I think we still need some sixteen-gauge wire, twisted pair."

"Ah yes, the wire," Santos said. He went over to a shelf on the wall, rummaged through a box, came up with a spool of wire.

"I'm in business," Stickney said.

"The other items, I should have those late tonight. I can bring them first thing tomorrow. The passports and the weapons, tomorrow afternoon."

"Can we say twenty-four hours?" Favor asked. The current time was about 2:20 p.m.

"My source for the documents won't be getting much sleep tonight," Santos told him. "How about six p.m. at the latest? Will that work?"

"But no later than six," Favor said.

"No problem."

Favor went with Santos to the door, shook his hand, shut the door behind him.

When he turned back to the table, Stickney was already at work.

TWENTY-ONE

Stickney was still busy with his project, tools and materials spread across the tabletop, when Arielle returned to the bodega.

She said that she had something to show them. But she didn't want to disturb Stickney's work, so she opened the laptop on a top of a shipping crate. They all gathered around the screen; even Stickney stopped what he was doing.

She said, "On Ronnie, the story is simple but not very encouraging. At 1052 on the day of his disappearance, he ended up inside the coverage zones of three towers. Those towers' zones overlap at an area roughly triangular, about two hundred fifty yards on a side. We know he was going to Optimo, and that makes sense. The Impierno building and the villa are both inside that overlapping zone.

"He did move in and out of that zone a couple of times, but he reentered it for the last time at 1106. During the next eleven minutes he received three text messages from his mother. No reply."

Favor said, "When did he leave that coverage zone?"

"He didn't. Well, the phone didn't. We can assume that the phone was taken away from him at some time that day, because at 1618 it transmitted the bogus text to his mother. Immediately after that, the phone went offline and completely off the grid. It hasn't shown up on the network since."

"Somebody pulled the battery," Stickney said.

"Most likely."

Favor said, "And Marivic?"

"We'll need maps for this," Arielle said. On the laptop Arielle pointed at screen captures made by Arturo Guzman, showing the path of Marivic's phone through the cell system's towers.

"Marivic did arrive in Manila. Records put her phone in two cells that cover the Philtranco bus station, followed by thirty-two minutes of apparently aimless travel through Pasay and Parañaque and Makati, the areas between the bus terminal and the airport, where she left Manila."

Mendonza said, "She left Manila by plane?"

"Yes, but not by jet. The phone was picked up by towers at the southeast side of the airport, the general aviation area. Around 0610, the phone began to pass through a succession of cells south of Manila, spending three or four minutes in each cell and moving into the next one. Obviously it was airborne. It flew about one hundred thirty-five miles an hour, three hours and forty minutes, on a heading of about one-eighty true. This flight path took it over the island of Mindoro, across the Sulu Sea, to where it landed along the western peninsula of Mindanao, twenty to twenty-five miles north-northeast of Zamboanga City. It spent approximately thirty minutes on the ground before it took off again. Distance of the first hop was five hundred miles, more or less."

"This sounds like a slow single-engine plane," Mendonza said. "The half-hour stop would be for refueling."

"Apparently."

"Wait a minute," Favor said. "Is there an airstrip twenty miles north-northeast of Zamboanga?"

"No."

Stickney looked closer at the map.

"That's a coastal area," he said.

"Seaplane," Favor said. "It wouldn't need an airstrip. Just a dock. They were carrying her on a seaplane."

"It looks that way," Arielle said.

"Zamboanga . . . You're getting deep into Muslim separatist territory," Mendonza said.

"Correct. Everything south of Zamboanga is in the autonomous Muslim region. And that's where it was headed on the second hop. It flew south over Basilan Island. Five towers on Basilan picked up the phone before it reached open water and fell off the network."

"Fell off the network?" Mendonza said.

"Once the phone got over open water, there were no more cell towers."

"And it was never picked up again?"

"Correct. The southernmost tower on Basilan lost it around 1130 that morning. It hasn't registered on the system since."

"Then the plane could have gone anywhere."

"Oh no," Arielle said. "I'm pretty sure I know where the plane landed."

She began to work with one of the maps on the laptop screen, anchoring the takeoff point above Zamboanga.

"It's basic trig, and a little deductive reasoning. I used the records from the towers on Basilan. I knew the coverage zones, and I knew how long the plane stayed in each zone. I also knew the airspeed from the first hop—one hundred thirty-five miles an hour. So, putting all that together and knowing the start point, I was able to line out the plane's flight path over Basilan, two hundred eighteen degrees, give or take a degree."

She tapped a key, and a straight red line appeared on the map.

"Even knowing the direction, you can't tell how far it flew," Mendonza said.

"True. But the destination would have to be an island. And along that flight path, anywhere near it, there's really only one island of any size."

She zoomed in on the map, to the red line, and moved the view along the line until a single island appeared in the otherwise unbroken field of blue.

She switched to an online view, Google Earth, a satellite image. At first the screen showed just deep blue, but as she zoomed in, an island took form. It was mottled white and dark, roughly a half-moon shape.

She said, "It's about forty hectares, almost ninety acres. The locals call it *berbalang*—that's a mythical flesh-eating ghoul. There's another name. In the early nineteenth century, eight British seaman were cast up on the island after a storm swamped their ship in the Celebes. Only one got off alive, three months later. His personal account was a publishing sensation in England, and he gave the island an English name. Devil's Keep, he called it. What a charming spot it must be."

Stickney said, "Any idea what's on the island? Why would anyone fly here?"

"It's supposed to be uninhabitable," Arielle said. "The last record of activity was a failed attempt at a coconut plantation in the nineteen fifties. But this is one of the most isolated spots in Southeast Asia. I don't mean just geographically. It's far from the shipping lanes, miles north of Malaysian territorial waters, and so out-of-the-way and so deep in Muslim territory that the Philippine Navy would have zero presence anywhere in the area. This is as close to a no-man's-land as you're likely to find. So if you ask what's on the island, the answer is: there should be nothing, but there could be anything."

When the rich feel a need to look closely at some remote part of the world, they don't usually travel there to do it.

They buy aerial photos.

Favor did this routinely with property that he was considering. Often he would do it even after he had visited the property. He found that the view from above provided context and scale that were hard to grasp from ground level. Usually he would try to find existing high-resolution imagery, if it wasn't out-of-date. But if he couldn't get what he wanted, he would commission a set of images, either aerial photos or satellite images, from the several commercial companies that offered custom high-resolution imagery from orbiting satellites.

That was how he tried to get a closer look at Devil's Keep Island.

First, Arielle searched the world's inventory of all known commercial suppliers of high-resolution ground imagery. She had done it so often, this required less than a minute. She had written a program that automatically queried all the indexes of available imagery, both free and for sale. The search turned up nothing beyond the low-resolution imagery used in Google Earth.

She contacted the commercial satellite operators individually, but the soonest opening was ten days away, and they couldn't wait that long.

Then she began a search for aerial photo operators in Asia. This required some research, since she was unfamiliar with the aerial imagery business there. But within twenty minutes she was on the phone with the manager of an aerial photography outfit in Kuala Lumpur, who said that he would add Favor's order to a queue that was seventy-two to ninety-six hours long.

"Double the fee if he moves us to the head of the queue," Favor said.

She conversed briefly with the man in Kuala

Lumpur and told Favor: "He can't do that, but he can bump us up a day. That's forty-eight to seventy-two hours, weather permitting. I think that's the best he'll go, Ray."

"What's the equipment?" Favor asked.

"Beechcraft King Air with an UltraCamXp. He suggests two flight runs at an altitude of three thousand feet."

Favor considered this. The King Air was a substantial twin-engine turboprop. At three thousand feet it was easily spotted from the ground. One pass at that altitude would be suspicious. After two passes, everyone on the island would know that they were being watched.

He said, "That won't go. I want one pass, eight thousand feet, straight from horizon to horizon. If anybody notices, it should seem to be random. I'll sacrifice a little resolution for stealth. We may drop in on that rock one of these days, and I don't want them stirred up before we get there."

Marivic Valencia stood on her wobbly perch and looked over the wall into the cell on the other side.

She could have done this at any time when Junior was there. The wall was the same height all around the room, and she could have looked over at Junior just as she looked out onto the hillside and the dock.

But she hadn't wanted to see Junior. Without the wall they couldn't have talked so freely, she was sure of that. Putting a face on that voice—and letting him see her—might have spoiled it.

But this was different. She had been checking over the wall since the orderlies first brought Ronnie in and laid him down on the cot. At first he was out hard, then shifting fitfully as he tried to get past the waning effects of the drugs. She knew how that felt.

Now she watched as he opened his eyes and stared up at the ceiling. He sat up unsteadily on the edge of the cot.

"Ronnie. Up here. *Ronnie*."

He looked up at her eyes, barely visible over the top of the wall.

He didn't seem surprised.

He smiled.

"Found you," he said.

TWENTY-TWO

Shortly before midnight, Ray Favor walked down the long hallway in the lower level of the Impierno building. He was headed for the Ultimate VIP Safari Suite at the end of the hall, and the massage attendant named Patricia was walking beside him.

She said, "Like MacArthur, you have returned."

He had asked for her automatically, without thinking. *PuhTREESia*. He would have preferred nobody at all: he needed two or three minutes alone in the room, and he had to find a way to get it.

"Just leaving the office?"

He wore black slacks, expensive loafers, a shirt with a button-down collar, left open. Mendonza had assured him that this was the look of a business executive in Manila, where a traditional jacket and tie marked you as a stuffy outsider. And he was carrying a leather briefcase. The briefcase was the point of the charade.

He said, "Yes, it's been a long day."

"And now you want some relaxation," she said as they approached the room.

"Yes."

"All right. I will help you to relax." She opened the door for him, let him enter. She walked in after him, shut the door, and locked it from the inside. She put her hand out, motioning for the briefcase.

"You don't need that here," she said.

He kept it, putting it down on the floor against the nearest wall.

"I would like a drink," he said. "Will you get me one, please?"

"Of course."

"Scotch whiskey, no ice. Water on the side."

He took some cash from his pocket and held it to her, thinking that she would take it, leave the room and go to the bar to bring his drink. It was all the time he needed.

But she shook her head and waved off the money.

She reached for a telephone on the wall.

"The room boy will bring it," she said. "You can pay when you leave."

Room boy? Christ, Favor didn't need this, someone knocking at the wrong time.

He said, "No, it's all right."

"All right? No drink?"

"Maybe later."

She put down the phone and stood looking at him. Perplexed. Maybe a little impatient.

This was not going well.

She turned away, took a clothes hanger from a hook on the wall, and handed it to him.

"I will prepare the bath," she said. She turned toward the shower room. The shower room with its wall of glass.

He said, "I have a request."

She stopped, turned back to him.

"What is your request?" Definitely impatient now.

"I would like to watch you in the shower."

"You mean washing? You wish to watch me bathing?"

"Yes," Favor said.

She seemed to find this amusing. She broke into a laugh, put a hand to her mouth to cover the giggle.

"It's one of my pleasures," he said. "To watch a beautiful woman bathing."

This happened to be true. Favor also liked to watch a beautiful woman brushing her teeth, combing her hair, eating a chocolate cupcake. To Favor, the most ordinary act became fascinating when it was performed by a beautiful woman.

Patricia stopped giggling.

She said, "As if I'm alone. And you are hidden, and you are watching me. Yes?"

"Yes," he said. "That's it."

"I understand," she said. "You are *pakipot*. You understand *pakipot*? Like, shy?"

"That's it," Favor said.

She reached for his arm, tugged him over to the massage table. It faced the glass wall of the shower room.

"Sit," she said. "Relax."

He sat up on the table. She went to a bank of light switches on the nearby wall. Tapped one—a bright light came on in the shower room, shining down from the ceiling. She tapped another, then another.

The lights went off in the main room. Only the single bright overhead light of the shower room broke the darkness.

He heard the padding of bare feet on the floor.

Nearly a minute passed, with just a soft rustle from near the shower room door.

She stepped into the light.

She was naked, her hair pinned up. She turned on the water of the shower, tested it, stepped beneath it. The water ran over her bare shoulders, down the curves of her body.

She was turned away from him. Letting him look, giving him plenty of time to feast his eyes. She reached for the soap, still deliberately angled away from him.

Favor climbed down from the table. He went around to the wall, felt for the briefcase, found it, opened it. He felt around inside, took out a metal penlight. He shielded it with his body and turned it on.

In the open briefcase was Stickney's device. It was the section of PVC pipe, capped at both ends, perforated by about a dozen drill holes. Near one end, a timing device. At the other end, glued in place, was a small battery-powered alarm clock. Braided wire ran from the back of the clock, down through a hole in the pipe.

Favor looked back over his shoulder. Patricia was soaping herself now, with deliberate, languid movements. Playing to him.

Favor carried the open briefcase to a corner of the

room. From there, he was almost out of sight from the shower. At the top of the wall was a metal vent. Air-conditioning: he could feel the cool air as it blew out in a hush.

One of the features that made the Ultimate VIP Safari Suite attractive to Favor was a plush armchair. He hadn't seen a chair in any of the other rooms. He brought the chair over, stepped up on it. The vent was now at his eye level.

Two screws held the vent cover in place. He unscrewed them, dropped them into his shirt pocket, then removed the cover and leaned it against the wall. He shone the penlight inside the vent. It was a rectangular aluminum duct, a few inches high and about a foot and a half wide. From inside the wall it bent ninety degrees to the left, and when Favor pointed the light that way, he could see where it joined a larger duct about five feet away.

This was a main duct of the building's air-conditioning system—he was sure of it.

He bent down and picked up Stickney's device and a black metal tube. He gently placed the device inside the opening, pushing it toward the intersection of the main vent as far as he could reach.

He placed the black tube into the vent. It was photo equipment, a monopod—like a single leg of a tripod—used to steady a camera for offhand shots. Favor pulled out section after section, each time pushing the device closer to the larger vent. The fourth section extended the tube to six feet, and when Favor gave the fully extended tube a last push, he felt the device hit the far wall of the main duct.

Perfect.

He quickly retracted the monopod, took it out. He replaced the vent cover, screwed it back on, and closed the briefcase.

He returned to the massage table and looked toward the shower. Patricia was still in the light, under the streaming water. Still turned away from the table. She was washing her right arm, the arm bent in front of her, turning it as she soaped it with her left hand.

She looked over her shoulder, straight at where he would have been sitting.

Favor knew that she couldn't actually see him in the darkness, but she was focusing where he was supposed to be. It was a stunning look, earthy and provocative and inviting.

She held the look for several seconds before she glanced away and continued to wash.

Favor watched for about a minute. Maybe longer.

He was carrying some cash in the pocket of his trousers. He took it out, a folded packet of one-thousand-peso notes. He counted them. Fourteen.

He thought, *Thank you so much*.

He laid the bills on the table and left the room.

HARVEST DAY
–2

TWENTY-THREE

Favor woke around 5:30 a.m., buzzed with an aimless and unfocused energy. He told himself that he should sleep a little longer. He would need the rest.

Often when he woke too early he would think about the hours ahead, how he planned to spend the time. It was a useful trick for clearing his head, and sometimes he would doze off, sleeping on his plans for the day to come. But not now. Thinking about his plans for the day just amped up the buzz, knowing what they intended to do before the next sunrise.

He got up, pulled on nylon shorts and a thin T-shirt. He laced up his running shoes. He left his cell phone on the table but brought the back-door key, and headed out into the streets of Tondo.

Eddie Santos rose just before sunrise. He scribbled *Good morning!* to his daughter on a notepad and left it at her usual place at the table; she would see it when she had breakfast. Then he picked up his wallet and car keys and went out.

Totoy Ribera began his day by stopping for a breakfast of fried eggs and rice and sausage, taking the chance to fill his stomach while he could.

He expected to be in his car for hours, still looking for whoever was behind the Nissan sedan and Tres Agilas and all the other shell entities that enveloped them. By the end of the previous day he had felt locked in a maze of corporate names and addresses, all fruitless, a convoluted trail that seemed to loop back onto itself. But he wasn't quitting. This wasn't even completely about the Americans (who hadn't surfaced for almost two days). This was personal, some unseen wise guy taunting him with his cleverness. Totoy couldn't wait to get his hands on the wise guy.

Marivic Valencia woke around this time too. A scuffle in the other cell woke her.

She didn't know how long it had been going on, but it lasted only a few more seconds before she heard the door close on the other side of the wall.

"Ronnie?"

"Yeah." Disgruntled.

"Are you all right?"

"I'm all right. But they were rough with the needles."

She said, "Needles?"

"Twice. Once to take blood from my arm. Once to give me an injection."

"NO!" she cried.

Favor ran south through Tondo's streets, then across the Roxas Bridge over the Pasig and past the thick stone redoubts of Intramuros, the old walled city of Manila. He ran through the city park called the Luneta, past the Manila Hotel, past the steel shafts of the fence around the U.S. embassy, perched on a shelf of land that angled into Manila Bay.

He ran on the broad sidewalk along the bay front, past gleaming hotels on one side and the still water of the bay on the other, with the high green ridges of the Bataan peninsula in the distance. A man, sleeping on palm fronds, opened his eyes and looked up as Favor passed.

Favor ran the full length of the curving bay front, past the Manila Yacht Club and the headquarters of the Philippine Navy. Where the seawall ended, at the green lawn and white walls of the Cultural Center of the Philippines, he stopped and checked his watch. He had been running for thirty-one minutes. A little over five miles at six minutes per mile.

He turned and ran back the way he had come, but the return trip took longer. He made a stop along the way. When Favor returned to the bodega, the time was almost seven a.m. and he was sweating from the heat of the day.

Mendonza and Stickney were seated at the table, drinking coffee and eating breakfast. Arielle, too, was at the table, but she was intent at her laptop.

Two large canvas bags sat on the floor of the bodega.

"Eddie Santos been by?" Favor asked.

"Second installment on the wish list," Stickney said.

"Now we just need the firearms and the paper. And Ari's worm."

Without looking up she said, "Ari's worm will be ready."

Favor said, "Ari, if you can take a break, I need to know about a dude named Franklin Kwok."

Now she looked up. "Would that be the rich dude Franklin Kwok?"

"Apparently."

"Hong Kong. Shipbuilding is the family business, but since he took over, Franklin has expanded into construction and chemicals and agricultural commodities—especially construction, I think. He's somewhere on the *Forbes* list. Not right at the top, but not anywhere near the bottom, either. He must be about your age. He has a touch of the flamboyant about him. He dates actresses and drives fast cars the way they're supposed to be driven. Kind of unusual for serious Hong Kong money. They usually keep their heads low."

Favor said, "I need an introduction."

"To Franklin Kwok? Ray, I rarely say this, but you may be playing out of your league."

"Probably," Favor said. "But I want to sit down with him. Right away. He has something that we need."

"What's that?"

"A rat hole," Favor said.

They all understood. To the members of the former Bravo One Nine, a rat hole was a haven. A refuge. It was any place where they could disappear and regroup in safety when their cover was compromised.

A rat hole being the place where rats go when someone unexpectedly turns on the lights.

When One Nine was active, they had never operated without at least one rat hole. Sometimes they would have several, a sequence of places where they could fall back and hide, buying some time before they retreated to the next one in the string.

The love motel had been a rat hole of sorts, but it had been improvised, and rat holes weren't supposed to work that way. Too chancy. Rat holes were supposed to be set up in advance, waiting.

"Jeez, Favor, a rat hole. It's about time," Arielle said.

"Is it a good one?" Mendonza said.

"It's a beauty," Favor said. "Like nothing you've ever seen."

Franklin Kwok motioned Favor to a seat at his table.

They were in the dining room of a golf club south of Manila. Kwok wore a golf shirt the color of lapis lazuli, mirror sunglasses, and a Rolex watch with a gold band only slightly smaller than a boxer's championship belt.

"Sit," he said. "Have a drink. Do you know what you want to eat? I recommend the yellowfin."

The introduction had been arranged by Favor's banker in Hong Kong, who knew Franklin Kwok. But this wasn't surprising. Most bankers in Hong Kong knew Franklin Kwok.

"I'm happy to meet you," Kwok said after they had ordered lunch. "But I have to tell you directly, I'm not selling. I didn't build it to sell."

"I knew it must be a custom job."

"Custom? I built it! It's my design, one of a kind. I was even in there getting my hands dirty when I had the time."

Favor wrote two numbers on the back of a business card, several digits each. He passed the card to Kwok.

Kwok took off his sunglasses and held the card up to read. "What are these figures?"

"The first is my estimate of the fair market value in U.S. dollars. The second is the amount I'm prepared to pay."

"Twice as much as the first," Kwok said. "I like the way you think. The first is close. The second . . . Look, if you're willing to spend this much, you can build one of your own. I won't let you have my plans, but I'll give you a few ideas to get you started."

"I don't have time for that," Favor said. "I need something that's ready to go right now."

"Need?" Kwok said. "One doesn't *need* something like this. Desire, yes. But not need."

"I need it," Favor repeated. "My friends and I are engaged in a certain enterprise. It's not for profit— not what you might think—but it entails an element of risk. This could save our lives, me and my friends. I'm not being dramatic. That's a fact."

"Tell me," Kwok said. Now he was interested.

Favor spoke: not all the details, but enough that Kwok would understand.

"Fascinating," Kwok said when Favor had finished. "This is perfect for your purposes."

"I thought so."

"No, I mean *perfect*. Even better than you could know."

"I may not even use it," Favor said. "But I want to know that I have it."

"And for how long would you want to know that?"

"I expect that the problem will be resolved in a couple of weeks. Maybe just days."

Franklin Kwok thought for a moment.

He said, "Are you a gambler?"

"Not the casino kind."

Kwok laughed. "I know what you mean. The stakes that really matter, you don't bet those at a roulette wheel."

He dug into a pocket and came up with a coin. He held it up for Favor to see. On the face it showed the national heroes Apolinario Mabini and Andres Bonifacio; on the reverse, the Philippine national seal.

"You call it," Kwok said. "Win the toss, it's yours for one month."

"And if I lose?"

"If you lose . . ." Kwok flipped the coin into the air.

"Tails," Favor said.

Franklin Kwok caught the coin and slapped it onto the back of his left hand without revealing it.

"If you lose," he said, "maybe you should take it as a bad omen, and consider abandoning your enterprise."

He lifted his hand, just enough to peek at the coin.

He looked down on the faces of Mabini and Bonifacio.

"This must be your lucky day," he said, and he swept the coin into his pocket. "Let me tell you exactly what you've got. No, better yet—let me show you."

TWENTY-FOUR

In Nice, France—seven hours behind Manila time—the sun was just rising as Ilya Andropov's most important client extracted himself from the limbs and bodies of the four young women who slept sprawled, mostly naked, on his oversize bed. He sorted out the arms and legs and rumps and breasts, clearing the tangle enough that he could crawl to the edge of the mattress.

He was in his fifties, a big man gone soft, his back and shoulders and barrel chest matted in graying body hair.

He was breathing hard as he sat up at the edge of the bed.

The jostling awoke one of the women. Lisette was her name. She was twenty-two, a sun-washed and tanned-all-over blonde. At different times she called herself, or had been called, a model, actress, party girl, whore. Just words, and they fit all the other women on the bed as well. They belonged to the female swarm that gravitated to the huge house on the hill above the city, with its infinity pool and its fast cars and endlessly flowing champagne, and the pricey gifts, and the prodigious quantities of drugs that were never out of reach.

And, really, all you had to do for it was be there, and be yourself, and be prepared to show a little indulgence to the man who called himself Uncle Teddy.

She watched him now as he stood and made his way over to the water closet and leaned over the toilet, bracing himself against the wall with one arm while he pissed.

She looked at his face as he walked back over to the bed. It was misshapen, out of balance. Normal from the centerline to his left ear . . . but the right side, the cheekbone to the jaw, was caved in and scarred. To Lisette it looked as if it had been badly broken and then put back together by someone who didn't know what he was doing. An accident, she supposed. It had left one eye slightly off-axis, just enough that you would notice when you looked at him straight on—enough that the swarming females all called him Cockeye Teddy, though never in his presence.

He walked over to the bed and stood looking down at the sleeping women. His dick was within arm's length of Lisette, and she reached up and gave it a casual tug. She knew there was no chance that he would respond. The dick didn't really work, but he liked to pretend that it did, and that he was voracious and desirable. Another indulgence.

He let her fondle it for a few seconds, then said, "Not now, my little dirty-leg slut. There's no time."

He reached into the bed and began grabbing wrists and ankles, shaking them, saying, "Let's wake up, come on sleepyhead, time to get up," speaking in his laughably awkward French. He clapped his hands loudly. "Let's go, girls. Time to leave. The party has ended."

Lisette didn't understand. In the weeks since she first came to the house, it had been an endless rolling feast of pleasure and the senses. The party never ended.

She said, "Leave?"

"Yes," he said. "I have to get dressed. Uncle Teddy is going away, and you can't come with me."

TWENTY-FIVE

The passports were ready for Eddie Santos about an hour later than promised. They were from Canada, for Jules Touchfeather; from the Philippines, Roberto Dugay; from Haiti, Claudette Monfort; from Trinidad and Tobago, Arnold Goforth. The quality was good, and Santos knew that Favor would be pleased. But he also knew that Favor was expecting the paper and the weapons no later than six p.m. The time was nearly five p.m., Manila's afternoon rush was swelling by the minute, and Santos still didn't have the pistols.

They were hidden at Santos's beer pub, in the northern suburb called Valenzuela. Santos drove there furiously, drawing on his lifetime knowledge of Manila's streets, avoiding congestion by using alleyways and obscure shortcuts every time traffic seemed to slow.

The time was almost 5:30 when he reached the beer pub. It was a Filipino version of a workingman's bar, with about a dozen outside tables and more inside. Santos found a space out front, parked, and hurried in.

Santos waved a quick hello to the beer pub's day manager and kept on walking. No time for chatter. He picked up two bar towels from behind a counter, went to the back room, closed the door. The floor hatch was beneath a tall stack of cases of Red Horse ale, and Santos had to move the cases one by one. The back room was sweltering, and Santos was soon damp from perspiration.

He pried up the floorboards with the tip of a pocketknife, and he reached in and found the pistols and a box of ammunition. He had acquired the weapons and stashed them there weeks earlier. It was like putting money in the bank—the demand for quality firearms was constant.

He wrapped a towel around one of the pistols, then wrapped another towel around the second pistol and the ammo. He replaced the boards and moved several cases of Red Horse over the spot.

He was sweating hard now. He went out quickly, holding the wrapped guns and ammo in the crook of one arm, checking the time on one of his phones as he walked. It was 5:43, and the bodega in Tondo was fifteen minutes away even under the best conditions. Santos was ready to call Favor, tell him that he would be late, but he decided to hold off until he knew for sure.

He put the phone in his pocket and looked up as he approached his car.

Totoy Ribera was standing in his path.

Totoy said, "You. You fucking little hustler. I should have guessed."

Just after seven p.m., Elvis Vega came by the bodega with dinner. Favor asked him if he had heard from Eddie; Vega said no, not since the early afternoon.

Vega left, and they ate. Arielle was at the laptop, munching as she worked. At 7:15 she said to Favor, "Here you go, hotshot. Don't lose it."

It was a USB flash drive, about the size of her thumb.

"Plug it in, that's all," she said. "The software does the rest. It'll take a few seconds."

"How do I know if it worked?" Favor said.

"I'll know. I'll be online. If it loads, it should connect back to me within a few seconds, then I'll tell you."

They were going to set up a conference call on their phones, Bluetooth headsets, using the phones like radios.

She said, "Nothing from Eddie?"

"Not a thing."

"Does that bother you?"

"Not enough to cancel tonight." He thought for a moment, and corrected himself: "There is no canceling tonight. We're committed."

Stickney said, "Anyway, the passports are in case we screw up. The guns are in case we really screw up. We don't have the guns or the passports . . ."

"So let's not screw up," Mendonza said.

"There you go," Favor said.

"I met them thirteen years ago," Santos said. "They came to me. They said they knew me through mutual friends."

"Who were the friends?" said Totoy.

"I never figured that out."

"You never asked them?"

"They aren't the kind of people you ask a lot of questions."

"You think they would have been angry?"

"I think they would have disappeared."

Totoy had taken Santos to a vacant apartment. At first Santos was relieved. It could have been police headquarters: possession of a firearm without a permit was a serious crime in the Philippines. It could get you years.

Then, alone in the apartment with Totoy, Santos realized that the headquarters might have been safer.

He also was not sure that they were alone. Santos got the sense of someone else in the next room, behind him. He didn't hear or see anyone, but something in the way Totoy spoke—something intangible—gave Santos that idea.

Totoy was standing, Santos seated in a chair, the only piece of furniture in the place.

Totoy held out the passports.

"Where did you come up with these names?"

"I used their names. That's what they call themselves."

Totoy took out photocopies of the passports from the hotel check-in, and gave them to Santos.

"What about this?" Totoy said.

Santos studied the photocopies. "I never heard those names before."

"What are the true names of the other two?"

"To the best of my knowledge, they are Jules and Roberto. I never ran a background check."

Santos had decided that he would give up only so much. His story would be a half-true concoction of fact and lies. Plausible lies, he hoped. With each answer, he was weighing how much to yield, how to camouflage the truth with realistic fabrication.

Part of this was loyalty. He wasn't close to the Americans, but they had trusted him, put their lives in his hands. His life and business relationships were built on discretion, and if his disloyalty became known, he would lose the trust of all who dealt with him. Betrayal was bad for business.

And there was an element of pride. He disliked being coerced. He believed that he was better than Totoy Ribera, smarter and more solid if not as vicious.

This was a high-wire act, but he wouldn't be bullied by a lesser man.

"What was the nature of their activity when they came here thirteen years ago?"

"I never knew for sure, but I believed that it was clandestine."

"Clandestine? Like spies?"

"They're an odd sort of spy. But yes, I guess so."

"Spying for who?"

"I never knew. I told you, they're pros."

"And why did they return?"

"I think they were here mostly on a holiday. But they had some small business to attend to. I have no idea what it was. I think they ran into some difficulty, though."

"How did you know that?"

"When someone asks for weapons and forged documents, you can usually guess that they're in some trouble."

"When were you supposed to deliver these goods?"

"About an hour ago."

"Where?"

This was the big one, Santos told himself. If he could put this one over, he might get out of the jam with honor intact. About the gun charges . . . he knew that Totoy most likely would keep the guns for himself, and without the guns there was no evidence of a crime. Whatever difficulty remained could be smoothed over with a large dollop of cash.

He said, "They were supposed to call me to arrange a meeting."

He knew that his phone—now in Totoy's possession—had been ringing, and he guessed that it was Favor or one of the others.

Totoy said, "I want to ask you a very important question. But before I do, I want you to look out that window, down in the street."

Santos went to the window. They were on the third floor, and he looked down. At first he wasn't sure what he was supposed to see, but then a light came on in a car at the curb, and he saw Anabeth in the backseat, with one of Totoy's goons up front.

This changed everything.

"She's at Assumption, I understand," Totoy said. "Not bad for the daughter of a cheap little chiseler."

"What do you want to know?" Santos asked.

"Where are they?"

"They're in a bodega in Tondo. They're waiting for me."

"That's much better. Now, you think about this. What should I know about these people? What can you tell me that will give me some advantage in dealing with them?"

"I can tell you, but you won't accept it," Santos said.

"Tell me."

Santos cleared his throat. He made sure to speak clearly, so that he could be heard by anyone else who might be listening.

He said, "I have no idea why they're here. I have no idea what's at stake. But I can tell you this. I wouldn't want them against me. If I had something they wanted, I wouldn't fight them over it. I would smile and I'd hand it over, and I would pray to God that they would just take it and go away."

At 9:15, Favor said, "We might as well be getting over there."

"It's about that time," Mendonza said. "Traffic— you never know when you'll get hung up."

They took both vehicles. Mendonza and Favor rode in a Mitsubishi Montero SUV with darkened windows. In the backseat of the Mitsubishi were the two large canvas bags from Eddie Santos. Stickney took the other car, a Hyundai sedan. Arielle opened the steel roll-up door and they drove out, and when they were gone, she pulled the door down and locked it.

She sat by the laptop, at the steel table inside the bodega, and she waited.

About fifteen minutes later, her phone rang. Favor. Her phone rang again. Stickney. She set it up as a three-way conference call, then called Mendonza to set up the fourth leg of the call.

They were all connected.

Stickney parked the Hyundai on Amorsolo Street, across the street from the villa. Seconds later, the Mitsubishi pulled up beside him. Mendonza was driving, with Favor in the backseat.

Mendonza left the Hyundai. Favor swung open the door to let him in, and they drove off, around the block, and parked at the cross street beside the Impierno building.

The time was now 9:47. They waited six minutes. At 9:53, Mendonza took out another phone, purchased the day before from a street vendor, and he called a number that he had programmed.

It was the City of Manila, Emergency Services.

In rapid Tagalog, he said, "I want to report a fire. Impierno nightclub, corner of Amorsolo and Salas streets. Better hurry, it's a bad one."

They sat and watched the building. Everything was normal. The valet attendants took away cars and delivered them. The doorman opened the front door for men who casually came in and out.

Favor lowered his window by a few inches. At

9:59, the first faint wail of emergency sirens drifted in through the opening.

Favor said, "Stick, you're on."

Stickney got out and crossed Amorsolo. He was carrying a cloth shoulder bag; inside the bag were half a dozen bricklike objects wrapped in black paper. He passed in front of Impierno, walking briskly to the corner of the high concrete wall, about where the old woman sold newspapers during the day. The sidewalk was empty now, and Stickney stopped and looked up, directly into the security camera that was fixed at the top of the wall.

He took out one of the black bricklike packages, sparked a flame on a disposable cigarette lighter that he carried in one hand, and lit a paper fuse that extended from the black paper.

Stickney threw the packet over the wall. He walked briskly along the sidewalk, lit another black package, and threw that one over the wall too.

The sirens were louder now in the Mitsubishi. Mendonza pulled out from the parking space, and he drove across Amorsolo Street, parking on the sidewalk beside Impierno.

The time was now ten o'clock.

In Impierno, in the air-conditioning vent of the Ultimate VIP Safari Suite, the device that Favor had planted came to life at its programmed time. It sparked and began to emit clouds of gray smoke through the holes that had been drilled in the PVC pipe. At first the smoke was thin, curling out of the perforations, but within a few seconds it blew out thick and heavy. This was the low point of the main cooling duct—Favor had looked for it when he scouted the building—and the airflow carried it up and into the main room of the Impierno stage.

Out on the sidewalk along Amorsolo, Stickney lit one more black brick and tossed it over the concrete wall. Then he crossed the sidewalk, looking for an opening in traffic, and he ran cross the street to where the Hyundai was parked.

As he started the car, Stickney spotted a white man emerging from the side gate, onto the walkway between the villa and the Impierno building. Stickney slammed the door of the Hyundai and pulled out into Amorsolo, disappearing up the street.

A ripping explosion erupted at that moment on the grounds of the villa, a rolling, continuous series of detonations inside the wall.

The noise came from the first of the three bricks that Stickney had lit and tossed over the wall. The bricks were five-hundred-count packages of ladyfinger firecrackers, fitted with a forty-five-second delay fuse. Even before the first one had finished, the second one ignited and began to explode.

In Impierno, smoke billowed from vents into the main showroom and the private rooms at the back. It was faint at first, and few noticed it. What hit most people then was the smell. It was the stench of rotten eggs, hydrogen sulfide. It immediately permeated the rooms, followed by the smoke, causing patrons and employees to panic.

Three fire companies arrived: two pumper trucks and a hook and ladder. They met the crowds that came streaming out the front door and the side emergency door.

Winston Stickney, having made a loop of three blocks, pulled onto Amorsolo Street again and back into the parking spot that he had left less than a minute earlier. From there he had a view of the walkway and the door at the side of the building, the Optimo entrance.

He said, "Got your back."

He heard Favor's response in the Bluetooth earpiece: "Coming out."

Favor and Mendonza stepped out of the Mitsubishi. They were dressed, head to foot, in firefighters' turnout gear: helmet and balaclava and jacket and pants and bunker boots.

It was the gear from the canvas sacks, Eddie Santos's second delivery.

Each wore a breathing mask to cover their faces. Favor carried a fire ax. Mendonza carried a firefighter's wooden pike pole, with a gaff hook at one end, and a large crowbar. They walked along the sidewalk, crowded now with firefighters and customers and employees of Impierno, including several squealing, near-naked young women.

Inside the villa grounds, the third brick of firecrackers began to bang and snap.

Favor and Mendonza made their way through the

crowds, around the corner and down the walkway, up to the door in the side of the building. With a single swing of the ax, Favor knocked off the doorknob. Mendonza poked the damaged door with the end of the crowbar. He pried, giving it his weight, and the door popped open.

They went up the stairs, two at a time. At the top, Mendonza stopped and took out another of Stickney's smoke bombs from inside his turnout coat. It needed no timer; he ignited it with a nine-volt battery, and set it on the top step.

He took up position at the top of the stairs, holding the pike pole ready for use.

Favor stood before the thick glass door at the landing, the entry to the offices. He swung the ax, and the glass exploded. He cleared the remaining large shards with a few swipes of the ax, and he stepped inside.

Just before ten p.m., the security staff at the villa was down to two Filipino guards, one at the walkway gate, the other manning the vehicle gate at the back alley. Two of the five Russians were at work in the lab in one wing of the house, as they always were at this time, after the arrival of the airfreight shipments. Ilya Andropov was in his office. Anatoly Markov was at the security console, idly checking the monitors, with the fifth—a gaunt, sharp-featured young man named Vladimir—dozing on a sofa in the room.

Markov noticed Winston Stickney tossing the

first of the bricks over the wall. Markov got a good look at him and recognized him.

He shouted: "Goddamn, it's the American. Vlad, go get him!"

Vladimir Raznar woke on the sofa, uncomprehending.

Markov was still shouting, yelling for Andropov and the two in the lab, yelling about intrusions in the perimeter. He shouted again at Raznar, and this time Raznar understood and ran out to the side gate and up the walkway and the sidewalk, looking for the American.

The two from the lab came out, and Markov sent them onto the grounds to find whatever had come over the wall.

For a few minutes, events overtook them. There were the firecracker explosions, and the fire trucks, and the customers and the girls filling the sidewalk, mingling with the firefighters who struggled to hook up hoses. Markov and Andropov watched all this on the monitors, until Andropov noticed the two firefighters on the inside stairs, up at the top of the landing.

He pointed out the shot. "Toly, something's wrong here."

"It's a fire," Markov said.

"Go see what's happening."

"Boss, it's a burning building."

"I don't see any fire," he said. "Go! And take this."

It was a pistol, a 9mm automatic.

Markov took it, tucked it into his waistband, and hurried out the door.

———

Favor ignited another smoke bomb when he entered the Optimo offices, and placed it under one of the desks.

Using a flashlight, he went to a PC at one of the nearby desks and turned it on.

Smoke filled the office as he waited for the machine to boot.

He said, "Ari, you ready?"

"I'm waiting."

He found a USB port at the front of the machine and plugged in the flash drive. "It's in."

Stickney said, "Al, one coming your way. With pistol."

Mendonza was on the landing, waiting at the top of the smoke-filled stairway. He held the pike pole at the ready, blunt end forward. As a figure emerged from the billowing smoke, Mendonza swung the pike at shin level, taking the man off his feet. The pistol flew as the man smacked hard into the floor, face-first. Mendonza swung the pike again, down across the man's back, knocking the breath from his lungs.

Mendonza kicked the pistol across the floor and turned back to the staircase, pike pole at the ready again.

Favor said, "Ari, anything?"

"Nothing," she said. "It's been thirty seconds. That must not be a network machine."

"Shit."

"Try the rooms in the back," Stickney said.

Favor unplugged the drive, shut down the PC,

and made his way through the smoke to the back of the room.

The flashlight's bright spot found a door to his right. He tried it. Locked.

He swung the ax, and the door splintered.

He stepped in, found the PC and the power switch.

He turned it on and waited for it to boot.

Stickney said, "Al, two more. One with a long gun."

Favor plugged in the drive. "Ari, it's in."

Mendonza stepped down into the thick smoke of the stairwell. He held the pole out in front of him, waited, and jabbed hard at the first shape he saw in the smoke. It was the barrel of a shotgun, and he knocked it aside with one flick of the pole, then went hard at the belly of the man behind the gun.

The blow knocked the man back, off balance, into the second one behind him, and they both fell backward down the stairs. Mendonza pressed forward down the steps, holding the pole out in front of him. The outline of a pistol appeared in the smoke. Mendonza knocked it aside and jabbed with the blunt end of the pole, looking for windpipes, abdomens, groins.

Ari said, "We're in."

Favor pulled out the flash drive, pressed the PC's power button, and left the room. He crossed through the office, over the broken glass, down the stairs. He stepped over the two sprawled figures on the steps, to where Mendonza waited near the door, looking up for him.

They walked out of the smoke and into the night.

"Out," Favor said.

Stickney watched until they had disappeared into the tumult on the sidewalk, swallowed up, and he pulled out of the parking space for the last time and drove away.

Favor and Mendonza made their way through the crowd, back toward the Mitsubishi. Mendonza got in on the driver's side, Favor through the passenger door. Before he ducked inside, he pulled the mask away.

Nearby was the group of young women from behind the fishbowl window, and when Favor removed his mask he saw that one of the women was watching him.

It was Patricia.

She met his eyes, flashed him a grin, naughty and complicit: *Ah, so you did this,* the grin seemed to say.

He returned the smile, then dropped into the seat and closed the door, and they drove away.

With the chaos at Impierno receding in the mirrors, he said, "Ari, are you getting what you wanted?"

"I'm getting it," she said.

"Good. Because I don't want to try that again for a while."

He laughed.

And he said: "Well done, well done, well done."

TWENTY-SIX

On the laptop screen at the bodega, Arielle
Bouchard watched the directory listing for the Optimo network scroll up in front of her.

The characters were Cyrillic. Russian.

Arielle had studied it for a couple of years as a
college undergrad. She hadn't used it much since
then, but figured she had enough to get by. She
began to review the list, looking for subdirectories
that seemed interesting or important, checking their
sizes and selecting those she wanted for download,
trying to get the most important ones earliest in the
queue. The connection could be cut at any time.

She heard Favor's "Out" in her earpiece, and a
little while later he was asking her whether she was
getting what she wanted, and laughing, and murmuring *Well done, well done, well done.*

They kept the phone connection open. She heard
Mendonza and Stickney discussing their locations,
learning that they were about two blocks apart on
Roxas Boulevard, with Stickney slowing down so
that Mendonza could catch up.

She kept opening directories, checking their contents, sometimes opening individual files.

At a corner of the screen was a counter that kept

track of the data that had already been transferred, tracking it in megabytes. The number kept rolling over, growing by the second. A pulsing light on the laptop indicated network activity, data being received.

She opened a directory, looked at some of the files within it.

Something was odd here. The directory contained medical files. Dozens. Another directory contained thousands of lab results, protein analyses.

In her earpiece Favor was suggesting that they stop to eat, bring back some food. He asked Ari whether she was hungry.

"No," she said, distracted, and "Yeah, sure, whatever you get is fine with me."

She was absorbed in the files, the medical records. Favor and Mendonza and Stickney were discussing restaurants, what was nearby and what they wanted to eat. The chatter in her ear was distracting, but if she dropped the call, she would disconnect the others too. So she took out the earpiece and put it on the table in front of her, and kept opening files and directories, disturbed by what she saw.

The buzzer sounded at the back door. She got up, went to the door, put her eye to the peephole.

Edwin Santos.

She unlocked the door, started to open it, and said, "Hey, Eddie."

The door flew open. Two Filipino men rushed in, guns drawn.

They caught her off guard, one of them knocking her down and pushing her to the floor while the second took a combat shooter's stance and swung his pistol around the building.

Two more men rushed in behind them, then two more, all of them in shooter's stances, yelling, "*Down on the floor! Put down your weapons!*"

Finally Eddie Santos appeared, stumbling inside with his hands behind his back. Arielle was down on the floor. One of the intruders had a knee at her back and a pistol to her head. But her face was turned toward the door, and she recognized the man who shoved Santos inside and stepped in behind him. She had seen him in the photos that Alex Mendonza shot outside the PAL terminal. Totoy Ribera was his name.

He looked around the room, then down at Arielle.

He said, "Just you? When will the others return?"

She showed him a shrug.

He said, "All right. If that's how you want, all right."

He sent two of the men out to park the cars where they wouldn't be seen.

"Yes. We'll wait," he said. "All the better. This will work out fine."

Mendonza and Favor caught up with Stickney along Roxas Boulevard. Favor motioned Stickney to stop and park, and they all got out and gathered near the curb.

Favor took out his earpiece and put it in his pocket. The others did the same.

Favor said, "Did you hear that?"

Totoy Ribera and the six men of his crew took up positions inside the bodega. Totoy was barking the orders, arranging the men in a rough semicircle, with fields of fire that converged on the door.

Santos and Arielle were seated on the floor near the table, both cuffed with plastic restraints. From where she sat, Arielle could see the laptop screen, the download counter still turning over. Nobody seemed to notice.

Totoy and the gunmen waited. Long minutes.

A car horn sounded outside, two quick taps on the button. It sounded close, just on the other side of the steel roll-up door.

The men all looked that way, toward the front.

Then came the sound of a key in the roll-up door, someone unlocking it. Several of the gunmen shifted positions, looking for cover. They all swung their guns toward the sound.

The door came up. It revealed the Mitsubishi, motionless, backed up to the door. The lights were on, engine was running. Nobody was in sight.

Several seconds ticked by.

The sound of rapid gunfire exploded from inside the Mitsubishi, a ripping sound like a clip being fired off in an automatic weapon, and the interior pulsed with rapid bursts of orange light.

In the bodega, one of the gunmen fired at the Mitsubishi, punching a hole in the rear window, and then everyone opened up, jerking off shots as quickly as they could, firing nonstop, creating a single, sustained, deafening roar of gunfire.

Bullets tore through the Mitsubishi, puncturing the body panels, smashing the windows.

Nobody heard the back door opening. Nobody saw Favor come through the open door in a crouch, his movements fluid and precise.

He pounced on the gunman closest to the door, knocked him unconscious with a single blow to the back of the head, then wheeled and sprang toward his next target. Mendonza and Stickney were through the door now, too, coming in behind Favor.

Mendonza crossed the floor with improbable agility, his mass perfectly balanced as he stepped in among the gunmen. He crumpled one with a vicious elbow to the side of the head. Without breaking stride, he smashed another in the face with the heel of his hand, launching a spray of blood and spittle and loose white teeth as the gunman spun and dropped.

Stickney seemed almost casual in his movements. He stepped in behind a man who was blasting the Mitsubishi with continuous fire from a 9mm automatic pistol. Stickney reached in from behind him, snaking an arm around his throat while grabbing the wrist of his gun hand. Stickney shook the gun loose, jacked the man's head back, and levered him hard into the floor, facedown.

The assault was swift and furious. The gunmen were so intent on the Mitsubishi that they were overwhelmed before they saw what was happening. Only Totoy Ribera reacted. As the gunfire slackened, he glanced to his left and found Mendonza advancing toward him.

Totoy swung his pistol around. The weapon was still in motion when Mendonza's roundhouse kick exploded into Totoy's midsection, doubling him over, dropping him to the ground.

He was the last to go down. Only Favor and Mendonza and Stickney were left standing. They stood tense and poised, ready to spring, but the only movement was from a gunman who writhed on the floor, hands clamped around his face as he tried to hold back the flow of blood.

Firecrackers continued to pop in the Mitsubishi for several seconds. Then the shattered black hulk went silent, and the only sounds were moans and mumbled curses from the gunmen who remained conscious.

Favor and Mendonza and Stickney relaxed.

Favor opened his new balisong to cut the restraints from Arielle and Eddie Santos. The blade sliced through the tough plastic without resistance. He helped them both to their feet.

He said, "Time to move out, my friends. Let's grab what we need. Al, you want to collect the hardware?"

Mendonza and Stickney went around the room, patting down the sprawled gunmen, picking up weapons and dropping them into a basket that Elvis Vega had used to deliver dinner.

Arielle went to the steel table and fitted the laptop into the padded case. The download indicator was still pulsing when she disconnected the cable.

Favor said, "Eddie, you coming?"

Santos shook his head. "I'll deal with this. I'm a little old to run away from home."

"Your choice."

Mendonza knelt over one of the gunmen, lying prostrate on the floor, and bent to pat down the legs of his trousers.

A few feet away on the floor, Totoy Ribera suddenly turned over on his back and came up holding a pistol. The muzzle swung toward Mendonza.

The four Americans all saw the movement, and they all reacted.

Arielle, farthest away from Totoy and on the wrong side of the steel table, could only yell, *"Al—"*

Favor, three or four steps away, flipped open the balisong as he started toward Totoy.

Mendonza instinctively rolled away from the gun as Totoy pulled the trigger. The gun boomed, the muzzle belched flame.

The shot missed. Totoy continued to swing the weapon, tracking Mendonza for a second shot.

A large dark hand flicked out and grabbed the barrel and pushed it up and away, pointing it toward the ceiling as the gun erupted again. The hand belonged to Stickney, who had been standing near Totoy's head. Stickney jerked the pistol free and turned it on Totoy.

All this in the interval between two ticks of a clock.

With one hand Stickney held the pistol at Totoy's head. The other hand flashed up, a palm-out *Stop!* signal to halt the knife that Favor had raised as he moved toward Totoy.

Favor stopped.

Totoy's eyes went wide, and he sucked in a breath. He stared past the muzzle, into the eyes of the man he had assaulted a few days earlier.

For several moments the bodega was completely still.

Totoy slowly exhaled.

Favor straightened, looked around the room.

"Anybody else?" he said.

They left through the open door at the front, walking past the shattered Mitsubishi, to the Hyundai parked nearby. The Hyundai was untouched. They drove off through streets that were now mostly empty.

Six blocks down the street, they passed a police patrolman on foot, then two more a block later.

As Mendonza drove, they sorted through the pistols. Most had just two or three rounds left. One was empty. There was enough ammunition to load one clip, and Favor tucked the pistol into the waistband of his trousers, under his shirt.

"We'll have to lose the car, grab a taxi," Favor said. "They'll be looking for us."

"You think that was an official PNP operation?" Stickney asked.

"Probably not. I think he was making a strong-arm play. But we have to consider ourselves fugitives. They lit up that neighborhood, and somebody has to be the bad guy. And we did commit felonious assault on a police captain."

Favor noticed that Arielle seemed subdued. She hadn't spoken. She was holding the laptop case in both arms, a distant expression on her face. He wondered if she had been shaken by the raid.

He said, "Ari . . . you okay?"

She said, "I need to sit down somewhere and look at these files. I was just getting started when the cops showed. And there should be lots more. I had files piling up the whole time. I really need to see all of them, Ray."

"Right. Under the circumstances, I think the rat hole is our number one priority. Then we can sort things out, decide what we do next."

She said, "I *really* need to look at those files."

"You will. I promise."

She nodded, but she didn't seem satisfied. Her face seemed troubled. She held the machine tight. "They're in Russian. I need you, Stick. Your Russian is way better than mine."

"You got it," Stickney said.

Up ahead was Claro M. Recto Avenue, a major thoroughfare. Mendonza found an empty spot about half a block away, and they parked.

Within a minute, they had flagged a taxi.

Favor got up front with the driver; the others squeezed into the back.

"Out for the evening?" the driver said.

"Actually, we're going on a trip," Favor said.

"Ah, the airport."

"No. Manila Yacht Club."

TWENTY-SEVEN

The clubhouse was dark when they arrived. Favor paid the driver, and when the taxi was gone, he led the others to a locked gate where a security guard sat with a shotgun in his lap.

Favor had a key to the gate and a letter from Franklin Kwok authorizing his use of the boat in slip 22. But he didn't need the keys or the letter. Kwok had already told the yacht club staff about the arrangement. The guard opened the gate, which led down to a pier beside the clubhouse.

From a few berths away, slip 22 seemed to be vacant. Only when they got closer did the form of a boat become visible. It was a black V-hull speedboat with dark tinted windows.

The rat hole.

They stood at the dock, taking it in.

Mendonza had been around boats all his life. He said, "Holy shit, Ray."

"Save the applause until the end," Favor said. "Otherwise you'll just wear yourself out."

"I've never seen anything like it."

"Nobody's ever seen anything like it. Franklin Kwok wanted to be top dog at any marina he visited, anywhere. So he built himself forty-eight feet of the baddest long-range oceangoing speedboat in the world. Twin turbocharged diesels, eighteen hundred horsepower. Range is six hundred miles at cruising speed, which is fifty-five miles per hour. It'll hit ninety wide open, but the ride gets a little rough over fifty or so."

Arielle said, "Will I be able to use the laptop?"

"There's a forward cabin. It's small, but it'll work. And the boat is stable. I suggest we cruise out to the entrance of the bay. That'll give you a chance to look at those files. Then we'll find a quiet place to anchor and we can talk it over."

"Good," she said. "Let's go."

They climbed in near the stern, then crossed a short deck to the cockpit. At the front of the cockpit, beneath the steeply raked windscreen, was a broad console with a set of control wheels. Two thickly padded chairs, each with a harness and lap belt, sat at the wheels. At the back of the cockpit were four more padded chairs, also with belts and harnesses.

Arielle and Stickney went through a hatch that opened onto the cabin. It was minimal: a small table, a small galley, an even smaller head. Upholstered benches, just wide enough for sleeping, ran along both sides.

Arielle and Stickney sat at the table, with the laptop open in front of them.

In the cockpit, Mendonza studied the console and found the switch that powered up the panel. A status screen appeared, and beside that a navigation screen. More switches powered up more screens.

Radar. Forward-looking infrared. Favor cast off the lines from the bow and stern, and Mendonza punched a button that brought the diesels to life. Even at idle, they thrummed with an ominous power. Favor took the second seat up front as Mendonza backed the boat out of the slip and steered it slowly beside the high breakwater, then out the narrow opening and into the bay. Mendonza gently advanced the throttles. The engines answered at once, rising to an easy lope that was enough to lift the nose and send the boat surging over the water. Just like that, their connection with the land was severed. Favor looked back and watched the lights of the waterfront receding. They were leaving behind Manila and its complications, flying free, untouchable now.

Glass crunched beneath his feet as Ilya Andropov stepped through the empty doorframe at the Optimo headquarters. Behind him came Magdalena Villegas, carefully picking her way through the shards until she stood with Andropov in the office.

"They came in here for a reason," Andropov said. "Look around—look good. See if anything is missing. Tell me what's out of place. Something isn't the way it was when you left this evening."

He watched her as she went around the room, checking desks and file cabinets.

After a couple of minutes, Markov came up the stairs. He was holding the device that had been built by Winston Stickney, the pipe and battery and timer.

He said, "This was in one of the vents. Looks like a smoke generator." He handed it to Andropov.

"This is pro work," Andropov said, examining it. "Not just the device. All of it."

"Who are these people?" Markov said. "And why do they have a hard-on against us?"

"I don't know." Andropov said. "But we'll get some answers when we see what Totoy has scooped up."

"So you've heard from him?" Markov said.

"No. Haven't you?"

"He doesn't answer. I left a message."

Andropov walked into Magda's office and found her standing beside her desk. Except for the smashed door, nothing in the room seemed to have been disturbed.

"What did they take?" he said. "What was done here?"

"Nothing."

"They came in here for a reason. Something happened. What was taken?"

"I keep nothing important here," she said. "If it matters, it goes into the system. You know that."

He needed a couple of seconds to realize what this must mean.

"Son of a bitch," he said. He began to shout: "Markov, the network! They got the fucking network!"

He strode out in a hurry and almost ran into Markov, who was holding out a cell phone.

"It's Totoy," Markov said. "You won't like this."

Manila Bay was almost thirty miles across, measured from the city's waterfront to the entrance of the South China Sea. The speedboat could have covered the distance in well under twenty minutes, but the bay was cluttered with traffic, including dozens of outrigger fishing boats, some marked by no more than a lightbulb or two, and Mendonza wanted to keep the ride as smooth as possible for Arielle and Stickney and the laptop below. So Mendonza kept the boat throttled back to about 40 miles an hour, and they ran that way for about half an hour, until the bay began to narrow, with long arms of land closing in on both sides, pinching in to form the mouth of the bay. An island, long and steeply humped at one end, lay ahead, in the gap between the two arms.

The island grew larger, and Mendonza slowed the boat almost to an idle.

Stickney looked up from the hatch. His face was grave. He said, "Are you anchoring? We're not done yet."

"That's fine," Favor said. "We're just looking for a place to put in."

Mendonza brought the boat in close to the shore. He was steering mostly by the infrared video display in the cockpit: the island was still, and completely dark. He brought the boat around to a concrete dock. It seemed to be old; chunks had fallen off the sides, exposing rusted reinforcing rods.

It was the only human structure in sight. Beside it was a beach of dark sand and gravel, and behind it was a saddle of land, forested, at the foot of the high, craggy hump.

Favor jumped up onto the dock and tied up the bow line.

Mendonza cut the engines, and there was silence, broken only by the water gently lapping against the hull and the concrete pilings.

Favor looked around and said, "Al. This is Corregidor."

"Yes, it is," Mendonza said.

Corregidor: it was a touchstone of the Second World War, an island fortress where American and Filipino forces had held out for months against daily bombardment and shelling from the Japanese who had captured all the rest of the bay and the land that surrounded it.

Hundreds had died here during the siege, then thousands more during the island's recapture by airborne troops three years later.

"We want a quiet place to talk, it doesn't get any quieter than here," Mendonza said. "And this is the mouth of the bay. From here, we've got more or less a straight shot south to Devil's Keep, if it comes to that."

"Let's see," Favor said.

He looked down into the cabin. Stickney and Arielle were still at the laptop, talking. Arielle was pointing at the screen, her voice low, animated. Favor couldn't hear what she was saying.

Favor and Mendonza sat back in the chairs. They chatted for a while about the boat and Franklin

Kwok and their raid on the Optimo offices. About half an hour went by before Arielle came up from the cabin, with Stickney behind her.

Something was wrong, Favor thought. Their faces were grim.

Favor said, "Ari? Stick? You got something?"

"They're organized," Stickney said. "They've kept a record of everything. So yes. We have it all. Flight logs, duty rosters, the manifest for the monthly supply boat to the island."

Favor looked closer at Arielle.

Her eyes were glistening.

Tears? Was Arielle *crying*?

"I always thought I was shockproof," she said. "I mean, the four of us? You'd figure there's nothing we haven't seen. I thought I knew the very worst that people can do to one another. But I was wrong."

HARVEST DAY
–1

TWENTY-EIGHT

They're Russians," Arielle said. "A mob, no doubt.

"And they're in the heart business. . . .

"Human hearts.

"They're transplanting healthy hearts to people who need new ones, and who can pay for it. Really pay. They do the transplants down there on the island. They started slow, three in the first two months, but it's been picking up. Five in the last month and a half, seventeen in all. And two more scheduled in the next couple of days. They have the whole setup—the surgical suite, post-op care facilities, a lab. They built it from scratch, and it must've cost them millions, but they probably paid it off in the first couple of procedures. We're talking millions of dollars for each surgery. Whatever they figure the traffic will bear. When you're selling life, you can name your price."

"Jesus Christ," Mendonza said.

"Let me tell you about heart transplants," Arielle continued. "They're wonderful, but there are a couple of major problems. One, there aren't nearly enough healthy donor hearts to fill the demand. Most countries, the waiting list is a year or more. People die waiting for hearts.

"Then there's rejection. Our immune systems are

built to repel foreign substances. The mechanism is the system of human leucocyte antigens: HLA. It's genetic. There are two hundred different antigens, and about thirty thousand different possible HLA sets. When the body encounters tissue with an HLA set that's different from its own—like with a transplanted organ—it goes to war with the foreign tissue. Never mind that the organ is essential to life. The body will literally kill itself to get rid of a heart that looks like it doesn't belong. Half of all transplant recipients experience a rejection episode in the first year after surgery. You can avoid that, or at least reduce it, by transplanting a heart with a similar HLA profile.

"The problem is, when you're on the list and you get that call to come in for surgery, you have no idea how well you match up. The heart is good for three hours after death. There isn't any time to worry about matching. If you're next on the list, and you can be there right away, you get a heart. Then it's a roll of the dice. A bad match, you're probably in for a rough ride.

"The Russians have solved both those problems. They're not waiting for hearts. They're *taking* them. But not at random: they have HLA profiles on their transplant clients, and they look for hearts to match. That's the purpose of the blood tests. They do the lab work in Manila, every night. If an applicant's profile is a close match to a client, she gets an offer for a job abroad and a bus ticket to Manila. But she doesn't go abroad. She just goes to Devil's Keep, and the only part of her that ever leaves is the heart that goes on beating in somebody else's body."

"By the way," Arielle said, "the employment agency part is for real. Optimo is a front, but it's a working front, just in case anybody happened to check. They have branch offices in Tacloban, Vigan, Naga, Laoag, and Calbayog—all small to midsize provincial capitals with airfreight service to Manila. And all of them, frankly, full of people who want to work abroad. People who would basically be disappearing anyway. Because that's what they do when they take that overseas job in Qatar or Singapore or wherever. To the people they leave behind, they're as good as gone. But if that's the only chance you've got, you jump at it. You do what you have to do.

"I guess that's what bothers me most about this. In material terms, these people have next to nothing. All they really have is each other, and life. And these sons of bitches are taking that away and selling it to the highest bidder."

Favor saw that she was finished. He said, "You're sure about all this?"

"Oh yeah, we're sure," she said. "There's a certain amount of connecting the dots required, but all the pieces are there. We have the clients' medical records. We have HLA typing results for thousands of Optimo's applicants. We have the maintenance and flight records for the floatplane that they use to ferry the victims from Manila, and for the private jet that picks up the clients and brings them to

Malaysia—Kota Kinabalu, it's the nearest international port of entry—and for the helicopter that takes them from Kota to the island. Oh, and we also found downloads from the helicopter's nav system. Devil's Keep is definitely the destination. That's where all this is going down. They have two surgical teams living on site—presumably one for the removal, one for the transplant—and a post-op recuperation facility."

"Only hearts?" Mendonza said.

"That's where the money is," Arielle said. "There's already a black market in kidneys, some Third World countries, poor but healthy people selling off one of their two kidneys to raise money. But the going rate is in hundreds of dollars, not millions. It's all about supply. Most of us have one more kidney than we need. But hearts . . ."

Favor said, "Stick, what's your take?"

"I don't follow the medical details as well as Ari," Stickney said. "But it all holds together for me. I buy it."

Mendonza said, "What about Ronnie and Marivic?"

"The records don't show names, just code numbers," Arielle replied. "But looking at dates, we're almost sure that we've identified Marivic and that she's on the island. And another donor entered the system the day after Ronnie went missing. We surmise that it's him. He's on the island too."

"They're alive?" Favor said.

"They're alive, but I think the clock is ticking. Beginning forty-eight hours before the surgery, the victims are put on an immunosuppression drug regime.

You want to minimize the chances that T cells from the heart will attack the body of the recipient. The records show that Marivic is scheduled to start the regime tomorrow . . . well, we're after midnight, so it would be sometime this morning. When that happens, she's forty-eight hours from surgery."

"What about Ronnie?"

"About Ronnie . . ." she began. But her voice choked, and tears welled up again.

Stickney said, "They started Ronnie on the routine yesterday morning. He's due for the second round of injections today. After that, he's on a twenty-four-hour countdown. The recipient for his heart is already en route from the south of France, and is expected in Kota Kinabalu later today."

Arielle gathered herself up and finished the thought. "Surgery is scheduled for ten a.m. tomorrow morning. For Marivic's recipient, twenty-four hours later. So the thing is, Ray, we need to talk about what we're going to do, but we can't talk too long."

Stickney asked how quickly they could reach Devil's Keep.

"The island is about eight hundred miles," Mendonza said. "Figure fourteen hours' running time at fifty-five miles an hour. Any faster, you'll just get pounded to jelly before you get there. And that's assuming good weather and reasonable conditions. We'll have to refuel at least once. Probably Zamboanga. I'd have to look at the charts. If conditions are decent, I can put us in the vicinity sometime late this afternoon."

Stickney said, "The problem is, just being in the neighborhood doesn't accomplish anything. We have to figure out what we'll be able to do once we get there. The island has a six-man security detail. It's on the personnel roster. We can assume that they're not nice men, and that they're well armed, and that they won't just hand over these kids, who are worth way more than their weight in gold."

"How are we fixed for ordnance?" Mendonza asked Favor.

"The boat carries a twelve-gauge shotgun," Favor said. "And we have the pistol."

"We don't even know the layout of the island," Stickney said.

"We could sure use those aerial photos," Mendonza said.

Arielle said, "The aerials are supposed to be available sometime today."

Stickney said, "Ray, how do you see it?"

"It seems pretty obvious to me," Favor said. "Two kids are about to have their hearts ripped out, and we're the only four people in the world with a chance to do anything about it. I don't know what we'll do when we get there. Maybe we can't stop it. But it's too soon to worry about that. Let's get there first, then we'll think about what's not possible."

They all nodded agreement, and without a word they prepared to leave.

Arielle stowed the laptop in the cabin and strapped herself into a seat at the back of the cockpit. Stickney took the chair beside Mendonza: he wanted to learn the boat so that he could take the wheel and give Mendonza a break sometime during the night. Favor released the lines, threw them aboard, and climbed in. He strapped himself into a chair beside Arielle.

Mendonza entered the coordinates for Devil's Keep into the GPS navigation system and designated it as the destination. He backed the boat away from the pier and accelerated toward the open water beyond Corregidor.

Arielle said, "I forgot to ask. Does this beauty have a name?"

"She's *Banshee*," Favor replied.

"It's Irish," Arielle said. "A wailing female spirit of the night."

"That's what Franklin said."

"Also a harbinger of death."

"Yeah. He said that too."

"Whose death, though? That's the question."

"That's always the question," Favor said.

They were past the island now, through the mouth of the bay, pulling away from the headlands of Bataan on one side and Cavite on the other. This was the South China Sea. Open water. Mendonza turned the wheel, and the boat swung to the south. Mendonza pushed the throttles forward, and the boat rose up and seemed to leap forward, a stunning surge of power, and they hurtled into the darkness.

"How did all this happen?" Andropov said.

He was standing with Totoy Ribera in the ops room at the villa.

"They're good," Totoy said.

"*We're* good."

"Yes, but this bunch . . ."

"What?"

Totoy paused. He didn't want to inflame Andropov any more.

"Spit it out," Andropov said.

"What the little hustler said this afternoon? It's starting to sound pretty good to me. I don't know why these people are coming after you, but if you have something they want, maybe you should consider handing it over and hope it makes them happy."

Before Totoy could finish, Andropov was already shaking his head, an emphatic no, no, no.

Totoy said, "I'm just thinking practically. An end to the difficulty. They go away, business resumes just as before."

"To hell with that," Andropov spat. "To hell with the little hustler for saying it. To hell with you for bringing it up."

His voice rose with each phrase, so that he almost shouted the last few words. But he gathered himself inside, tamped down the anger.

Truth was, Andropov had already considered this possibility. But it was impractical. Impossible. The intended recipient of the boy's heart was already en route from Nice, and would expect full satisfaction at the end of his journey.

Even if he had wanted to make a deal and hand over the kids, Andropov had nobody to deal with. The Americans had disappeared again. They seemed to have a knack for that, vanishing and reappearing at the time they chose.

"You can put that idea out of your head," Andropov said, his voice calm again. "It's a little late for that."

TWENTY-NINE

They got lucky with the weather. The skies were clear and the seas were calm. To save fuel, Mendonza kept the speed around fifty miles an hour, and after a couple of hours he saw that they'd be able to make Zamboanga without refueling.

Around noon, they pulled into a small marina. While an attendant fueled the boat, Arielle got out onto the dock and found a spot where she could set up the laptop and the satellite transceiver. She needed a stable platform for the uplink. That was impossible on the boat, so this was her first chance to check for the aerial photos online.

The others watched from the boat. They needed those photos.

Arielle sat cross-legged with the case in front of her. She unzipped the case, removed the computer and the flat, book-size antenna. At this location, just a few degrees north of the equator, the Inmarsat Broadband Global Area Network Asia-Pacific satellite was almost directly overhead; she aimed the antenna almost straight up.

A weak electronic tone rose out of the laptop's speakers. She began to adjust the antenna in increments, tilting it slightly toward the southern sky, and the tone grew louder and more high-pitched.

It shrieked.

Connected.

She worked the keyboard for a few seconds, shielded her eyes against the sun, looked closer.

She shook her head.

No.

While the boat refueled at the city dock in Zamboanga, the floatplane was doing the same at its base about twenty miles up the coast. It carried four: Andropov, Anatoly Markov, who was flying it, and two other members of the Manila crew. This left only one Russian at the Manila headquarters, but Andropov wasn't concerned. He believed that Manila didn't matter anymore, as far as the four Americans were concerned. The action would be on the island, and it would come soon. The most important transplant yet to be performed on the island—by far—was to take place in less than twenty-four hours. Its recipient would be landing in Kota Kinabalu around sunset, and Andropov believed that the Americans would do everything in their power to interfere.

He knew that this was improbable, in realistic terms. But the very existence of the Americans was an improbable event, and here they were.

Anything was possible.

Andropov knew that they must be out there somewhere, somehow finding a way to the island, and he intended to be ready when they arrived.

THIRTY

The sea grew restless after they left Zamboanga. At first it pushed up easy swells, so broad and gentle that they seemed to be incidental distortions in the bright green surface. The swells began to roll, more abrupt, the troughs steeper and deeper. Then the swells became waves, two and three feet high, a hard chop that pounded the hull.

The sky was hazy now, and gray cloud tops were dimpling up on the far horizon to the east. The boat was alone, surrounded by open water.

Banshee easily handled the waves, but it was pounding through the water now, not skimming anymore. Mendonza was at the wheel. He throttled back slightly. The navigation display showed sixty-three miles to Devil's Keep, with at least three hours of daylight.

Favor stayed down in the cabin, where an LCD screen showed the boat's navigation panel. When the distance to Devil's Keep reached sixty miles, he came up and spoke to Mendonza.

"I want to stay at least ten miles off the island until the sun goes down," Favor said. "Due south would keep us out of visual and take us into the archipelago. I don't want to run into any habitation, but maybe we can find a quiet place to put in for a while. See if we can find somewhere for Ari to connect."

Mendonza turned the wheel slightly to the right, and immediately the boat's sharp nose swung around by about fifteen degrees. Favor and Mendonza stood together in the cockpit, watching the nose tick up and down as the hull shot through the chop.

After a few minutes, Mendonza said, "Ray, it's almost crunch time. What're we going to do?"

"I don't know yet," Favor said. "Let's see if we can get those aerial photos. That'll give us an idea."

"And without the pics? We don't know fuck-all about what's on the island. And it's not like we can do a quiet little recon, cruise around it a few times to check it out. This is a sweet boat, but it's not going to sneak up on anybody."

"We don't back off now," Favor said. "You decide this doesn't work for you, that's no problem. We can turn the boat around, I'll take you back to Zambo. No questions asked, no hard feelings. Ari and Stick, same deal. But I'm going to do this."

"You know I don't back off," Mendonza said. "I'm just asking."

"Fair enough," Favor said. "All else fails, I guess we wing it."

Mendonza looked over and saw that Favor was grinning. *Grinning.*

Mendonza couldn't help it—he found himself laughing out loud.

He said, "I guess it wouldn't be the first time."

———

About an hour later they spotted the tops of palm trees in the southwest horizon. Mendonza steered toward them. The trees seemed to rise up out of the ocean, finally revealing a ragged line of low coral islands, most no larger than an acre or two, connected by shallow white flats that lay just below the surface. Mendonza cut the engines back and idled down the string of islets until he reached the largest of the group.

He motored in close and anchored. The navigation display showed 14.2 miles to Devil's Keep.

The sea was calmer here in the shallows. Stickney jumped down into waist-high water. Arielle handed him the laptop case, then she climbed over the side and down into the water. She followed Stickney through the surf as he held the case high above his head, up onto a beach of powdered-sugar sand, over to a spot away from the trees.

Favor and Mendonza watched from the boat as Arielle adjusted the angle of the antenna, tilting it slightly in the bed of sand.

One last adjustment, and her hand left the antenna. Connected.

She turned to the laptop. Her fingers worked at the keyboard.

She looked up and spoke a word to Stickney.

Stickney turned to the boat and showed a thumbs-up.

The images were online.

The file was large, almost half an hour's

download. Arielle sat beside the laptop the entire time, drinking from a bottle of water that Stickney carried out to her, watching the data counter flash on the screen. When it was done, she packed the machine in the case and gave it to Stickney, and he walked it back through the surf and handed it up to Mendonza.

Favor pulled Stickney aboard, and they both helped lift Arielle aboard. She dried her hands on Favor's shirt and said, "Let's see what we've got."

She took the laptop down into the cabin and opened it on one of the padded benches. The others followed her down, nearly filling the cramped space, and they gathered around the screen.

She opened the file in an image viewer.

The screen showed the island's mottled half-moon shape, alone in a dark sea. At first it seemed identical to the Google Earth image that they had seen a few days earlier. But this image didn't blur as Arielle began to enlarge it. Instead, new levels of detail emerged with each tap of the key. The island now filled the screen, yet the image was perfectly sharp. It showed a cluster of three buildings at the south end of the half-moon, and several other smaller structures scattered nearby, some half hidden among the trees. It showed a white outboard runabout tied up at a stubby dock at the curved eastern side of the island.

She pressed another key combination and moved her index finger on the touch pad. The island seemed to tilt and spin. It showed elevation. This image was a composite of more than a dozen high-resolution photos taken at various angles during the aircraft's single pass. The process was called photogrammetry, extracting elevation data from 2-D photos to produce a near 3-D rendering. From directly above, the island appeared flat. But as Arielle moved the point of view, they saw that the western side of the island— the straight side of the half-moon—was actually a cliff.

The island didn't look like a half-moon anymore. Instead, it was as if a plump cookie had been broken in two, with one half laid down in the sea, the broken edge dropping sheer to the water.

Mendonza pointed at the screen and said, "There's a chopper landing pad. Is that a fuel tank beside it? Can we get in closer?"

Arielle zoomed in, close enough that they could make out the dark hose wound along one end of the tank.

Stickney said, "A pipe coming out of the ocean up to this outbuilding, more pipes coming out to the structures. Can you get in tight here? They're running a desalination setup. And this would be the generator, off by itself so the noise doesn't drive them crazy. They're in here for the long haul."

Favor was leaning in close to the screen, studying it, taking it in.

Arielle said, "Ray? Is there anything you want to see up close?"

"Yeah," he said. "Here by the dock. And over here, beside this tree."

He was pointing to specks in the image. She

zoomed in tight, and the speck near the dock resolved into the standing figure of a man. He was looking out to sea and holding a weapon. The long slim barrel was plainly visible. The second speck became a man seated partly in the shade of a tree, with the barrel of a long gun gleaming in the sunlight.

Favor said, "What time was this shot, Ari?"

"The time stamp says just after nine this morning."

"Nine o'clock in the morning, they're alone on a rock with fifteen miles of empty water in every direction, and they've got the guns out. These people are serious about keeping the world away. But I guess I'd be paranoid, too, if I had that much to hide."

They left the cabin without discussing plans. Mendonza said that it was dinnertime, so he went into the food stash and brought out the cans of beans and sardines. They ate it cold, straight out of the can, and Stickney got a laugh when he said how grateful he was that Favor went first-class on the amenities.

When they were finished, they sat out on the deck. The sun was down now, leaving just a red smudge in the western sky. A breeze blew out of the north, and the boat rocked gently with swells slapping against the hull. Nobody had much to say. Arielle thought they were all aware of Devil's Keep somewhere out in the darkness to the southeast, and of the reality in the images down on the laptop.

She knew how this was going to play out; it was

obvious in the photos, she thought. She knew that Stickney and Mendonza saw it, too, but were reluctant to mention it.

The truth was that the risk in rescuing the two teenagers—or trying to rescue them—was not going to be equally shared. One of them alone was about to lay his ass on the line.

That would be Ray Favor.

Mendonza and Stickney weren't going to mention it, Arielle thought. She didn't want to talk about it, either, but she knew that somebody had to start. She supposed that this was her part in the script.

She broke the silence. "I'd like to hear some ideas about how we approach this thing with the island. I mean, given what we saw in the images."

Mendonza jumped in right away.

"The direct approach," he said. "There's the dock; here's a boat and it's fast as hell. We go in pedal to the metal, bail out of the boat as soon as we hit the dock, spread out."

Favor said, "No offense, Al, but I don't think you're seeing this clearly." He was playing his part now: the relentless voice of reason. "This boat will be noticed. I don't know how soon they'll pick us up. A mile out, maybe two. That's enough. They'll be waiting for us, and we'll be outgunned for sure. Come on. We'll be lucky if any one of us gets out alive, much less bring back those kids."

Stickney said, "We go in the middle of the night, we may be able to get off the boat and into the buildings before they know what's happening."

Favor said, "I don't think so. They post guards during the day; we have to assume the guards are there at night too. Everything about this says that they're hard-ass pros. They know what they're doing. I don't care what time of day or night, if we rumble straight in there, we'll get cut to pieces."

Mendonza said, "You have a better idea?"

"Yes I do," Favor said. "They watch the front side of the island, the dock, because that's where you'd expect somebody to come. But the back side? That cliff? They won't expect that."

"I don't climb cliffs," Stickney said. "I don't suppose Al climbs cliffs, either. Ari, I don't know."

"No," she said. "I'm not a climber."

"I am," Favor said. "Here's how I see it. We move out when the moon goes down. That's a little after two, according to the software. Bring the boat in slow and quiet, maybe within half a mile of the island. I swim the rest of the way. Climb the wall, up over the top. They won't have a clue. Then, you know . . . then I do my thing."

"What about us?" Mendonza said.

"Lay back a couple of miles and watch close," Favor said. "I'll let you know when to come."

"How will you do that?" Stickney said.

"I'll figure it out. You'll know."

The others were silent.

Favor said, "This makes sense. You all know it. This is how it has to be. I won't do it any other way. This is it."

The script was almost finished now, Arielle

thought. They had gotten to Favor insisting on his own sacrifice. Demanding it.

"Ari hasn't had anything to say about this," Stickney said.

"That's right, Ari's been quiet," Favor said. He looked at her. "What do you think about all this?"

Just one line remained now in the script, and she knew what it was.

She just wasn't ready to say it yet.

Instead she said, "You'll have to be perfect. Your margin for error will be zero. You slip off that wall, you're fucked. One wrong step on the island, you're fucked. There are no rat holes when you leave this boat."

"The holes always run out eventually," Favor said.

His eyes said, *Come on now. Don't you dare let me down.*

She said, "I don't like it, but I don't see any better way."

And that was it, the final line, bringing them to where they all knew it had to go.

"Good," Favor said. "We have a plan."

"Tomorrow is a special day," Andropov said. "And this is the most important shift you'll ever spend on the island. Very soon we may have intruders who'll try to bring down everything we've worked for, and I expect you to find them and stop them."

He was speaking to eleven men: six regular members of the island's security team, the two orderlies who usually dealt with the prisoners, plus Markov and the two others from Manila.

They were seated on the floor, in the hallway outside the operations room, in the main building. At the end of the corridor was the surgical suite, with the operations room and the pharmacy and the armory and the surgeons' ready room in between.

Two of the six-man island security crew exchanged a disbelieving glance. Yuri Malkin and Kostya Gorsky had been on the island since the start, and nobody had come close to threatening the operation.

Literally, nobody even had come within sight, except the two local fishermen, and Yuri had dealt with them easily enough.

Yuri raised a hand.

"Sir, will they be coming in great force?" he said. "Will it be by plane or by sea? Can we expect airborne?"

He was twitting Andropov, but Andropov took it seriously.

"There should be no more than four," he said. "Three men and a woman. I don't know how they'll arrive. They're clever as hell."

All of the men seated on the floor were combat veterans, specialists. Even the two orderlies were warriors—former commando medics with Spetsnaz, the fearsome Russian special forces.

That made a force of eleven. Three men and a woman taking them on—they wanted to see this.

"Are you sure we don't need reinforcements?"

said Kostya Gorsky. Someone snickered behind him.

"Just do your jobs, stay alert," Andropov said. "The perimeter posts all have night-vision binoculars. Use them. Draw some greenies from the pharmacy if you think you'll have trouble staying awake. We'll go back to a reduced crew after daybreak. I'm not concerned about the daylight hours. It's tonight that worries me."

Markov read off a list of post assignments. He had originally designed the island's security arrangement: four watch posts at the edges of the island, looking out in four directions, plus two posts in the interior that were rarely used. Tonight all six would be manned, with a seventh sentry outside the main building.

Markov stood at the door of the armory, handing out weapons as he called the assignments. As each man took the weapon, he also pulled a miniature radio transceiver from a box on a table. They fit into the ear. All shared the same frequency, a communications net, so that anyone on duty could speak to anyone else.

"Surin, post one. Karlamov, three. Gorsky, five."

Most of the weapons in the armory were AK-47 rifles. But two stood out from the others. They were Dragunov sniper rifles, more accurate than the assault rifles, and fitted with infrared telescopic sights, thermal imaging, that let the scopes cut through darkness and fog.

Markov was down to the last two assignments.

He said, "Vladimir Raznar will handle the radio in the ops room." Markov handed the first Dragunov to Raznar, a former Red Army sniper.

And Markov said, "Yuri Malkin, post two."

Post two sat alone at the top of the cliff at the west side of the island. It looked out in the direction of the Sulu archipelago and had the widest field of view of any post on the island.

Markov said, "On your toes tonight, Malkin," and handed Yuri the second Dragunov. It was the rifle that Yuri had used to kill the two fishermen. He was the best shot on the island—better even than Raznar, the ex-sniper—so the rifle and the post were his by logic.

They all dispersed.

The door of the ops room opened.

Karel Lazovic stood inside the door. He was a tall man in his fifties. His facial features were classically European aristocratic, and his voice was deep, commanding. Lazovic was the island's primary surgeon, and since surgery was the island's sole purpose, he was in charge most of the time. But the lines of authority shifted subtly with Andropov present, and Lazovic's tone was respectful as he spoke: "Can we have a word?"

Andropov nodded and stepped into the room and closed the door.

Lazovic said, "I've been on the radio with Kota Kinabalu. Our recipient is having trouble sleeping, and I don't want to start him on a sedative this early. He's anxious to start and wants to move up the surgery as early as possible. I told him that four a.m. is the soonest."

"That's up to you."

"The medical end is up to me. But the security end is up to you. How serious is this threat?"

"I take it very seriously," Andropov said.

"Seriously enough to postpone the procedure?"

"That's a big step," Andropov said.

"Yes, it is," Lazovic said. "But I need to know that there will be no interruptions once we start."

Andropov took several seconds to answer.

He finally said: "We'll handle it."

"Good," Lazovic said. "Then I'll tell Kota we're on."

When they had finished talking it out, Favor told the others that he was going below for a while. He said he wanted to get his gear together and study the aerial images some more. They all understood him to mean *I'd like some time alone,* and they stayed up on the deck while he went down into the cabin.

But about an hour later, Stickney ducked his head in and paused at the narrow hatch. Favor was sitting in front of the laptop, staring at the screen.

"Come in," Favor said.

Stickney said, "You're taking on a load here, bucko."

"That's the way it worked out."

"Just one thing I want to be clear about," Stickney said. "This deal with karmic accounts and paying off the debt—it sounds good on a slow afternoon. But it's just words. It isn't real."

"It's real," Favor said. "I know that, and you do too."

"You are not obligated."

"I think I am," Favor replied. "But that's okay. This is what I'm supposed to do. I want to do this. You shouldn't try to take that away from me."

"You're a good man," Stickney said.

"Not yet," Favor said.

About half an hour after Stickney's visit to the cabin, Arielle, too, left the deck and slipped down through the narrow hatch.

The cabin was dark. The laptop was put away in the case.

Favor was stretched out on one of the benches, asleep.

Arranged on the opposite bench were the balisong knife and a neatly folded wet suit, with a mask and fins and snorkel resting on it. Something about Favor made her look closer, something in the way he slept. He was stretched out almost full length, legs slightly bent, one arm tucked beneath his head.

She watched him for a few seconds before she realized: he was relaxed.

He was breathing evenly. His body was limp, his face was calm.

She couldn't remember the last time she had seen him this way.

Ray Favor was at peace.

HARVEST DAY

THIRTY-ONE

When Favor woke, he went straight from deep sleep to fully alert. No yawning and stretching, no groping for awareness. His eyes blinked open and he was instantly in the moment.

The time was one a.m.—exactly when he had wanted to awaken, to the minute. The boat was rocking, harder than when he had gone to sleep. Waves were slapping the hull, louder than before.

He stripped naked, stepped into the wet suit, pulled it up to his waist. He laid the balisong along the inside of his left forearm and secured it there using adhesive tape that he tore from a roll in the first-aid kit. Then he pulled the suit up over his arms and shoulders. It was a size too small, but the rubber was thin, and it stretched enough that he could zip it up across his chest. He flexed his arms. The knife felt snug between his skin and the taut shell of the suit. The largest pair of surf shoes was also a size too small, but he jammed his feet inside and fastened the Velcro straps.

They were all awake in the cockpit, waiting for him, when he came up from below with the mask and fins and snorkel in hand.

"Morning, Ray," said Mendonza.

"Ray," said Stickney.

"Hello, Ray," Arielle said.

The greetings were casual. Almost as if this were just another morning. Almost.

Favor looked out and saw whitecaps on black water. The moon was a smear behind clouds.

He said, "I realize we're still early, but why don't we move out and take it slow? I'm ready to get out of here."

Stickney pulled up the anchors, and when he was back in the cockpit, Mendonza moved the throttles forward and swung the long hull to the southeast, toward the island.

The panel showed fifteen knots. At this speed the engines burbled softly, the hull slicing through waves that were now three to four feet. Favor sat quietly with the fins in his lap, the mask and snorkel hanging around his neck. His face was impassive.

The moon's blur was fading when the navigation screen showed five miles to target. At three miles out, Favor stood and looked at the navigation panel and then outside. The darkness was almost total, just the dimmest of illumination from starlight through the clouds. *Banshee* was running without lights, and in the cockpit there was only the muted glow of the hooded screens.

The wind was picking up now, buffeting the windows of the cockpit. It was from the south. That was good, Favor knew: it would carry the engine sounds away from the island, into the empty water to the north.

He said, "Take it in to one mile, or until you can see the island. Whatever comes first. If you can see the island, they can see us."

A mile and a half out, he spat into the mask and rubbed it into the glass—a crude trick to prevent condensation—and stood in the hatch behind the cockpit. He said, "Five knots. Bring it around when you hit the drop point. I'll know it's time to bail."

He stepped out onto the rear deck. At that moment, lightning pulsed silently in the southeastern sky. A squall line. It silhouetted the hulking shape of the island.

Favor said, "Shit, that'll highlight us for sure. I'm out of here." He pulled the fins over his surf shoes and fitted the mask over his brow and nose. The boat was swinging around, stopping. Arielle came out into the deck.

She said, "Watch your ass, tough guy."

He met her eyes through the glass, nodded, then stepped to the edge of the boat and held his palm against the mask so that the fall wouldn't dislodge it.

He front-rolled over the side and into the dark water.

Lightning throbbed again as he plunged.

He curled, rolled head up, and kicked for the surface. Thunder was rumbling when he broke into the open air. He swam several strokes, turned, and looked back. Arielle was watching, saw that he was clear, and gave Mendonza a rev-it-up signal. The engine's rumble seemed loud to Favor as he bobbed at the surface, but within a few seconds the boat was out of sight, and seconds more after that the rumble was swallowed by the wind.

He was alone.

Again the lightning. It was directly behind the island. Favor counted and got to five before the thunder arrived, a low rumble.

He put his head down in the water, breathed through the snorkel, and he began to swim.

Ilya Andropov was timing it too. When the first flash came, he was standing at a window in the operations room in the main building of the complex. He began to count, and was just about to hit four when the thunder clattered in. Four miles, maybe a little less.

He said, "What's the speed of storms in these parts?"

From his desk, the radio operator said, "Most of them are fast. Real fast."

He cupped a hand at his earpiece, listened, and spoke to Andropov:

"Chopper's twenty minutes out. It'll be close."

Andropov walked out, across the corridor, into the scrub room where the surgical team sat waiting. Two surgeons, including Karel Lazovic, an anesthesiologist. two surgical nurses, two orderlies.

"Thirty minutes," Andropov said from the door, then turned and walked away.

"Thirty minutes" was not just timekeeping: it was a command, and the two orderlies understood it. One of them picked up a hypodermic kit, and the two of them left the room.

Boris Godina and Sasha Batkin were their names. Godina was a hulking man-mountain: tall and massive. Batkin was small, slight, wiry. They were often assigned to the same details, and the sight of the odd pair provoked grins around the island. But only from a distance. Both were Spetsnaz-trained in hand-to-hand combat. Godina was especially feared, as much for his dark temper as his physical size and power. He was mean and massive and viciously schooled. Nobody screwed with Boris Godina.

Now Batkin and Godina walked along the corridor and out of the building, down to the high-walled concrete block structure that everyone on the island knew as the Guest House. Batkin had a key ring with three keys, one for the pharmaceutical locker and one for each of the doors to the cells. These were among the few locked doors on the island. He flipped a wall switch that turned on the lights in the first of the two cells, picked out the correct key, and swung the door open.

Both Batkin and Godina had combat experience. They knew exactly what was going to happen soon to the boy in the cell, but they were unfazed. One way or another, they had brought dozens across the threshold between life and darkness, either dealing violent death by their own hands or tending mortally wounded comrades as they slipped away. This was just more of the same.

The boy lay on his cot, head lolling. He was out.

At least he was supposed to be out. They had kept him sedated since the trouble the previous morning. But there was fight in him yet. He began to struggle as they lifted him off the cot, one at each arm. He writhed and pulled.

They couldn't bring him in this way. Godina pinned his arms behind his back, and Batkin fixed the hypodermic and injected him with more sedative, a double dose. All this time his sister was making a fuss in the other room, shouting and wailing, enough to wear on their nerves. So they hauled him outside and held him up while they waited for the drugs to kick in.

In a few minutes his legs buckled. Then they carried him in, one at his shoulders and the other at his feet, his body sagging between them.

They didn't bring him through the main corridor to the operating room. Instead, they carried him around to the south side of the building, through a door to a prep room with a bare steel table on rollers. Lazovic was waiting there. He stood to one side while the orderlies strapped the boy onto the table and cut away his shirt, exposing his chest. When they were done, they moved aside and Lazovic stepped up to the table. He was holding a marking pen with a thick black tip. He touched the tip to the boy's bare skin and inscribed a single line, about a foot long, down the middle of the chest.

Favor was a strong swimmer, a high school distance champion in the pool. He often swam two or three miles in Lake Tahoe in the early mornings before the casual boaters and water-skiers put their craft in the water. Now the distance to Devil's Keep was just under a mile and a half. The fins added power to his kick, and the buoyancy from the salt water and the foam rubber of the wet suit seemed to make him weightless in the water.

This should have been nothing. But the waves were high and growing higher. Rolling in off his right shoulder, they were pushing him back and trying to sweep him past the island and into the open sea. To counter the current, he altered his course to the southeast, making for a point off the southern tip of the island.

The lightning was brighter and more frequent now, and when he looked up during one extended string of bursts, he found that he was still being pushed north. He turned again to the south. Now he was plowing directly into the waves, digging up the steep faces with his arms and then kicking hard down the back sides. More lightning, more thunderclaps, loud and furious, coming within a one-count of the flashes, the squall line passing over the island.

The cliff was closer. He knew that he was making distance now, and he pushed harder, fighting up through the waves, almost bodysurfing as he kicked down into each trough, immediately digging up the next face. He was barely conscious of the storm as it moved overhead. His face was down in the water as he breathed through the snorkel. Each flash threw a pale glow deep into the water, and he was distantly aware of the booming thunderclaps: they sent a shiver through the water that he felt against the exposed skin of his face.

The current grew stronger as Favor closed on the island. The waves were higher; they broke over him, driving him down into the turbulence and filling the snorkel. He cleared it a few times with sharp exhalations that blew out the seawater, but it continued to fill after nearly every breath. So he gave up the snorkel and spat out the mouthpiece as he kept stroking against the current. A low churning sound now filled the space between thunderclaps. It was the sound of waves crashing against rock. He looked up and saw the cliff face looming overhead. The surging water had him now, pushing and tossing him. His strongest kicks and strokes barely kept his head above the surface. He felt himself lifted and dropped, shoved and lifted and dropped again, then thrown one more time.

He was being tossed toward a pile of rubble at the foot of the cliff, sharp-edged chunks of stone the size of dressing tables and refrigerators. He tried to kick away, but an onrushing wave flung him into a rock that jutted out of the water.

Favor managed to turn aside and take the wave head-on. The move saved him. When he smashed against the rock, he took the blow to his back instead of his face. It knocked the breath from him and stunned him. The backwash pulled him down and tumbled him over a slope of submerged stones; he got his arms up over his face in time to absorb the jolts.

He fought the instinct to ascend. He knew that the next wave would take him again, and he might not survive a second crash at full force against the rocks. So he stayed down and wrapped his arms around a submerged boulder, and waited until he felt the wave surge over him. Then he shot up and forward, finding a few seconds' lull in the fury. He kicked and stroked and came in just behind the breaking wave. It was a barely controlled crash. He covered up and let his arms absorb the force, then kept moving, scrambling upward.

The following wave smashed in around his legs, but he felt its force drain away as it receded. He hauled himself up onto a tilted slab, and when he was sure that he was beyond the reach of the crashing surf, he stretched out on the flat stone surface, facing up toward the sky.

He gasped and heaved and sucked in air by increments until he could finally breathe again.

Rain was falling. He hadn't noticed. But he could see it now, gleaming streaks in the lightning flashes, and he could feel it pattering against his cheeks and taste it as it washed the salt water from his lips. He reached up and pulled away the mask to let the rain wash over his face.

His right arm seemed to work okay. Elbow and wrist and fingers. Yeah. He began a cautious inventory of the rest. His left arm hurt, but it was the bruise-and-contusion kind of hurt, not the stabbing pain of a fracture. He noted that the knife was still in place. Left leg, right leg . . . all good. He breathed easily.

He told himself that he was lucky. Real lucky. He could have broken his back.

The rain continued to pelt him. He knew that he should be moving up the cliff, but he was tired. Not just tired, he thought. Drained. Completely exhausted.

He told himself that he needed to rest for a while before he continued. He lay on the slab. He would have napped, except for the noise. There was the pounding of the waves, and the thunder's intermittent roar, and the spattering of raindrops against the flat rock near his ears.

Then another sound. It came from somewhere across the water. At first it was just a whispery thrumming, hardly louder than the rain on the stone. But within a few seconds it grew louder and more intense, a rapid insistent rapping that he could hear above the surf, then suddenly as loud as the crashing of thunder.

Chopper!

It was nearly above him, coming in fast. The bright beam of a spotlight lanced down through the rain, heading straight for him. He bailed off the slab and crouched beside it. A heartbeat later, the hot white shaft of light exploded across the slab where he had been lying, then vanished beyond the cliff.

Favor knew that it wasn't searching for him; it was moving too fast for that. From the sound now, somewhere beyond the cliff, it was hovering, dropping down: a landing approach.

But had someone spotted him anyway?

Probably not, he decided. During a landing in this weather, the pilot would be preoccupied. And the backscatter from the spotlight on the rain would have helped to obscure him down on the rocks.

But if the helicopter carried a passenger from Kota Kinabalu, then the surgery might be happening at any time.

He pulled off the fins and mask, wedged them out of sight beneath the slab.

He clambered up the rubble pile until he was at the base of the rock wall. The rubble hadn't been apparent in the aerial photos. He thought that the photos must have been shot at high tide. The rock seemed to have fallen off in sharp-edged chunks. This meant that the face was probably fractured with long vertical seams. And there should be indentations that the rubble pieces left when they fell away. There must be handholds. Ridges. Steps.

A seam was directly in front of his face, running upward, but it disappeared into blackness when he tried to follow it up. He couldn't see more than three or four feet in any direction.

He stepped back down the rubble pile, so far back that water surged around his calves when an incoming wave exploded against the rocks. He turned toward the rock face and stared up into the blackness and tried not to blink.

He waited.

Lightning flashed behind him, a ripping bolt that illuminated the rock face as bright as daylight. The brightness pulsed for little more than a second, but the afterimage seemed to linger on Favor's eyes, and he tried to memorize it. He was looking for a route, the pathway of holds and cracks and creases that would take him to the top.

The cliff wasn't high by his standards. He estimated 120 feet, not even a quarter the height of Lover's Leap. But he knew a dozen routes on the Leap so intimately that he could close his eyes and imagine each move, every reach and traverse that he would string together to connect the bottom of the wall to the lip at the top.

Now he had to do the same in darkness, on a wall he had never seen.

He continued to stare up, and he waited.

Again lightning flashed behind him, a heartbeat of brightness before the wall went black again.

He stood through four bursts of lightning. Five. Six. Each time he added a few more details, links to the chain.

Then he thought he had it. He waited for one more flash, a quick check to be sure that the reality matched his mental image.

The lightning flared and died.

Favor stepped up to the wall. He reached up into the darkness with both hands, and each hand fell on an invisible hold.

He began to climb.

Andropov thought that the patient should stay in the helicopter until the storm passed, and Lazovic agreed. They radioed this message to the chopper.

Seconds later the reply came back: "No delays. Patient says that a little rain won't hurt him."

Lazovic shrugged, and Andropov sent the two orderlies out with the Gator to bring him in. They rigged a plastic tarp over the canopy and drove off down the hill.

At first Favor had the lightning to help him as he climbed. In its intermittent flashes he was able to glance at the stretch of rock wall immediately above him, checking that brief glimpse against the mental image that he had burned into memory. So far the route was holding up, the holds and cracks coming where he remembered them.

And there were plenty. The fracture pattern had created small shelves and pockets with space to let him grip with his full hand or to plant nearly the entire sole of a foot. In daylight, in good weather, this would have been pure pleasure.

In the dark and the rain, it took all his focus and strength and nerve.

He was about halfway up when the rain slackened. Although the rock was still wet and slick, he was at least able to look up without getting raindrops in his eyes. But the lightning, too, was slackening. The squall was moving away and losing intensity. The pulses of light were weaker and further apart.

Near the top, Favor found a nice ledge. Three or four feet wide, nearly a foot deep. Lovely. He estimated that he was fifteen feet from the top—one more set of moves. He breathed, rested, relaxed. And he kept looking up into the blackness above, waiting for a last beat of lightning that would confirm his memory of the rock above.

He waited.

He waited.

Minutes passed, long enough that he knew there would be no more lightning.

He tried to retrieve the image from the last flash of lightning, the rock face beyond the shelf where he now stood. A pull up to a knob, to a crack, to another knob, across to a long, narrow sill that angled upward, to a last shelf just two or three feet from the top.

He ran through it once more in his mind. Then he moved, drawing himself upward, feet dangling. He hung with his left arm, reached upward to the knob *there* to the crack *there* to the second knob *there* to the angled sill *there*.

The sill was no deeper than the length of his toes. He crabbed along it until he could go no farther.

He was more than a hundred feet from the bottom, with his calves bearing nearly all his weight as he balanced on the narrow sill.

He craned his neck and looked up. He could see where the wall ended. The edge of the rock face was absolute black against a sky that showed the pale glow of starlight against the clouds. The top was no more than five feet from his fingertips. One more hold was left—the last shelf.

It should have been just overhead. Reach up, grab the shelf, pull up and scramble over the top.

He slid his right hand up the face, as high as he could reach.

No shelf.

He strained upward, lifting on the tips of his toes, calves tensing. His fingertips found just smooth rock.

No shelf.

Once more he looked up, but he could see nothing beyond his up-stretched arm. His fingers dissolved into blackness.

He told himself that the shelf had to be there, inches above his fingertips.

He had to act. His calves were trembling. There was no alternate route, no going back. He had just the featureless black between his fingertips and the top of the cliff, and the memory of a shelf that had to be there.

Or not.

He relaxed the tension in his calves, then launched himself upward.

His toes left the sill as he leaped. He lost all contact with the wall. For an instant, he hung in space, twelve stories above the rubble pile and the ocean, right hand reaching into the darkness as he arrived at the peak of his thrust.

He slapped at the wall. His fingertips found the shelf.

He grabbed. Held. His left hand shot up and grasped the shelf.

Without a pause, Favor pulled hard against the shelf, rising up, going hand over hand as he rose above the lip and vaulted over the top.

He landed silently, in a crouch, ready to react to sound or movement. But he saw nothing, and the only sound was the muted drone of the generator down toward his left.

He knew from the aerial photos that he was at the top of a slope, in an area of sparse brush and grass and coconut trees and banana trees. Straight ahead, at the bottom of the slope, was the helicopter landing pad, and beyond that the edge of the island and the dock. To his right, downslope, was the main group of three buildings. A couple of bright specks showed through the trees, lights from windows.

To his left, also somewhere below, he heard a low voice. Two voices. He guessed that they were thirty or forty yards away.

He looked in that direction and saw only darkness.

He rolled back the left sleeve of the wet suit, exposing the balisong. He pulled the tape away carefully, to keep from making a sound.

He opened the knife, swinging out the split sides of the handle and fastening them.

Holding it lightly in his right hand, he moved toward the sound of the voices.

At first Yuri Malkin stayed at his post while he watched the storm roll in from the east. It was shaping up to be a spectacular show, the first excitement on the island since he popped the two brownies and sank their skinny little boat. Fortune hadn't brought any more curious locals, and the prig

Lazovic prohibited any diversions with the female guests in the blockhouse—as if it mattered! After midnight, on a shit pile of rock in the middle of the ocean, Yuri had to take his entertainment where he could find it.

And he had the best seat in the house. He was under the thatched roof of the guard shelter that sat at the topmost point on the island, near the edge of the cliff. The spot had been chosen because it gave a clear view across miles of sea to the west. But the view to the east was nearly as good. He could stand in the shelter and see over the tops of the trees, across to where the bank of clouds was tumbling and roiling, lit up from behind by the lightning, booming and flashing like a distant cannonade.

At first he divided his attention, looking away from the oncoming storm to briefly scan the sea with the night-vision binoculars in the shelter. But as the storm got closer, he gave that up—apart from the two fishermen, he had never seen a craft approach within five miles of the island—and turned his back on the dark expanse of water to fully take in the storm. The thunderhead was growing, and it seemed to be headed straight for the island. Hell, straight for his guard shelter. The wind was picking up, the palm tops shaking. A blue-white bolt sizzled down from the leaden cloud and danced for a second on the ocean.

Great shit!

Then Yuri realized what was happening. He had the best seat in the house because he was standing on the highest point for at least twenty miles around.

He grabbed the Dragunov and started down the slope. To the left, down through the trees, was another shelter. Most times it was empty. But to-night, with the reinforcements, it was occupied by his sometime pal Kostya Gorsky. Yuri tramped down the hill and found Kostya's AK pointed at him as he came out of the trees.

"Goddamn, it's you," Kostya said.

"Who else would be coming down the hill?"

"You shouldn't be walking around," Kostya said as he lowered the rifle. "The Manila boys have everybody nervous. You could get shot. What are you doing here?"

"Fucking Andropov tried to turn me into a lightning rod," Yuri said, and they both laughed.

Rain began to fall, fat drops that smacked hard into the earth. Yuri and Kostya stood in the shelter and watched as the storm crashed in over the island. They smoked a couple of Kostya's cigarettes. While the rain fell in sheets, they talked about the Manila assholes, and how shitty the food was these last few days before the monthly boat, and how they both wanted to rotate into the Manila crew so that they could live in luxury and diddle whores anytime they wanted.

They turned to watch the helicopter as it hurtled over the brow of the hill from the west, plunging through the storm, descending. They watched as the Gator ground up the hill, carrying the client to his appointment.

They started talking about football, soccer, the Russian Cup tournament. Football was the one topic that divided them. Yuri was from Moscow and had been a Dynamo fan all his life. Kostya, from St. Petersburg, was disgustingly loyal to his hometown Zenit club. As usual, the jibes were good-natured at first and then turned edgy. They were arguing when Yuri realized that the storm had passed and the rain had ended.

Kostya stood and announced that he had to take a crap. "Create a steaming likeness of Moscow Dynamo" was how he put it. He walked off into the darkness. Yuri knew that he should return to his post, but he wanted a couple of cigarettes for later, and he decided to wait so that he could bum them when Kostya returned.

A sudden noise in his earpiece startled Yuri. It was Andropov, taking roll of the security detail.

"Karlamov?" he said.

"Karlamov here," a voice answered.

"Surin?"

"Surin here."

"Gorsky?"

Yuri heard the answer simultaneously in his earpiece and nearby in the undergrowth: "Kostya Ivanovich Gorsky present!"

"Malkin?"

"Here," Yuri said.

"Any unusual activity at your position, Malkin?"

"Ah, no, sir, everything is normal," Yuri said.

Yuri heard a rustling in the brush in Kostya's direction. Then the rustling stopped.

In his earpiece, Andropov finished calling roll. He said, "Stay alert," and he was gone.

Where Kostya had disappeared, there was silence.

After about a minute, Yuri said, "Hey numb nuts, come give me a couple of smokes. You can whack off later."

There was no answer.

Yuri said, "Kostya?"

And a few seconds later: "Kostya? You all right, buddy?"

No answer.

Yuri could see nothing in the direction that Kostya had gone. He lifted the Dragunov and brought the telescopic sight to his right eye.

The scope was night-vision, thermal-infrared. It detected variations in heat. The scope worked in darkness, even through fog, with hot spots shown as light against dark: the hotter, the brighter. Even on a tropical night, the human body would show clearly against the cooler background.

Yuri pointed the scope in the area Kostya had gone. He scanned at about shoulder height and saw nothing.

He lowered the barrel of the gun a few degrees, pointing the scope down where a standing man's feet might be. That was how he found Kostya: about ten yards away, on his back, legs splayed.

Heart attack was the first thought that came to Yuri. But in the same instant, he took in the odd angle of Kostya's head, twisted at an unnatural angle.

A hand clamped over Yuri's face, an arm reaching

in from behind. Yuri's training took over. He reacted instinctively, shoving the butt of the rifle behind him, trying for a blow to his attacker's abdomen to make him release his grip.

But the attacker was waiting for the move. He shifted, and the rifle butt found just air.

Uh-oh, he's good, Yuri thought.

The hand was still firmly on his mouth. It was the left hand, Yuri thought. And the right . . .

Well, Yuri knew what the right hand was about to do.

So he wasn't surprised to feel the pressure at the top of his spine, the sudden roaring pain as the tip of the knife blade pierced the hollow behind his neck, angling upward toward the brain.

Real good, Yuri thought, and the blade slid in to the hilt.

Cockeye Teddy lay sedated on a bed in a presurgical prep room. The OR actually had two of these rooms, reached by separate doors from outside: one on the south side of the building that was used to prepare the unwilling donors, the other on the north side, for the patients. The arrangement was designed so that the client was kept separate at all times from the source of the transplanted organ.

Lazovic entered the room, checked the handwritten notations on the medical chart that hung from the foot of the bed. He pulled back the sheet that covered the patient up to his neck, revealing the bare chest, shaved smooth within the past few minutes.

He touched a black marking pen to the skin and traced a single line, about a foot high, in the middle of the chest.

In a corner of the room, Ilya Andropov was checking his security detail, calling them individually on the radio net.

"Surin? . . . Gorsky? . . . Malkin? . . . Any unusual activity at your position, Malkin?"

Lazovic waited until Andropov was finished, then said, "Is there any reason we shouldn't proceed?"

"Apparently not," Andropov said.

"Then let's proceed."

Favor dragged the second body out of the shed, back into the undergrowth, and laid it beside the first.

He picked up the Dragunov, examined the scope. He brought it to his eye and made a slow 360-degree scan to be sure that he was alone.

Infrared thermal imaging, he saw. Generation 4—the Russians weren't scrimping on the goodies. He wondered how many more like this were on the island.

The two dead men wore almost identical clothing, dark T-shirts over dark fatigue-style pants. He went through their pockets. A key ring, two keys. Cigarette lighter. Spare ammo magazines.

Favor's wet suit had no pockets. And it was hot. He was sweating under the neoprene shell.

He peeled it off quickly and stripped the clothing from the first body. He pulled on the pants, then the T-shirt. He put the lighter and the keys in one of the pants pockets.

He picked up the Dragunov. It was a potent tool, with a killing range that extended from one end of the island to the other. He didn't need it yet, but it was too good to leave behind. He dropped the spare magazine into another pocket.

He moved out of the undergrowth, to a spot where he could see more clearly. He lifted the rifle and looked through the scope, making another long, thorough sweep across the dark mass of the island before him.

He picked up four ghostly white figures.

One, on the far left in his field of view, was a man standing alone in one of the thatched-roof shelters. Favor knew that this man must be near the northern tip of the island.

About ninety degrees to the right was another lone man, this one seated near the dock, facing out to sea.

Farther to the right, and nearly out of his vision, was the helipad, where two men were refueling the chopper. Favor knew that the main group of buildings—his ultimate target—was still farther to the right, to the south of the helipad. But it was out of sight, through the trees and on the other side of a hump of land, and he wasn't ready to go there yet.

Operating alone, Favor knew that he had to keep his back secure. That meant clearing the area north of the helipad before he advanced on the structures to the south.

Favor slung the Dragunov over his shoulder. Wearing a dead man's clothes, with the knife held ready in his right hand, he stepped out into the darkness to the north.

Like all the others on the perimeter, the guard at the north end of the island had the use of night-vision binoculars that would easily have detected the approach of a man from one hundred yards or more. And, like the others, he had orders to watch the sea.

When the rain stopped, he left the small shelter and stood at the edge of the rocky shore with the binoculars around his neck. Looking constantly through the glasses was tedious and—he thought—completely unnecessary. But he did raise the binoculars every few minutes and scan the sea from left to right and sometimes back again.

He was doing that when he heard someone walking behind him, legs brushing against the high grass that fringed the shore. The surf was loud, so he knew that whoever was coming up must be close already. But this didn't alarm him. He was sure that the interior was secure. The danger, if there was any, would come from the sea.

He put down the glasses and turned. He saw the outline of a man dressed exactly as all the guards were dressed, with a Dragunov slung over his shoulder.

Who had been issued a Dragunov?

He said, "Yuri?"

The approaching figure was three strides away, and he closed the distance quickly but without rushing.

"No," said the figure, and the knife sliced through the darkness.

When they finished refueling the chopper, the pilot and the medic sat together in the open cabin door, legs dangling, looking out toward the shoreline and the dock. The pilot held an AK-47, cradling it self-consciously. A second AK lay beside the medic on the cabin floor.

The orderlies had brought the rifles when they drove down to get the client in the middle of the storm. One of the orderlies had passed the rifles up while the other helped the client into the front seat of the Gator.

"What's this?" the medic had said.

"Your weapons. Also, refuel as usual, but don't depart until you receive permission from Andropov. You are to assist the security detail if necessary."

"I'm a medic, he's a flier. We aren't responsible for security."

"You are tonight."

So now they sat at the open cabin door, rifles in their laps, waiting for permission to leave. The control panel was powered up, and the volume on the radio was cranked to the maximum. They wanted to hear that time-to-go notice when it came.

They expected it at any time. The night seemed completely normal.

Then the medic said, "I smell jet fuel."

"I don't smell anything."

"Did you have a spill?"

"Of course not."

"I smell fuel," the medic insisted. "Don't you?"

"You're crazy," the pilot said. But he drew in a deep breath through his nose.

He said, "Maybe."

He breathed in again and said, "I'd better check."

He put the rifle aside and reached into a pocket of his cargo shorts for a small flashlight. He turned on the light and hopped down to the ground.

The pilot started around to the front of the chopper. The bright spot of the flashlight beam bounced on the ground in front of him as he walked, and then he turned along the chopper's nose and disappeared from sight.

The medic sniffed the air. Jet fuel? Suddenly he wasn't sure. An intermittent breeze was blowing from over the water, and when it picked up—as it did now—it was in his face, and he could smell only the ocean's salty dampness.

The flashlight reappeared where the medic had last seen it, then moved around the nose of the helicopter, not pointed down at the ground now but held higher, angled so that the beam caught the medic full in the eyes.

The light was very bright in the darkness, and the medic turned his face away and said, "What did you find?"

He got no answer. The light kept coming, not bouncing anymore but fixed on his face, blinding him. The medic said, "Hey, asshole—" and put up his left hand to block the glare.

The light went off, and in the next instant the medic took a hard blow to the head that knocked him back. His left arm flew back, and in that instant another hard blow came under it, slamming against his chest. It was not like any punch he had ever felt— it punched *into* his chest—and as the life drained out of him, he thought, *No, not that* . . .

Favor walked quickly around the nose of the chopper, back to where the body lay on the packed dirt of the helipad. He hooked his arms under the shoulders, dragged it to the open door of the helicopter, lifted it in. He dragged it to the back of the cabin where the second body lay, blood pooling.

He went out and got the Dragunov where he had left it. He crouched near the nose of the chopper and looked through the scope, up the hill toward the clump of buildings. The nearest one was within two hundred yards. It seemed dark and quiet.

He shifted his attention to the second building up the hillside. He could make out the outline of incandescent lights behind three shuttered windows, and the rifle's scope picked out the figures of three men near the building, one of them standing in a doorway.

Favor didn't think that he could reach the building without being seen. The hillside was mostly open, broken only by a thin scattering of palms. And to his left, still looking out over the water, was the sentry near the dock. He, too, would be hard to approach: between the helipad and the dock, there was virtually no cover.

A voice came over the radio in the cockpit. It was Russian, spoken too quickly for Favor to understand. Seconds later, the same phrases, the same voice, only this time more insistent. Up on the hillside, the light went off behind one of the shuttered windows and the shutter opened. A man was standing at the window. He held a rifle. At the top of the rifle receiver, where a telescopic sight would be, Favor could make out a blocky shape that looked a lot like the thermal imaging sight on the Dragunov.

As the rifle swung toward him, Favor scuttled up into the cabin.

He would be invisible there. The Plexiglas window would block his body heat.

In a pocket beside the pilot's seat was a loose-leaf binder of aeronautic charts. Favor took the book and ripped out several pages.

On the wall of the helicopter's cabin was a slim steel cylinder with a valve and a pressure gauge. A clear plastic breathing tube ran off the valve. Oxygen.

The cylinder was held in place by locking metal straps that came open when Favor released them. He grasped the neck of the cylinder and pulled it free.

He was ready to announce himself.

The cataclysm erupted when Andropov wanted another roll call, a security check. He had the radio operator start with the helicopter, which was on a different frequency from the radio net.

Vladimir Raznar was the radio operator. He

called down to the chopper for a status report. No response.

He called again. No response.

Andropov said, "Put a scope on them."

Vladimir turned off the lights in the room and picked up the Dragunov. He pushed open one of the shutters, just enough to give a clear view of the chopper.

He said, "I don't see them." He kept looking through the scope for several seconds, then said, "Something's funny with the ground around the chopper."

"You're picking up a heat signature?"

"No. The opposite. It's *cool* down there."

"What do you see in the chopper?"

"I don't. But I'm telling you, something is really funny down there under the bird."

Andropov got on the radio and spoke to the guard at the dock.

"Sergei, what do you see at the chopper?"

The guard turned and looked back up the hill to the helipad. He was using his night-vision binoculars.

"Nothing," he said. "Nobody, nothing."

"Go up there and take a look."

Vladimir kept looking at the dark blotch below the helicopter. It seemed to be spreading.

He said, "I think I know. . . ."

In the helicopter, Favor squatted behind the bulkhead that separated the cockpit from the cabin. He tore the breathing tube away from the valve on the oxygen cylinder and turned the valve all the way open. Pure medical grade O$_2$ began to hiss out.

He tossed the cylinder out the door, onto the ground below. It made a muffled *clank* as it hit.

Down by the dock, the sentry named Sergei had just turned to walk toward the chopper. The soft *clank* got his attention. He stopped and brought the binoculars to his eyes once again.

He saw Ray Favor raising the Dragunov, bringing it level so that the barrel seemed to disappear. There was only the front glass of the scope and the black dot of the rifle's muzzle, and they were both pointed directly at Sergei.

Favor fired, and the sentry went down.

The crack of the gunshot ripped through the night. The muzzle flash briefly lit the cabin's interior. Andropov, standing behind Vladimir, saw it blaze, strobe-like. Vladimir, looking through the thermal scope, perceived it as a white fog on the Plexiglas window.

In the chopper, Favor slung the Dragunov and jumped to the ground. He landed in a puddle of jet fuel. A few feet away, the steel cylinder was still expelling oxygen.

The fuel was flowing from a drain valve in the tank beside the helipad. The flow was hard enough that the hardpan earth, already wet from rain, didn't absorb it all. The fuel was pooling, and the pool was spreading.

Favor bent down low with the torn map pages in one hand and swiped the paper through the fluid. He was quick, but not in a hurry. He knew that the helicopter's fuselage blocked the view from the hill.

He began to move away from the pool in a crouch, trying to stay behind the chopper's shield for as long as possible. Five, six steps to the edge of the helipad.

He jumped into a drainage ditch that ran beside the pad.

He stayed low and crawled a few yards along the ditch. There was no fuel in the ditch: he checked the ground to make sure.

He pulled the rifle in close and removed the thermal scope. It was mounted with a quick-release mechanism, designed so that it could be swapped with an ordinary telescopic sight in daytime. He pulled a small lever on the side of the mount, and the scope popped free. He put it aside. He was done with it. In a few seconds it would be useless.

Then he balled the fuel-soaked paper, wadding it tight in his hands.

He took the lighter from his pocket and lit the wad. It caught right away. He tossed the flaming ball out of the ditch, toward the helicopter and the pool of fuel beneath it.

The fiery wad of paper flew up into the dark sky, then started back to earth.

And now Favor was up and running like hell.

Up in the window, Vladimir almost got off a shot in that instant when the scuttling man emerged from behind the chopper. But the move surprised him, and the pale white figure disappeared into the ditch an instant before Vladimir could get the crosshairs on him.

But before the interloper vanished, Vladimir did get a look at the rifle slung behind him: a Dragunov. He knew it was probably Yuri's weapon and that it was supposed to be with him up at the top of the hill, but he didn't waste time thinking about how it had gotten down here.

He just thought: *Ah, a sniper duel. This should be fun.*

Then the flaming wad of paper flew out of the ditch, hot white in his scope.

Fucked, he thought.

The wad of paper never reached the ground. It ignited the fumes that hung over the helipad, and was instantly consumed in the fireball it had created.

The helicopter had a jet turbine engine and burned Jet A fuel, more stable than gasoline. It is a kerosene-like fluid, and in open air it usually burns like kerosene on a wick, sooty and not very hot.

But the oxygen that spewed from the tank changed all that. It created a volatile mixture that burned hot and bright as a blowtorch, feeding off the fuel that had soaked into the ground and off the fluid that continued to gush from the tank.

The sudden inferno lit up the entire island, and it

overwhelmed the heat sensor on Vladimir's thermal scope. He was slow to pull back from the eyepiece, and for an instant the screen was as bright as if he were staring straight into the sun.

Favor was about fifty feet away when the fuel ignited. The concussion nearly knocked him to the ground as he ran, and it came with a tsunami of heat that felt as hot as a candle's flame held to the palm. He continued to run, not away from the fire but around it, skirting the edge of the helipad, swinging around until he was clear of it, with a view of the hillside again. Then he dropped to the ground, into the classic prone position of the marksman.

The hillside was lit almost as bright as day, and Favor quickly spotted each of the four targets he had seen through the thermal scope.

He sighted along the barrel.

The Dragunov was a weapon of the old Red Army, intended for hard use in primitive conditions. To keep it useful even without the delicate optics of a sniper scope, its designers had given it basic iron sights.

As Favor sighted along the barrel, his eye found the blade and notch from the first rifle he had shot when he was a boy.

He knew what to do now.

He sighted first on the window with the half-open shutter. Someone inside reached for the shutter, closing it. Favor put a shot into the shutter at the spot where the head had appeared an instant earlier.

He swung over to the first of the three men standing around the building as if dazzled by the fireball.

Favor notched the blade on the guard's chest, going for center mass. He fired, and the target dropped.

Favor swung fluidly, and the front sight came to rest on the second guard, center mass. He fired and the target went down.

The third man reacted. He ducked and disappeared into the doorway where he had been standing.

Favor had no more targets—none that he could see. He wondered how many were left. He knew where he could find more: the second building up on the hill seemed to be the center of activity. That was where he wanted to be.

He reloaded, stood, and ran back the way he had come, behind the burning helipad, keeping the flames between him and the hill. He ran toward the dock, to the body of the guard he had just shot there. He crouched at the body, looking up at the hill—still no movement—and took the AK-47 and spare clips of ammunition.

Favor ran to the dock and put down the Dragunov and the ammo that he had been carrying. He thought that Mendonza would know what to do with it.

The noise from the fire grew suddenly louder. Favor glanced over and saw that fuel was gushing from the helicopter's tanks. He threw himself down on the dock, and an instant later the chopper exploded, flinging body panels and mechanical pieces in every direction.

A fireball rose into the night sky. Favor waited for pieces of the helicopter to stop falling around him, then picked up the AK and started up the hill.

Banshee at that moment was four miles from Devil's Keep and closing fast.

When Favor left the boat, Mendonza had dropped back and circled to the south until he was about six miles southeast of the island, looking toward its low front side. He wanted to stay out of sight but close enough that he could catch whatever signal Favor might send. He figured that Favor would start a bonfire or maybe get his hands on a flashlight. *Ray will figure out something,* he thought, but he didn't expect anything like the bloom of flame that erupted to the northwest, illuminating the island against the dark horizon.

"That's our boy," he said. Stickney and Arielle scrambled for seats. Mendonza looked back just long enough to see that they were fastening their harnesses. Then he turned the engines over and shoved the throttles all the way forward.

Anatoly Markov was the target who ducked inside the doorway of the main building. Markov heard shots and saw one of the guards fall—hit—before he dropped and crawled inside, an instant before Favor could line up his sights for another shot.

Markov found the hallway empty. He opened the

door of the ops room on his right and found Andropov and the radioman Vladimir Raznar both down on the floor. The rear wall was splattered with gouts of blood and brain tissue, and Markov knew that it must have come from the ex-sniper; the back of Vladimir's head was gone. Andropov was beneath Vladimir, and when Markov pulled the body away he saw that Andropov was in bad shape. The side of his cheek had been ripped open, exposing the shattered hinge of his jaw.

Markov saw a hole in one of the window shutters, now half open, and realized that a single shot must have done all this: passed through the shutter and in and out of Vladimir's head, striking Andropov in the cheek.

The slug had lost energy, otherwise Andropov would have been dead, but it still had kept enough punch to screw him up good. Andropov's eyes looked uncomprehending as Markov pulled away Vladimir's body. Andropov tried to speak, but his mouth wouldn't move, and his right arm made flailing motions, but his left side looked strangely inert.

Markov dragged Andropov out of the room and into the hallway, where he could lay him out. The big orderly, Boris Godina, appeared at the door of the operating room and said, "Dr. Lazovic wants to know what the hell is happening here."

"Tell Lazovic I don't *know* what the hell is happening. Get Sasha Batkin and come here. We have to organize a defense."

Godina hurried out, and Markov began calling names on the radio net, trying to get information.

He got no responses. He believed that there was a problem with the system. *Surely not everyone is down,* he thought.

The two orderlies, Godina and Batkin, came to the door.

To Batkin, Markov said, "Get an AK and go fetch the girl. Bring her here. Then secure the south door of the building."

To Godina, Markov said, "See what you can do with Andropov, then secure the north door. I'll guard this hallway."

Markov tried the radio again.

He said, "Malkin. Malkin. Are you there, Malkin?"

No response.

"Gorsky? Report your situation, Gorsky."

Only silence.

Surely not everyone . . . Markov thought.

He tried one last name, almost as an afterthought. By now he was sure that the system must be screwed up.

"Karlamov, this is base," he said. "Come in Karlamov."

The quick response in his earpiece startled Markov.

"Karlamov here."

Of the seven men who had been sent out to sentry posts that night, only Viktor Karlamov was still alive.

He had been sent to the far south end of the island. This post was more than three hundred yards from the dock, and when the fire exploded on the helipad, Karlamov saw it through the trees as vertical slivers of brilliant orange. He heard the barking of the sniper rifle that followed the explosion, and got down low behind some cover, but no shots came his way. Karlamov couldn't see what was happening, and he couldn't be seen.

Remain at your post until ordered to leave was a soldier's fundamental. So was *Maintain radio discipline.* Karlamov knew that the island was under attack. He wanted a better idea of what was happening, and he was eager to join the fight, but his years of military training kept him rooted to his post and kept him silent as he listened to Markov calling to the other guards.

Then Karlamov heard his name called.

"Karlamov here," he said at once.

"Karlamov! What is your status?"

"I'm at my post. Nothing to report. Ready for orders."

"Nothing in your area?"

"Nothing," Karlamov said, then he paused and added, "No. Wait a minute. I hear something."

A hammering drone was drifting in from the ocean southeast of his position. It was faint at first but quickly getting louder. He moved to one side until he had a clear view out across the water.

Then he saw it.

He said, "It's a boat. A fast one. Real fast. It's headed for the dock."

"Jesus, reinforcements," Markov said. "You have to stop them."

Karlamov considered the speed of the boat, the distance from his position to the dock, and the ground that he would have to cover.

"I won't make it to the dock in time."

"Then stop them where you can. *But stop them.* Understood?"

"Understood," Karlamov said.

He set off down the long slope toward the dock. Karlamov soon had a choice of two routes. To his right was a shallow gully that entered a grove of coconuts, long untended, choked with undergrowth. Karlamov knew that the gully led down to the dock: in fact, it was a more direct route, though slower, because of the tangled brush and fallen logs in the grove.

To his left, skirting the grove, was his usual route. It would bring him through the cluster of buildings to the main path that ran down past the helipad to the dock.

But the fire still glowed hot and bright. Karlamov knew that he would be illuminated on that open path—exposed and all lit up. He remembered the purposeful rifle fire he had heard from that direction a few minutes earlier, and he thought of the silence on the radio net as Markov ticked off the names of the other sentries. None of them had answered after that rifle quit booming.

The gully would be a pain in the ass, especially in the dark, but the trees and the brush would cover him as he worked his way down.

With his rifle in his arms, he turned to the right,

moved down the gully, and entered the old coconut grove.

Stickney tightened his harness straps as Mendonza brought in *Banshee*, thundering hard. To Stickney it seemed crazy fast. The island and the blazing fire loomed, growing larger, filling the windscreen.

But Mendonza held course and speed, then cut the engines back at the last moment. The hull settled deep into the water, digging in, as Mendonza swung the wheel and brought the boat in broadside against the dock.

It drifted in and thumped against the pilings. Almost before it had stopped moving, Mendonza was out of his seat, running forward. He threw a coil of rope that lay in a recess near the bow. He jumped up onto the dock, looked around, and snugged the line against a cleat.

Arielle unstrapped from her seat and went below. Stickney opened his harness, too, and joined Mendonza on the dock.

Stickney said, "Ray?"

"I don't see him," Mendonza said.

Stickney took in the hellish scene on the island, lit by the fire. He saw a body near the dock, then two more up on the hillside near the clump of buildings. The fire was still so intense that he could feel its heat across the length of a football field. He became aware of the stink of charred flesh and knew that at least one body must have been been burned in the flames.

He thought, *Ray . . . this. My God, all this. . . .*

Arielle came up onto the dock, carrying the shot-gun and the pistol. She quickly took in the scene and pointed up the hillside to the buildings.

"We want to be there," she said.

"Definitely," Mendonza said. He walked a couple of steps over to the rifle on the dock. He picked it up, quickly examined it, brought it over.

"Bet Ray left this," he said.

"Close quarters, I'd rather have the pistol," she said.

Mendonza said, "Yeah, I'll want the shotgun in-side a building." He laid the rifle on the dock. Not exactly at Stickney's feet, but close enough to reach.

"Let's hustle," he said.

Stickney knew that *Let's hustle* meant them, not him. He wasn't a part of this—not now, not with death all around them and the promise of more to come.

He didn't belong here. He didn't belong with them.

Definition of "useless": A man at a battle with a pledge never to kill.

Ari seemed to sense what he was thinking. She said, "It's okay, Stick. Someone has to stay with the boat."

"That's right," Mendonza said. "We'll need the boat. Anybody comes, you cast off and back the hell out of here."

Stickney watched them start up toward the build-ings.

He spotted movement up on the hill. A man—not

Favor—came out of the largest building, running in a crouch. He was carrying an AK-47—even at this distance, Stickney recognized it. The man disappeared into the smaller structure nearby, the building lowest on the hill.

Stickney knew that Ari and Al had seen him too. They were now double-timing. Mendonza was pointing as they ran. Stickney could imagine him saying, *You take that side, I'll go in this door.*

Stickney looked down at the rifle, a couple of paces away. He found himself walking over, picking it up, examining it. Finding the safety.

He couldn't say why. The weapon drew him in. The moment drew him in.

He held the rifle and watched his two friends as they hurried up the hill.

The Russians moved into position for another spasm of violence.

In the main building, the huge orderly named Boris Godina decided that he couldn't do anything for Andropov. There wasn't much bleeding, but Godina knew that a bullet fragment must've gotten into the spinal nerves at the back of his neck, because Andropov was paralyzed on his left side. Godina stood and walked into the armory across the hall.

The orderly named Sasha Batkin left the main building and crouched low as he covered the few yards down to the blockhouse. He noticed the boat, and the men and the woman down at the dock, and thought that they had spotted him too. He knew that he had to move fast now, bring the girl up, and get back to the post he was supposed to secure.

He slipped into the blockhouse, turned on the lights, propped the AK against the wall.

He dug out his keys to the cell door and turned the key in the lock.

Viktor Karlamov was in the coconut grove, trying to stay hidden as he moved down to the dock, when he looked off to his left and saw a man and a woman through the trees. They were hurrying up the hill. Karlamov knew that they must be from the boat. He had to stop them.

He turned left and maneuvered through the trees. He moved quietly, picking his way past dried palm fronds. The man and the woman didn't hear him. They continued up the hill, and as Karlamov came out of the trees, he thumbed off the safety and stepped in behind them with a clear shot at their backs.

Sasha Batkin pushed open the cell door, looked for the girl, and found the muzzle of an AK-47 inches away, pointed at his chest.

Batkin looked into the face of the man holding the AK. It was like staring down into a well, black and empty and infinite. Batkin felt himself falling into that well, falling forever. Gone gone gone.

Batkin saw the twitch of the trigger finger. He never heard the burst that ripped him apart.

———

The burst echoed down the hillside. Mendonza and Arielle looked up to where it had come from.

Stickney looked up the hillside too. He saw Viktor Karlamov step out of the coconut grove about twenty yards behind Mendonza and Arielle.

Karlamov brought his AK to his shoulder, into firing position.

From the moment he saw Karlamov emerge from the trees, Stickney had about a second and a half to react.

He didn't think about what he was going to do. He felt.

He felt Al and Ari, and Ray unseen somewhere up on the hill. He felt bonds and debt. He felt love—more love than he had ever known from anyone in his life. More love than he had ever felt.

He lifted the Dragunov to his shoulder.

Favor was leading Marivic Valencia out of the cell, putting his hand out to her as she stepped around the body that lay in the doorway, just a reassuring touch to let her know that she was okay. But she seemed to be fine. Her hand was light and steady.

"Sir," she said as she left the cell, "now my brother, please."

Then the shot.

It was a single rifle shot from the direction of the dock. Favor stepped out and looked down the hill and saw Mendonza and Arielle turning, and saw the body on the ground a few steps below them, and saw Winston Stickney still sighting down the Dragunov.

Stickney slowly lowered the rifle, then abruptly tossed it away, flinging it

Oh Stick, Favor thought.

Favor motioned to Marivic Valencia, pointing down the hill to Mendonza and Arielle, and said: "That way. Hurry."

Then he started up the hill to the big, low building, the one he had been bound for since he first saw it.

In that building, the orderly Sergei Godina was rushing through the surgical prep room, outside the operating suite, when he literally ran into Favor coming through the door from outside. Both were carrying AK-47s but had no chance to raise them. They used the rifles as staffs, pushing and parrying. Godina knocked the rifle from Favor's grasp, but Favor reacted quickly, launching himself hard into Godina's midsection before Godina could raise his own weapon.

Favor clutched at him, slammed him into a wall, putting his weight and momentum behind it. They fell to the floor together, grappled, rolled . . .

. . . and Godina came up on top, with both hands at Favor's throat, trying to clamp down, the pads of his thumbs looking for Favor's larynx as Favor bucked and writhed beneath him.

And then the balisong was suddenly in Favor's hand, the blade flashing and snapping into place.

Favor swung the blade and buried it to the hilt in Godina's back. But Godina seemed to ignore it, and his grip tightened. Favor's hand jerked back and forward, this time sinking the knife into Godina's left arm.

Godina screamed and released his grip.

Now Favor was loose. He threw Godina off and leaped forward, ripping with the knife, sweeping and stabbing, a fury of motion, slashing at the arms that Godina raised to fend him off, then thrusting downward as Godina faltered. Favor bellowed, the blade rising and falling, sinking into Godina's chest, again and again and again.

Godina stopped struggling. Favor drew the blade up once more . . .

. . . then held back.

He stood.

He was a feral creature now, grim and fierce, panting, snarling, slathered in blood. Murderous.

He picked up one of the rifles.

On the floor, Godina pawed at one of Favor's ankles. He held the fabric of Favor's pants and looked up at him with an expression of shock. *How could you do this to me?*

Favor kicked the arm away without looking back, strode forward toward the swinging doors of the operating room, and threw them open.

In the hallway at the other side of the surgical suite, Anatoly Markov pushed a desk out of the ops room, into the hallway. He turned it over, crouched behind it, and pointed the AK at the door. The safety was off. His finger was on the trigger. He was ready to fire at the first movement.

Ilya Andropov was on the floor behind him. Andropov had been quiet, but he now began to grunt and thump the wall with his free hand. Markov ignored him at first, then finally looked over his right shoulder at him and said, "Ilya, please." Andropov's eyes went wide—pleading, Markov thought. He wondered what that was about.

Markov felt a pressure at the back of his head.

It was the muzzle of a shotgun.

From behind Markov's head, a voice said in English: "I don't know if you understand me, but you can save your life right now."

Markov understood. He laid the rifle down, very slowly.

THIRTY-TWO

A green curtain divided the operating room, drawn nearly three-quarters of the way across. When Favor burst through the swinging doors, every head on the near side of the curtain turned to look at him. Every head that was conscious and could move.

Lazovic and his assistant, two nurses, the technician who sat at a heart-lung machine—they all stopped what they were doing and turned toward Favor, the fearsome apparition that he was. Favor, too, paused as he entered the room. He looked around. He saw the patient unconscious on the table, mostly covered in surgical sheets. Two clear tubes ran from his chest to the heart-lung machine, blood flowing out and in through the tubes.

"Where's the boy?" Favor said.

Nobody spoke. Nobody moved. The only sounds were the electronic beeping of medical monitors and the soft swish of blood as it moved through the heart-lung machine.

"Where's the boy?" Favor said. Louder now, heated.

Still nobody answered. But something in their silence, the way they stood, made him approach the table. He saw that the patient's chest was open, framed by the jaws of a stainless steel retractor that held it open wide. Lazovic's hands were in the opening, and when Favor looked closer he saw that the hands were cradling a flaccid, fist-sized lump of meat, partly enclosed in a membrane. Off to one side was a rolling cart, and on the cart was a stainless steel dish, and in the dish was a nearly identical fist-sized lump.

Favor realized that they were both human hearts. The one in the steel dish was pushed off to one side. An afterthought.

A discard.

So the one in the surgeon's hands, the one already in the patient's chest . . .

Favor circled around the head of the table and pulled back the green curtain.

Ronnie Valencia's body lay on the other side, on an identical table, his chest held open by an identical steel retractor, with a cavity in his chest where the heart should have been.

Favor raised the AK and leveled it at Lazovic's midsection. He intended to kill Lazovic . . . kill all of them.

From across the room, Winston Stickney said, "Ray, don't."

He had followed Favor up the hill, into the building.

Favor shouted, "Do you see this, Stick?" He pointed at Ronnie's body with the muzzle of the rifle, then swung it back on Lazovic.

"I see. More dying won't bring him back."

"They're killers . . . they're evil."

Stickney's shoulders formed a sad shrug of agreement.

Lazovic spoke: "Whatever we are, the patient doesn't deserve to die. If you kill us, you'll kill him."

Lazovic's hands were still buried in the chest, but he inclined his head, nodding toward the head of the unconscious patient.

"You can see, his life is in our hands," Lazovic continued. "Not just at this moment or for the next hour. He'll need our care for at least the next couple of weeks before he can leave the island."

"I don't give a shit about him," Favor said. "He's as evil as any of you."

"Is he?" Lazovic said. "He wanted to live. That's his great sin. He used what he had, just to buy a few years. Can you really say you wouldn't do the same?"

Favor didn't answer. He was looking at Stickney. Favor thought of him picking up the rifle, raising it to protect his friends. What that must have required. He thought of Stickney throwing away the rifle.

Stickney looked inexpressibly sad.

Favor looked down at the patient, distantly noting the sunken cheek, the eye askew. He was unconscious, suspended between life and death, fragile. Completely vulnerable.

"We did what we came here for," Stickney said. "This place is done."

"Of course it is," Lazovic said. "We can't possibly continue."

"Shut up," Favor said. He pointed to Ronnie's body, the retractor in his chest. "Take that thing out. Clean him up. Wrap him in a sheet. I'm bringing him back to his mother."

He walked out, through a door and into the hallway where Mendonza was holding the shotgun on two Russians, one badly wounded, the other badly scared. Favor felt suddenly detached, drained. He looked curiously at the wounded man. He leaned in closer to examine the man's wound, and from the way he reached up to fend Favor off—one arm and leg moving while the other lay still—Favor saw that he was paralyzed.

Favor said, "Who did this?"

Mendonza said, "Not me. I guess it was you."

Favor stared at the injured man on the floor, his eyes darting, wild. He was finished, Favor thought, no future but a lingering death. Favor took out the balisong and opened it. It would be easy: slit the jugular and the carotid, finish what he had done. It would almost be a kindness.

Favor folded the knife and put it away.

Stickney came through the doors at the head of the corridor. He was holding the body, wrapped in a surgical sheet.

Favor said, "You got him, Stick?"

"I've got him," Stickney said.

They walked down the hill together, Mendonza following a few steps behind, holding the AK, checking back every few seconds.

Nobody followed.

Marivic was waiting with Arielle at the dock. She shrieked when she saw what Stickney was carrying. She knew. She followed, wailing, as Stickney carried the body down to the cabin and laid it out on the floor.

Mendonza climbed into the boat, and Favor was about to do the same when Arielle put out a hand, touched his arm.

She made a vague gesture to Favor, hands and face.

He understood.

He sat at the edge of the dock and lowered himself into the water, in over his head. He came up and rubbed his face and his arms, wiping off the blood. It made dark clouds in the water. He kept splashing and rubbing his exposed skin until he was clean, the water around him clear.

Then he climbed up on the boat, and Mendonza backed it away from the dock and pointed the nose to the north.

They reached Zamboanga around mid-morning. While Mendonza refueled, Favor called Lorna Valencia. He told her briefly what had happened before he handed the phone to Marivic.

From Zamboanga, Mendonza chose a route that ran along the north coast of Mindanao, through the Surigao Strait, and into Leyte Gulf. Marivic stayed in the cabin with the body, but Arielle went down in the late afternoon and brought her up as the dark green hills of Leyte slid by on the port side.

Mendonza slowed and brought *Banshee* in toward shore. Ahead they could make out the highway and the rutted road up to the village and, through the trees, the huddled huts and houses of San Felipe. Dozens of people were standing on the shore. As the boat got closer, Favor could make out Lorna Valencia among them, looking out, waves lapping at her feet.

Mendonza brought the boat in very slowly and let it run aground gently on the soft mud and sand of the beach.

Arielle brought Marivic to the side, but Marivic wouldn't leave until she saw Favor coming up with the body. Then she jumped down and ran to her mother. More people were streaming out of the village now, crossing the highway and coming down to the shore. Mendonza jumped down and put his arms up for Favor to lower the body down to him, and Mendonza carried Ronnie's body through the surf as Lorna wailed in agony and in joy.

The villagers gathered around Lorna and Marivic and Mendonza with the body in his arms, and they began a sad procession away from the shore, across the highway and up the broken road. San Felipe was bringing its children home.

AFTER THE HARVEST

THIRTY-THREE

Franklin Kwok was waiting the next evening when Mendonza guided *Banshee* into slip 22 at the Manila Yacht Club. Kwok asked them to stay for dinner, and sat rapt as Favor described in detail all that the boat had done, and what it had meant to them.

They bought tickets for a return flight to San Francisco the next day, the four of them traveling together, first-class. Favor worried about repercussions from their escape at the bodega in Tondo. They were traveling on their true passports, and he thought that warrants or stop orders might be waiting for them when they checked through Philippine immigration at the airport. But the officer on duty just pounded departure stamps onto the pages, and they walked on board and flew out without a hitch.

The hitch came in San Francisco. The hitch was saying good-bye. Mendonza had barely enough time to catch his connecting flight to Los Angeles, so with him it was quick and relatively painless: a brief embrace for Arielle, a shake of the hand for Favor and Stickney a few words of thanks, and he was gone.

Favor's vehicle was in Oakland, and he hired a limo to take him and Arielle across the bay. Favor wanted to get a limo to take Stickney home to

Mendocino, but Stickney just laughed and said no thanks, he had had enough of the high life for a while, it was just too damn stressful. He was going to rent a car.

So they said good-bye in front of the transportation desks at the arrivals concourse. Stickney gave Arielle a long embrace, and when Favor tried to shake his hand, Stickney grabbed him by the arm and pulled him close.

He said, "You did good, Ray."

"We all did good."

Stickney gave a sad shrug and turned and walked away.

It was the last time they ever saw him alive.

Six days later, Karel Lazovic stepped from a taxi and went to the pedestrian gate of the residential compound on Amorsolo Street in Manila.

The gate was unattended, and also unlocked. Lazovic lifted the latch and walked onto the grounds and into the main room of the home.

The room was empty. The banks of video monitors were dark.

He was looking through files in a cabinet when the last remaining Russian in the compound came into the room carrying a bowl of soup and a bottle of beer.

Dmitri Myukin was his name. Of all the Russians in the operation, he was the only one without security training or military experience. He was a lab technician, an expert in the instruments that they had used for protein analysis.

He was startled when he saw the man standing at the cabinets, and said, "Hey!"

Lazovic turned without haste.

Dmitri Myukin saw his face and said, "Oh. Yes."

"You know who I am, then?"

"Definitely, Doctor."

"Good. I want to see all the records for the last five days of the operation," Lazovic said, and added, "I mean the five days preceding the unpleasantness at the island. Can you show me that?"

"There isn't much. The usual daily reports and logs. That would all be on the computer. Paper, let me see . . ."

Lazovic stepped aside to let him get to the files.

"Some expense vouchers from the local employees, that's about it. Oh, and this."

It was the sheaf of copies from the hotel check-in records obtained by Totoy Ribera.

BOUCHARD, Arielle
STICKNEY, Winston

Lazovic stared at the papers for a few moments, then folded them and placed them in his shirt pocket. He said, "Thank you very much," and turned to leave.

Dmitiri Myukin said, "Uh, Doctor, that's the only copy. I should make one for the files."

"It's not necessary," Lazovic said. "This is of use to only one man in the world. And that's where it's going."

———

When he returned to Mendocino, Winston Stickney immediately resumed work on the project that he had suspended when he drove to see Favor at Lake Tahoe. It was a large abstract piece, using seven different metals, intended for the lobby of a school of engineering at a large midwestern university.

He always worked single-mindedly when he was in the shop, but now he was even more focused than usual. His housekeeper seldom saw him during her three-times-a-week visits.

On an early afternoon about two weeks after he returned home—a day when the housekeeper wasn't scheduled—he was grinding the edges of a shaft of high-chromium steel, a job that required all of his concentration to get the precise bevel that he wanted.

Movement caught his eye: a man walking past a nearby window, wearing the brown jacket of a UPS deliveryman.

Stickney growled under his breath. He often received UPS shipments, and he had told the local delivery office that he wasn't to be disturbed in the workshop. The experienced drivers knew this; he told himself that this must be a new one.

The bell rang at the front door of the workshop. Stickney's focus was broken now, and he thought that he might as well answer it and clue in the new guy.

He stopped and took a deep breath.

Patience, he thought, and he went to open the door.

———

About twenty-four hours later, Arielle walked into Favor's office, the corner room with the knockout view of the lake.

He was at his desk, intent at the monitor screen.

She said, "Hey, Ray. I'll be at home if you need me."

"Sure," he said.

"I think I'll grill tonight. I'm in the mood for some red meat. I picked up a couple pounds of some great-looking fillet tails. Thought I'd do that, grill some peppers. Get into a bottle of Montrachet. Hey, maybe two bottles of Montrachet."

He said, "Did you see the files on that Missoula property?"

"I saw it."

"Sweet stuff."

She said, "Ray. An invitation just flew over your head."

He looked at her, uncomprehending at first. Then he got it.

He said, "Right. Sorry."

He made a vague gesture at the monitor screen, the files from the Missoula property.

He went back to the screen.

She went out, got halfway to the stairs, went back to his door.

Trying not to sound like a female spurned, she said, "If I didn't know better, I'd think you lost the key to my place."

"No I didn't," he said. His voice was serious. "It's on my key ring."

She said, "See you tomorrow, Ray."

———

She had a house on the Kingsbury Grade. It was the original wagoneers' route to the lake, winding upward from the Carson Valley to the town of South Lake Tahoe. The home was just a few minutes from the lake, and a few minutes more to her office at the lodge. It sat on thirty acres and lay between two rolling folds of land that cut off all view of any other buildings. Behind the house was a steep hillside. In front, on the other side of the road, was a sharp drop-off to the valley more than a thousand feet below.

When she got home, she changed into hiking clothes, stuck a liter of cold water into a fanny pack, and went out and up the hillside. A hiking trail ran almost to her home, through the rock garden at the back. If Favor were coming to dinner, she would have skipped the hike to marinate the meat and prepare the vegetables and open one of the bottles of wine.

But he isn't, she thought, *so screw it.*

She hiked nearly back up to the top of the grade, then started down to be back before dark, covering a lot of ground in a hurry on the way down. Near the bottom of the trail, on one of the last switchbacks, she noticed a dark sedan rolling slowly down the road below. Two men in the front seat.

One was looking at her, she thought. Or maybe not. It was hard to be sure in the dusk.

Her house blocked the view of the road from there. The sedan disappeared behind the house, and she waited for it to appear at the other side, continuing down the grade.

But it didn't.

She knew that it must have stopped at the house.

She slowed but kept walking. She reached the rock garden at the back of the property, and slowed even more.

She was approaching the back door now, watchful.

A stranger stepped out from the north side of the house. She was already dropping, rolling, as he raised the pistol and fired. She came up moving, running, with a handful of sand and gravel. He swung the pistol to follow her, and seemed shocked to find her running straight at him, crouched low, flinging the gravel into his face as he fired.

And missed.

She hit him low, digging a shoulder into his gut, knocking him to the ground. His head barely missed striking a cantaloupe-size piece of granite.

She picked up the stone, raised it high with both hands, and drove it down onto his skull with all the force she could find.

She distantly registered the crunch of bone and the squish of soft tissue, ticking him off as dead, but she didn't dwell on it. She was looking for the second man as she reached back for the pistol that had to be near the dead one's right hand.

Nobody else along the north side of the house.

She thought, *The pistol. Maybe behind me.*

Behind me.

And there was the second one, no more than five paces behind her, gun coming up, not in a hurry but with the confidence that he had her, that it was all over now.

A gunshot jerked him off his feet, and he fell.

It was Favor.

She recognized the 9mm Beretta that she kept in her nightstand drawer.

Favor, damn. Waiting for her in bed.

He looked around and said, "Two?"

"Two," she said. "I'm sure."

He patted the pants of the man he had shot, came out with a wallet, which he opened. He found the driver's license. State of New York. Brighton Beach.

"Russian," he said.

They both understood what this meant. Russians coming after her—could be coming after any of them.

"I'll call Al," she said. "You call Stick."

She went to her back deck and called Mendonza. He picked up on the first ring. He said that he was in Minneapolis, in the suite of a boorish actor who wouldn't need a bodyguard if he weren't such a twit.

"I'll be watching," he said. "What about Stick?"

She saw that Favor was talking on the phone. So he must've gotten through to Stickney.

Looks like Stick is fine, she thought.

But something wasn't right with Favor.

He put away the phone.

"What did he say?" she asked.

"It wasn't him. It was his housekeeper. Stick is gone."

THIRTY-FOUR

There were no more attempts against them. Ballistics tests matched the bullet that had killed Stickney to one of the guns that had been used against Arielle in the backyard ambush.

Stickney's friends and neighbors in Mendocino organized a memorial service about ten days after his death. They did it among the redwoods behind his workshop.

Favor and Mendonza and Arielle didn't know anyone there. Favor almost didn't recognize the man that they were eulogizing: the kindliness and gentleness and warmth they described. Favor had always seen these things in Stickney, but only as the flip side of something dark and hard and ferocious. Favor realized that Stickney had re-created himself here, becoming the person that he truly wanted to be, putting aside the parts that he no longer wanted to claim and letting the rest flourish.

Favor thought about Stickney raising the gun on Devil's Keep to save the lives of his friends. He realized what an act of love and self-sacrifice it had been, summoning all the dark parts he had tried so hard to bury.

These people had never seen that side of him,

Favor thought; they couldn't imagine him doing what he had done on the island. As much as they liked and admired him, they wouldn't have suspected the greatness that was in him at that moment.

Good for them, he thought. *Good for Stick.*

Just one other person seemed as out-of-place as they did. It was a young man, maybe thirty, maybe less. He wore a charcoal gray suit and carried a slim leather portfolio. He was tall, straight, with an athletic build. Dark skin that nearly matched the mahogany tone of the portfolio.

He hung near the back, watching politely as Stickney's friends took turns talking about him and singing songs, and when the service was finished, he approached Favor and Mendonza and Arielle.

He said, "I represent a man named Simon. He would have liked to be here, but he knew that you would understand why that's impossible."

Simon. They knew Simon from Bravo. Simon *was* Bravo, as far as Bravo One Nine could tell. He was their trainer, their guide, their sponsor, their angel.

He said, "I can tell you who is responsible for the death of Winston Stickney, if you wish. But Simon has instructed me to tell you that this information shouldn't be used to satisfy idle curiosity. You should ask to see it only if you intend to act appropriately. That's the message, verbatim."

He looked at them, waiting for a response.

"I want to see it," Favor said.

"Yes, let me see it," Arielle said.

"Open it up," Mendonza said.

Arlo Addison was his name. He was near the end of his first year of training in the Bravo program, long enough to have heard the stories—the legends—about One Nine and its four members.

Stickney, Favor, Bouchard, Mendonza. Students and trainers often discussed them: not just what they had done, but how. The way they had worked, four personalities meshing and becoming one. It was a model of the Bravo concept.

Addison brought them to a picnic table, away from the rest of the mourners. He stood across the table from them, looked into their faces. He felt that he knew them.

He put the portfolio down on the table, keeping his fingertips on it, maintaining possession.

"The gunmen were working on contract to a man named Feodor Novokov," he said. "A Russian crime boss, one of the biggest and, for sure, one of the most brutal. The connection has been verified. Recordings exist of conversations. Don't be surprised; we're in the realm of national security now. Especially with the death of one of our own."

Addison opened the portfolio. Inside was a dossier on Feodor Novokov, and the one known photo.

"Novokov is a veteran of the Afghan war. So are many of his captains and soldiers. He was badly wounded, disfigured. He has been known to call himself Uncle Teddy—maybe in irony, I don't know, but he is frankly a creep and a pig, and also an extremely vengeful man. His health has been shaky, but only the good die young."

Addison stopped when he saw Favor's reaction. He was looking down at the photograph, the image of the man with the sunken left cheek and the eye askew.

Favor was weeping. But not in grief, Addison thought. Something deeper and stronger than grief, and far more terrifying. His body shook with a barely controlled rage.

Addison suddenly wanted to be far away, anywhere but here.

Favor was looking at the other two, speaking to them. His voice was cold.

"Never again," he was saying. "Never again. Never again. . . ."